Kiss Me on the Inside 2

Kiss Me on the Inside 2

Janice Burkett

www.urbanbooks.net

Urban Books, LLC
97 N 18th Street
Wyandanch, NY 11798

Kiss Me on the Inside 2

ISBN 13: 978-1-62286-912-1
ISBN 10: 1-62286-912-5

First Trade Paperback Printing July 2015
Printed in the United States of America

10 9 8 7 6 5 4 3 2 1

Distributed by Kensington Publishing Corp.
Submit Orders to:
Customer Service
400 Hahn Road
Westminster, MD 21157-4627
Phone: 1-800-733-3000
Fax: 1-800-659-2436

Acknowledgments

Being a Virgo, I have been blessed with a humble demeanor that allows me to appreciate the people God has blessed my life with.

I am acknowledging my three sisters—Marvalyn Bulgin, Patrina Graham, and Orlene Burkett—and my nieces—Lashawn, Sashee, Bryanna, Madison, and Elon—and also my nephews, Noel and Caylen.

People always say family can make you or break you, but in my case I want to thank my cousin, Karen Mitchell, for making this possible.

I would like to acknowledge Cynthia Clark, Tudy-ann Moodie, Gertrude Mckenzie, Petune McFalling and Jordonna Robinson for playing a role through different stages of my life, giving motherly love, sisterly love, encouragement, and a listening ear through good times and bad.

I will always give special thanks to my Heavenly Father for being my rock!

Dedication

My mother and father are my biggest motivators. I want to show my gratitude by dedicating this novel to my parents, Mrs. Ancella Robinson and Mr. Keith Burkett.

CHAPTER 1

"Bling, Bling! Give us a statement," the shouting paparazzi's voices came at Bling as soon as he stepped outside the courthouse with his lawyer in tow.

Bling pushed his way through the barricade that was formed around him.

"Bling! Why aren't you behind bars where you belong?" a female reporter stretched the microphone forward.

"My client is a free man," his lawyer nonchalantly proclaimed as he adjusted his tie.

Bling was looking dapper in his gray Armani suit. But he quickly came to the realization that it doesn't matter how well made or expensive his suit was, it wouldn't stop people from thinking he deserved to rot in jail. He was hoping his ride would be waiting outside, but he didn't see any sign of his friend Trey.

"How can they let a murderer walk free?" a male reporter's voice shouted at him.

Bling had questions firing at him, and he didn't care to give a comment or statement. Instead, he held his head down like a man that has lost his pride. *Where the hell is Trey?* he wondered, as the 80-degree temperature penetrated his skin. Trey was the only label mate that had his back while he was in jail when everyone else had put him in the wrong for taking Hype's life.

"Bling, how does your wife feel about you having an affair?" another female voice shouted at him.

"Bling, is your wife filing for a divorce?"

The question resonated in Bling's head. The thought of his wife filing for a divorce never crossed his mind because his plan was to make it right.

"Why don't you ask me yourself?"

Bling heard a familiar voice and raised his head to see his wife exiting a black-tinted Range Rover with poise. The paparazzi lost interest in Bling and their lenses focused on Denise. She was looking confident in a knee-length black dress with leather trim at the side with her Tom Ford shades protecting her eyes from the beaming sun.

A look of confusion captured Bling's face because he hadn't seen his wife after purposefully blocking her from visiting him in jail.

"Are you going to stand by your husband?"

Denise made her way to Bling and greeted him with a kiss on his lips, extending her arm around the small of his back. "Why wouldn't I stand by my husband? My vows were for better or worse," she spoke with authority.

"Babe, what are you doing here?" Bling asked through gritted teeth, barely moving his lips.

"Do you honestly think that I wouldn't be here to support my husband?" she replied to him while smiling for the cameras.

Bling didn't know what to make of his wife's showing up at the courthouse. Seeing her standing by his side defending him was mind-boggling.

"Are you saying that you will forgive your husband's infidelities?"

"Yes, that's exactly what I'm saying. I will, in fact, be a good wife," Denise declared.

"What exactly do you mean?"

"*I will indeed forgive everything,*" Denise gracefully stated as she displayed a wide smile for the cameras.

"My client and his wife will refrain from answering any more questions."

Bling held on to his wife's arm and scurried off to the vehicle but the paparazzi were still in hot pursuit.

"What about Keisha?"

The question stopped Denise in her tracks. She did an about-face and spoke with anger in her voice and fire in her eyes. "What about her? She was just a bitch for hire. Besides, if you offer a man food he will eat, but how can you compare the appetizer to the main course?"

Bling wanted to escape the commotion but the paparazzi bombarded them, blocking them from the vehicle. "You need to back up," Bling demanded.

"Or else what? You're gonna murder us like you did Hype?"

Bling held his composure and pushed his way into the vehicle and closed the door. "I didn't want you to be involved in this mess." He reached for his wife's hand.

"Don't you dare touch me," Denise declared as she scooted herself to the opposite side of the seat. "Do you think I'm really here to support your cheating ass?"

Bling was taken aback by her change in demeanor. "So were you just putting on a show for the cameras?" he curiously asked.

"It's called damage control. They needed to know that I wasn't at home being a damsel in distress."

"This is bullshit." Bling shook his head.

"The bullshit is you screwing your damn whore while I'm at home being naïve thinking that you love me!" Denise's voice was on high.

"I didn't mean to hurt you! I just . . ." Bling struggled to find the right words.

"Wasn't I freaky enough? Wasn't my pussy always shaved and waiting?" Denise's anger started to boil.

"Come on, Denise, you don't have to go there. I don't want to talk about this." It was as if Bling was shamed by her words.

"No?" She was livid. "You don't have the privilege of deciding what you don't talk about." She made her way over to him grabbing his shirt. "You need to tell me what the problem was."

"*I* was the problem!" He wanted the conversation to be over with. He was just granted his freedom, and fighting with his wife wasn't on the top of his to-do list.

"Wasn't I spontaneous enough for you?" She started undoing his belt.

"Stop it, Denise! Stop it!" Bling firmly grabbed her hands.

"Would you be telling that bitch to stop? Or would you let her take you into her mouth and have her way with you? Tell me!" she screamed at him.

"I don't want to talk about Keisha," Bling spoke directly to her face.

Denise's finger came up against his cheek hard. "Don't you ever say her name in my presence again!" She scooted away from him.

Bling brought his hand to his face hoping to soothe the burn, but it stung even more.

"You humiliated me, but you know what pisses me off the most?" She stared out the window. "The first time I met her at the appreciation ceremony when you signed your contract, I knew something was off. I remember vividly that you disappeared, both of you, because Hype was also curious of where that bitch had gone. I went searching for you but you were nowhere to be found. But you came back with that silly excuse about going outside to make a phone call. Then that whore strolls in with that silly grin on her face—and I hear rumors that you were screwing her in the damn bathroom. Where was your love for me *then*?" Tears escaped her eyes.

The vehicle was in silence. Bling didn't speak another word, neither did Denise. They both sat in misery trying to put the pieces to the puzzle together.

The vehicle came to a stop and a rustic voice spoke. "We are here, Mrs. Mills. Should I get the bag out of the trunk?" the driver asked.

"Yes," Denise replied, swiftly wiping her tears.

Bling glanced out the window and saw that he was at the Marriott Hotel. "Shouldn't we be going home?" His eyes met with hers.

"Well, you thought wrong." Denise exited the vehicle and Bling followed. "Thanks, Max." Denise took the Louis V. duffle bag from the driver.

"So you're just going to dump me here?" Bling queried as he stepped out of the vehicle.

Denise dropped the bag at his feet. "This will be your home until further notice."

"What?" Bling asked, feeling blindsided.

"Did you really expect to come home with me?" Denise spoke without compassion. "The room is already booked. Come up with a good reason why I shouldn't divorce your lying ass." Denise brought her Tom Ford shades over her eyes and stepped past her husband with her head held high.

Bling stood there with a look of emptiness in his eyes, watching the Range Rover disappear out of his sight. His right foot kicked his bag hard, as if he were a soccer player. "*Ahhhhhhh,*" he bellowed from the pit of his guts. His frustration could be heard far and near. Bling knew that even though he was free from murder charges he still had to be tried in his wife's court of cheating.

He grabbed his overnight bag by the straps and with each step he took, his reality sank in deeper.

"This hotel is now your home until further notice." He took another step and Denise's voice replayed in his head.

"Come up with a good reason why I shouldn't divorce your lying ass." The automatic door slid open, giving him access, and he took a deep breath accepting his reality.

"Welcome to the Marriott Hotel," the receptionist greeted him with a smile.

Bling was in no mood to be cheerful so he got straight to the point. "I have a room reserved."

"Your name, please?" she asked.

"Anthony Mills."

The receptionist tap-danced her fingers over the keyboard. "Room #303 is ready for you." She handed him the key card.

Bling didn't care to exchange another word. He just wanted to get to his room. As he approached the elevator the door opened, letting off a man yelling on his cell phone, barking orders to get the job done right. He pressed the button for the third floor, then took a step back and closed his eyes, taking in a moment of tranquility. The elevator came to its stop all too soon because Bling was in a zone. A young blonde cradling her poodle like a baby stepped in before he could exit, and he stepped sideways letting her on. The arrow on the wall pointed him in the direction of his room, and he walked off to his right. He slid the key card and the green light blinked, accepting his request to enter.

As soon as he stepped in the room, he tossed the bag aside and removed his suit jacket. The AC was on full blast. He had no complaint about that. Bling dropped his body hard on the bed, then positioned himself on his back, staring at the ceiling.

What do I say to my wife? How do I explain to her that my heart betrayed me too? My heart wasn't supposed to race for any other woman. But it ran wild for Keisha. Bling remained stoic as he reminisced on the day his wife came to visit him in jail.

***

"Why?"

He remembered her screaming at him as he desperately searched his soul for a logical reason that would comfort her without causing her more grief, but he only found the truth, and the truth would hurt her to the core. *I was tempted, and I couldn't resist.* But he didn't dare utter those words.

"I don't deserve this," his wife cried out to him.

He kept his head down because her eyes were sad, and he knew she needed him to console her. But instead of giving her comfort, he got up and cut the visit short.

"I hate you!" Bling remembered his wife yelling while she banged on the partition that separated them. But Bling remained emotionless, even though his heart ached. It wasn't because he didn't care but because he knew that behind bars he had to hold his emotions intact.

Bling became overwhelmed and a queasy feeling consumed his body so he got off the bed and headed to the bathroom where he washed his face, then stared at himself in the mirror. He was disgusted at the person that stared back at him.

"What the hell did you do?" he spoke to his reflection. "You had it good, but you fucked it up! What were her faults? Not being freaky enough?" he retorted. "What explanation can you face her with? Except that you are a man with no respect or loyalty for your wife. You cheated on your wife with a damn bitch for hire!" He was livid.

His fist connected with the mirror, but the mirror won the fight. "Holy shit!" Bling yelled as the glass penetrated into his skin. Without delay, his hand went straight for the water. "Fuck!" His pain intensified when the hot water scorched his wound.

The white towel that was situated on the sink became his Band-Aid. He wrapped his knuckles while grunting like an old man with arthritis trying to climb a staircase.

Bling caught sight of his reflection in what was left of the broken mirror and with his wounded hand he went to war again, throwing fists until there was no trace of the mirror left on the wall.

"I have to get out of here. I need to clear my head." Bling left the bathroom, and his feet were in motion to the door. "I wouldn't want to forget this." He grabbed the key card and left the room on a journey to set his thoughts free in the universe.

The automatic door in the lobby slid open, acknowledging his presence, and he embraced the fresh air by inhaling deeply. "Just what I needed," he declared. As he descended the few steps that led him away from the hotel he thought about his wife's change in personality. In fact, she was more like a boss lady instead of the submissive woman that she used to be. He was half a block in his walk when the sky opened up, and the rain poured down on him. "What the hell?" He ran back to the hotel. "Damn it," he expressed his vexation.

"Somebody got a little wet, I see," the receptionist called out to him.

Bling looked over at the receptionist who was making her way from behind the desk. "It's just water, no harm done," he spoke without enthusiasm.

"I can get you a towel," she offered.

"I'm heading up to my room. I'll be fine." He declined her offer.

"I have a better idea," she said with a smile on her face.

Bling viewed her name tag, then brought his eyes back to her face. "Jordonna, is it? I don't want to be rude, but I have a lot on my plate, so if propositioning me with sex is your better idea, I don't want to hear it. And I definitely don't want it." He walked away.

"Wow, don't you have a big ego!" She rolled her eyes at him.

"It is what it is," he spoke, looking back at her.

"Don't get ahead of yourself. I was just going to suggest that you have some rum and orange juice at the bar. My father often says it's a good remedy to fight off a cold." She raised her voice so he could hear her.

Bling brought his attention back to the receptionist. She was very attractive. She wore her Brazilian hair weave long with a side swipe to the right. Her cheekbones stood strong, defining her Jamaican ethnicity. She rolled her eyes at him and walked back to her post. Bling couldn't help but look at her ass because it jiggled with each step she took.

He had misread her intention, but that was the least of his worries. "I guess I'll go have a drink after all."

He tightened the gap between him and the bar and a person shouted in disappointment, "Mello, you suck." With that statement he knew the New York Knicks were probably losing the game. Bling seated himself and surveyed the room, then focused his attention on the 52-inch plasma TV that was mounted on the wall and the New York Knicks were, in fact, losing the game. He observed the bartender pouring from a full bottle of Hennessey and his palate wanted just that. "I'll take that bottle off your hands!"

"It can't be that bad," the bartender chatted back.

"You have no idea," Bling replied.

The bartender planted the bottle with a glass, but Bling took the bottle to his mouth.

"Think about your liver, bro," the bartender cautioned him.

Bling swallowed hard and rubbed his chest as the liquor burned while going down. "I'm drinking to celebrate my freedom. And secondly, my wife evicted me from our home. My marriage was next to perfect, but I wanted more, and I ruined it all." He took another long drink from the bottle.

"Women can be forgiving, man. Just be creative." The bartender was now a member of Bling's pity party, keenly listening to Bling's tales.

"How about if you help me come up with a creative reason for cheating on my wife, then killing my mistress's lover." He took another long drink.

"There's no coming back from that." The bartender slid a beer to another patron, who also tuned into Bling's tales.

"Well, for now, I'll just drown my sorrows." The 32-oz bottle was more than half empty.

"Aren't you . . . ?" The bartender pointed his finger. After taking a good stare at him, he said, "Aren't you that dude? That artist charged with—"

"Not guilty. I'm a free man." He tilted his head back, downing what was left in the bottle.

"I'm going to need your autograph, man. This is too good to be true." The bartender's hand dipped in the tip jar removing a dollar bill. Then he rummaged under the counter trying to find a pen.

"Woo! Burn, baby, burn." Bling hit his chest while getting off the stool. He took a few steps but couldn't keep his balance.

"We meet again," Jordonna exclaimed as she broke his fall.

"I took your advice," Bling said with a smile.

She brought him to his feet. "Which was . . .?" she probed.

"You said a strong drink will make me feel better." He stumbled backward.

"I said no such thing," she defended herself.

"My autograph," the bartender shouted as he made his way to the other side of the counter.

"Autograph, for what?" Jordonna interrogated as she struggled to hold him up.

"That's Bling, one of Top Dot Records's major artists," the bartender excitedly spoke.

"I need another drink," Bling mumbled.

"Regardless of who you are, you're in no position to drink anything but water, so have a seat. On second thought, I'll escort you to your room."

"Just sign for me, man," the bartender solicited holding the dollar bill and the pen.

Bling scribbled his name. It seemed as if he was still in preschool.

Jordonna struggled with him to the elevator. He was much too wasted for her to handle on her own. She was like an ant carrying a loaf of bread.

"Is that a victim?" the new receptionist on duty inquired.

"Victim of the bottle," Jordonna responded while pulling Bling into the elevator.

"Where are you taking me?" Bling slurred his speech.

"To your room," she replied.

Bling pushed all the buttons in the elevator and instead of going to the third floor they were on an expedition to the garage.

"Oops," he said while burping.

"You are a mess." Jordonna shook her head.

"I need to go home to my wife." Bling pointed his index finger in a scolding manner while bracing so he wouldn't fall. He was now unbuttoning his shirt. "I don't feel too good. Is it hot in here, or is it just me?" He was on his third button.

"Oh no, you don't. You better button your shirt before this door opens up. I wouldn't want anybody getting the wrong idea." She started to button his shirt, but for each one she closed, Bling opened another.

"I really-don't-feel-too-good." His stomach revolted, and he vomited all over Jordonna's blouse.

"Ugh!" She jumped away from him and was now unbuttoning her blouse. "And you better not get the wrong idea." She was out of her blouse and her pink push-up bra held her B-cups in place.

"I will not be tempted." Bling turned his back to her and took his shirt off.

"Boy, please, I'm not trying to tempt, seduce, or trap you," Jordonna said, turning her back to him.

They came to a stop, this time at the third floor. The door opened and a lady quickly covered her daughter's eyes.

"You two should be ashamed of yourselves," the woman scolded.

"It's not what you think," Jordonna stated while exiting, using Bling as a block.

Bling lazily tried to insert the key card but after the second futile attempt Jordonna took over and access was granted. She sprinted to the bathroom while Bling stumbled to the bed. "You can let yourself out," he bellowed.

"What the hell happened in here?" she hollered back, seeing the pieces of glass from the broken mirror.

"Put it on my tab." He spoke loud enough so she could hear him over the running water. Bling fell facedown on the bed kicking his shoes off his feet. "Why is this damn room spinning? I command you to stop right now." After a few minutes of silence Bling got up off the bed stumbling. "I need to use the bathroom and you've been in there for too long. What's your name again? Jon . . . don't tell me. Jordon, like the sneaker? Wait. I got it! Jordonna. You gonna let me piss on myself, woman!" He banged on the door.

"I just need the iron to dry my blouse, then I'll be out of here." Jordonna exited the bathroom.

Bling pushed past her unbuckling his belt. "Ahhh! Shit!" he yelled as a piece of broken glass cut through his sock. He wanted to piss his pants. In that moment Bling had to make a quick decision. Piss or nurse his wound. But with a clenched fist and tightened jaw he emptied his bladder without doing the ritual of putting the seat up. He drained his tank for what seemed to be an eternity, and he definitely wasn't shooting straight.

After a few more seconds his bladder was finally empty, and he pivoted on his right foot, limping to the tub where he took a seat and removed his sock. There was a visible piece of glass sticking from his foot. He pulled on the splinter. "Ahh!" He quickly realized that it was more than a small splinter. The shard of glass went deep.

"Is everything OK in here?" Jordonna came rushing to the door. "If you're hurting like that while taking a piss you really need to give your doctor a call."

Bling yanked the glass from his foot. The white towel at the side of the tub was now decorated with blood. He quickly placed his foot under the faucet, and the water turned from light pink to red.

"Do you want me to call an ambulance?" Jordonna asked with concern in her voice.

"No, I'm fine. Just pass me one of those towels so I can wrap my foot." Bling shuffled out of his pants, exposing his red boxer briefs.

Jordonna scanned his body from head to toe. His ass was firm, and his sculpted legs were strong. "I hope you're planning to keep your boxers on." She swallowed hard trying to suppress the urge to reach out and touch him. Jordonna handed him the towel and left the bathroom, not wanting to be tempted.

Bling wrapped his foot really tight. He removed his belt from his pants, using it to firmly secure the towel on his foot, then hopped out of the bathroom and took a seat on the bed, reclining his back on the pillow.

Jordonna glided the iron back and forth over her blouse keeping focus on her task. Bling was almost naked with only his boxers covering his package. Even if you were the pastor's wife you would be lusting. Jordonna's eyes drifted to his bulging manhood. He seemed to be well compensated.

"I'm feeling a little hungry, what about you?" he asked browsing through the hotel menu.

"I'll grab a bite on my way home." She refocused her attention on her blouse that she was about to burn through with the iron. "As soon as I'm done drying my blouse I'll be out of here."

"Well, can you at least let this crippled man order you dinner to say thank you?" Bling laid the menu on his lap.

"Thanks, but no thanks. I already took a risk by escorting you to your room. I can lose my job, so I think I should go before word gets around that I'm fraternizing with a guest." She rejected his offer without lifting her eyes to look at him.

"Aren't you off duty? So what does it matter what you do with your personal time?" Bling's eyes surfed the menu.

"Rules are rules, and I need my job." She remained professional.

"Well, think about it this way. You helped a guest to his room after the bartender served him alcohol way past his limit. So to protect the hotel from losing its liquor license you escorted the guest to his room, where he also got wounded by broken glass in the bathroom while taking a piss." He gave her an alibi.

"Interesting spin, but my answer is still no." Jordonna was reluctant.

"Come on. That's the least I can do to thank you." Bling remained persistent.

"What happened to the mirror anyway?" Her blouse was dry to her satisfaction, and she unplugged the iron and put the board away.

"It's a long story, but if you stick around for room service I'll fill you in." Bling tried to persuade her.

"OK, I will stay since you are so desperately in need of my company, but you have to tell me why your wife decided to dump you here at the Marriott—when maybe your ass should be at a motel infested with roaches and rats." She draped her blouse over her body, leisurely buttoning each button.

"On second thought, I think you might be bad company." Bling withdrew his offer.

"I see you have no sense of humor." Jordonna tucked her blouse in her pants. Even though she was off duty she wanted to remain professional. Besides, she didn't want him to misjudge her.

"Oh, was that supposed to be a joke? Well, let's just say I forgot to laugh," Bling replied with a straight face.

"Maybe you are too intoxicated to remember how to laugh," Jordonna jabbed.

"Was that another one of your corny jokes? How about suggesting something good on this menu?"

"The drunken chicken is a favorite of all the guests." Jordonna sat at the foot of the bed laughing.

"And the jokes keep coming." Bling was unimpressed.

"That's just a small price you have to pay for vomiting all over my clothes." She patted his leg.

Bling picked up the phone and dialed room service. "I'll have a grilled chicken breast sandwich with sweet potato fries, and my guest will be having steamed shrimp with broccoli and baked potato."

"Make that steak instead of shrimp because I'm allergic," Jordonna corrected.

Bling made the correction and ended the call. "I guess it's always wise to let a lady order for herself."

"So let me hear it. What got you kicked out of your house? I bet it was a nice house too. Since you're a big artist and all—"

"I broke her heart." Bling's answer was short.

"What exactly did you do? I need details."

"I cheated," his answer was another short but direct one.

"Is that it?" She was unfazed by his confession. "She should've known that comes with the territory."

"I'm not a cheater, and for the record, I love my wife." Bling fixed the pillows at his head.

"So much so that you fall between another woman's legs? Oh, let me guess, it was your wife's identical twin sister and you couldn't tell the difference." Jordonna added insult to injury.

"It wasn't like that." Bling tried to clear himself.

"Answer me this, why can't love fight for what it wants just as hard as temptation does?" Jordonna asked.

"I don't have an answer for that." Bling was stumped by her question.

"Picture this scenario." She fixed herself at the foot of the bed facing him. "Temptation comes in the bar strutting her stuff in a little black dress. She sits next to you and whispers in your ear. *'I wanna fulfill your wildest fantasies. I'll be your love slave. I'll drink from your fountain of love.'* Then she hikes her dress up a few more inches, giving you a glimpse of her red panties. Your dick starts to harden in your pants. She places her hand on your thigh close to your throbbing manhood, and your heart skips a beat. She raises her martini glass to her mouth and licks the salt from the rim seductively with her tongue, then takes a sip, and you watch as she swallows. She gets up slowly and places her hand on your dick and whispers in your ear, *'Meet me in room #303.'* Then she sashays out of the room in her six-inch Christian Louboutin Red Bottom pumps.

"You gulp your drink and scope the bar to see if anyone had seen what had transpired, and no one seems to have noticed. You place a twenty-dollar bill on the bar to cover your tab and hers and get up to pursue your temptress. Your phone starts to ring in your pocket and you look at it, and the name 'wife' appears. You clear your throat and answer the call. *'I'll be home shortly. I love you too,'* you replied to your wife's statement. The phone call deterred your intention, and you get to your car and turn the key in the ignition, intending to go home to your wife. But your mind drifted back to the temptress in the red panties, and you turn your car off and stroll to room #303."

There was a knock at the door. "Room service."

Bling was glad to end the conversation so he hopped off the bed and limped to the door. There was another knock and Bling limped a little faster. "Yeah, coming!" Bling opened the door and a Spanish lady with a half smile stood with a cart. "Thank you. I'll take it from here," Bling said smiling back at her, but the lady still stood there, and Bling knew she wanted him to tip her. "Sorry, but I have no cash."

"El cheapo," she said as she walked away.

"I'm starving." Bling resumed his position on the bed and the sandwich met with his mouth. He took big bites and swallowed hard.

"When was the last time you ate?" Jordonna asked, picking at her baked potato.

"This meal is gourmet in comparison to prison food." Bling stuffed the sweet potato fries in his mouth. Within minutes he was finished eating and reclined on the bed rubbing his stomach.

"Dinner was great." Jordonna lay her fork down.

"You barely touched your food," he pointed out.

"I guess I wasn't that hungry after all," she replied.

"Thanks for looking out for me at the bar. I'll tell the manager to give you a raise," he joked.

"Aren't you kind. I'll lock up on my way out." Jordonna draped her pocketbook over her shoulder. She got to the door, and Bling's snores were loud, causing her to turn and look. She went back to him waving her hand over his face in disbelief that he had already fallen asleep. Jordonna squeezed his nose, then let it go, and he didn't react to her toying with him.

"Got you!" she said with a smile. Her hand went into her pocketbook and came out with her phone. She snapped a few pictures, then stripped herself down to her bra and panties. She climbed into bed and gently placed her lips onto Bling's and snapped more pictures. She posed seductively many times, and when she had enough she started to run a video. She kissed his face, chest, and other places.

"Enough, girl, you might wake him," she said quietly, calming her anxiety. She went to put her phone in her pocketbook, but she quickly changed her mind.

Where can I hide this phone? She thought for a few seconds. *Under the bed? No. Somewhere he's not going to search.* She thought for a few more seconds. *I got it. The bathroom. I know he wouldn't want to get another splinter.* Jordonna carefully went to the bathroom and wrapped her phone in a washcloth and hid it in the trash can. She peeled tissue from the roll and dumped it on top. *Girl, you are too good,* she complimented herself. *Let part two of my plan begin.*

She came out of the bathroom and climbed into bed with Bling with a wide smile plastered on her face, knowing she had got him good. *This was too easy. I'll sleep now till he awakes. Then I'll make my demands.*

CHAPTER 2

"I gave you all of me." Denise sat on the bed sipping on a glass of Pinot Grigio that she gripped firmly in her right hand, browsing through her wedding album that sat in her lap. She was still wearing the same dress she wore to the courthouse, but she wasn't prim and proper; instead, she was sweltering in anger. "I catered to you; I did my wifely duties of pleasing you! But you weren't satisfied." She flipped the page and poured wine from her glass on a picture of them sharing their first kiss. "Love is supposed to be for a lifetime!" She slammed the photo album shut. "Ha, the joke's on me."

She refilled her glass and lackadaisically took a few steps stopping at the glass patio door and fixed her eyes on the pool. The rain was pouring down, and she watched the droplets disturb the serenity of the pool. "I thought I was doing a damn good job of getting down on my knees too." Her voice was composed. Her index finger traced the trail of a raindrop as it scurried down the glass door. "My intuition was telling me something wasn't right. But what did I do? I ignored it." Denise sipped from her glass. Her body was physically present, but her mind wandered far. She kept her eyes on the pool not saying a word. Tears escaped her eyes, and she broke her silence. *"I'll be at the studio late, honey; don't wait up for me, honey! I'm too stressed out, honey! Not tonight, honey!"* Anger consumed her once again, and in a rapid swing, she released the glass from her hand, connecting it onto the wall. The wine splattered, creating two streams that raced to the floor leaving an outline in the eggshell-colored wall. "I believed you! I trusted you!" she bellowed as she wept. Bracing her back against the door she slid to the floor, bringing her knees to her chest, then wrapped her arms around them. She steadily rocked herself to and fro, letting the outpour of her tears convey her grief.

"It all started when you signed that damn contract. That contract brought that bitch into my life!" she crawled on her knees to the nightstand drawer on Bling's side of the bed where she thought he kept the contract, but it wasn't there. Then she marched to the closet pushing a few hangers forward, exposing the safe. Denise turned left, right, left, and the safe unlocked. "You are a damn curse!" She snatched the contract and raced downstairs to the kitchen, lit the stove, and ripped the first page from the stapled contract, putting it to the fire and watched it burn. "This is for you humiliating me!" She burned another page. "This is for you taking me for granted!" She dumped the remainder. "I damn you to hell!" The contract was engulfed in flames, and within seconds, it turned to ash.

A vengeful monster had taken over Denise's body, and she wasn't going to suppress it, and like a fiend, she rummaged in the fridge and the kitchen cabinets for a strong drink to feed her rage, but she found nothing, so she scurried to the dining room where the wine rack was stocked with Bling's expensive souvenirs. "There's no better occasion than this." She took his most expensive bottle of cognac, opened, it with urgency, like an addict, and guzzled the harsh liquor.

The poised woman that represented her husband at the courthouse now resembled a lunatic. Her hair was now tangled and a mess. It desperately needed to be brushed or combed. The bottle met her lips. She tilted her head back as she drank, then lugged herself to the living room as if she was in a trance, retreating to the sofa.

"We're not ready for a baby, Denise," she mimicked Bling's voice. *"Let's wait until I'm done touring, then we'll have enough time to start a family."*

"Bullshit!" She tossed a cushion, and it landed on the piano in the corner playing a quick note. "You brought your damn mistress on tour with you while I foolishly counted the days down for your return."

She took another swig, then raised her eyes to the ceiling giving the impression that she was speaking to God. "Am I supposed to forgive him?" She raised her voice as her anger intensified. "Woman honor thy husband, that's what the good book said, right? Well, right now, I despise my damn husband. I want to torture him. I want him to hurt the way I hurt! I want him to cry the way I cry!" she sobbed. "Well, in all fairness, you did step in on my behalf. My husband's stealing bitch is exactly where she should be. Pardon my French." She raised her eyes to the ceiling again. "Should I thank you for that? Maybe not, 'cause you don't get your hands dirty, right?" she took another swig.

The doorbell chimed, but she made no attempt to answer it. Instead, she reclined on the sofa, but the person kept their finger on the bell causing Denise to cover her head with one of the cushions, trying to block out the sound. Then, whoever it was started pounding on the door, which infuriated her. She willed herself to get up and staggered to the door on a mission to eradicate whoever it was.

She pulled on the door hard, causing it to swing open. "What is it?" Her pitch was high. A tall, handsome man stood in her presence looking very refined with slightly slanted brown eyes that scanned her face looking for a clue as to why she was looking so disarrayed. His cool chocolate brown skin seemed to be withstanding the scorching summer temperature just fine. His neatly shaped sideburns ran along his well-defined jawline. His appealing cologne floated to her nostrils, calming her temper.

"I didn't mean to—" he didn't finish his sentence before Denise cut him off.

"Who are you?" she spoke in a tame tone, but unable to keep a firm stand, she staggered to the left but quickly managed to compose herself.

"I'm Trey, Bling's label mate. I didn't mean to disturb you," he apologetically spoke.

"Well, you did." She proceeded to close the door.

"Is he here?" Trey spoke quickly as the door closed in his face.

Trey pounded the door, and Denise reopened it. "If you pound my door again you might not have an arm to pound another one."

"Sorry to bother you again, but do you know if he'll be home any time soon?" Trey asked but found it hard to look at her.

"My cheating husband is staying at a hotel." Denise released her grip from the door and lost her balance. Trey took two quick steps rushing to her aid.

"Are you OK?" he asked out of concern.

"I'm just fine." She pushed him away, making her way back to the living room. Trey followed behind her.

"I said I'm fine!" she barked at him.

"Sorry." He threw his hands up and backed away. "I was just tailing you in case you fall again."

"Did he send you here to check on me? I know he did. Well, tell my cheating husband I'm holding up like a champ." She rekindled her affair with the bottle, downing more of the beverage.

"No. Like I said, I came here looking for him," he reassured her.

"I bet all you guys at the label was cheering him on." She got in his face. "He was the man, right?" She poked his chest with the bottle. "I know how you guys like to boast and show off. I bet you pounded fists every time he went on his rendezvous and filled you in on the details."

"I think this is my cue to leave." He backed up from her. "But I think you should get some rest and maybe put that bottle down. It's not suitable for a woman." He walked away. His statement was insulting to Denise, and she went after him like a rattlesnake ready to strike.

"Who the hell do you think you are?" Denise was in his face again. "I want to have a drink, and that's what I'm doing. I'm having a damn drink. I don't need you or anyone telling me what's suitable for a woman because as a woman, I did everything that I was supposed to do. I cooked, and you can see that I keep my damn house clean. I was a good wife to him, so if I want to have a drink to rid myself of my heartbreak I will!"

"With all due respect this is no drink for a woman. Besides, it seems you've had enough. I'm just saying . . . " He proceeded to the door.

"I'll decide when I've had enough!" she shouted at him.

"Yes, ma'am. Since you seem to have everything under control I'll leave you to your privacy," he said without looking back at her. "But if he . . . " Trey turned his body just in time to see Denise falling to the floor, and without hesitation, he ran back to her and lifted her to the couch where he lay her down.

"Do you think I'm beautiful, Trey?" she asked, trying to sit up.

"It's not my place to answer that, but I think your husband would say yes." He gazed at her sad eyes and felt empathy. Her beauty was undeniable even though she was disheveled and drunk. She brushed the bangs from her face and raked her fingers through her hair trying to beautify her appearance.

"Am I not special enough for my husband to be faithful to me?" Denise asked with tears escaping her eyes. The woman that once reigned with confidence was now plagued with insecurities.

"I'm sure your husband has his regrets." Trey tried to console her as he wiped her falling tears.

"Would you have cheated on me, Trey?" Denise spoke in a soft tone.

"No. I don't think I would." He swiped the hair from her face.

Denise brought her lips to Trey's and he pulled back, but her sad eyes connected with his heart and he indulged himself. Their kiss wasn't sensual—it was intense. Denise was under the influence and wanted to feel loved. Trey was consoling a woman who felt unloved, disregarding the fact that she was his friend's wife. Denise was all over him. Their breathing was heavy. She was like a hungry hyena ready to devour her kill.

"What are we doing?" Trey stopped himself.

"You're making me feel good." Denise wanted more, and she kissed him again.

"I can't do this to Bling." Trey mumbled his words as Denise's tongue tackled his mouth.

Denise was in control. She led and Trey followed.

"Make me feel good," she pleaded as she removed his white polo shirt revealing his tight abs.

Trey brought her to her feet and unzipped her dress, exposing her naked back. He placed kisses from the nape of her neck to the small of her back. Denise released her arms, and the dress fell to the floor. She turned facing him, and his eyes zoomed in on her breasts that were held captive by her black lacy bra. He extended his arms to her back and set her perky C-cups free.

"Love me the way I'm supposed to be loved. Please me like I was your woman," she begged.

Trey lifted her like she was a featherweight and sat her on the piano, removing her black panties that matched her mood. He parted her legs and her shaved haven was enticing to his eyes. He got down on his knees and tasted her. His tongue played music on her piano. He touched all the right keys, and she sang the notes.

"Oh yes," she sang in soprano.

"Umm," he moaned in alto, enjoying his friend's wife.

Trey had taken her to a place where she felt only pleasure. The hurt she felt from Bling's infidelity was masked with sensual bliss. Her body was enjoying every moment. Her mind was elevated to a place of solace. Her hips swayed as she created a rhythm to his beat. Her mind was held captive by undignified gratifications, and selfishly, she reveled in the moment. Denise wanted to be desired. She wanted comfort, and Trey was the fly that got caught in the web.

"Don't stop," she panted wanting more when Trey came up for air.

He placed his muscular arms under her, lifting her to her feet, bending her in the doggy position with her ass poking out at him. Immediately, he dropped his trousers, and his rock-hard manhood thrust at her like an arrow zooming in on its target. His anticipation heightened. He was ready for her. He spread her legs, positioning her to receive his hardened manhood.

"What the hell is this?" Denise's sister Madison interrupted.

Denise and Trey hit several keys on the piano, and it played an awful combination creating a dreadful sound. They hid their naked bodies as their heart beat rapidly, pounding their chests.

"What are you doing here, Madison?" Denise asked her sister in a panic.

"I came to check on my sister, and from the looks of things, it's a good thing I did because you are up to no damn good."

Trey was on his knees extending his arm from behind the piano, trying to reach his shirt.

"Did it cross your mind to call first?" Denise questioned.

"Did you think about locking the door?" Madison followed Trey with her eyes as he hightailed it out of the house. She took Denise's dress from the floor and approached her sister who was still hiding behind the piano.

"You were on the news looking so poised, but I know you were putting on a front, and like the caring sister I am, I came to check on you. I even brought a bottle of wine for us to drink your sorrows away, but I see you found other ways to do it." She stood in front of Denise who was curled up into a ball and tossed her dress to her.

"I can't believe I did that." Denise hurriedly covered her body.

"You should be glad it wasn't your husband who witnessed what I just saw. That would have turned the tables. You couldn't guilt-trip him into giving you half of everything. By the way, who the hell was that, and have you lost your damn mind?" Madison asked placing her hand on her hip.

Denise hurriedly stepped into her dress. "I don't want to talk about it."

"Were you drinking?" Madison smelled the liquor on her breath and fanned her nose while trailing behind her. "You better talk." Madison grabbed her arm.

"I messed up big time." Denise was on the verge of crying.

"From what I see, you scored big time. Did you see the body on that man? You really should've gotten some of that," she teased.

"He's my husband's friend. Now I'm a whore just like her." Denise walked to the kitchen and started a fire under the kettle.

"Is something burning?" Madison asked, sniffing the air.

"Yes. Bling's contract," Denise answered.

"Did you really burn his contract?" Madison said in amazement.

"I was so upset I wanted to burn everything having to do with that bitch." Denise sat at the table with her head down.

"You burned his contract, you slept with his friend. What more are you going to do?" Madison questioned.

"I didn't sleep with his friend," Denise corrected.

"Denial is not a river in Egypt," Madison said while taking down the tea cups.

"You came just in time to stop the train wreck that was about to happen," Denise spoke with her head still on the table.

"You think he will keep it a secret?" Madison asked, taking two tea cups out of the cabinet.

"I didn't think that far ahead." Denise lifted her head. "I wasn't thinking. I was just so angry, hurt, betrayed . . . I'm no better than him."

"Don't you dare compare yourself to him. Bling had an affair. He willingly cheated on you multiple times. You are better than him." Madison massaged her sister's shoulders trying to ease her stress.

"I cheated, and he cheated, so we're even. I would be very hypocritical to punish him now. I have no grounds to be upset anymore. I want to save my marriage," Denise declared.

"Over my dead body. His actions were premeditated, and yours was on an impulse. You better not let your guilt get the best of you." She removed the kettle and filled both cups with the scalding hot water, dropped the tea bags in, and brought the cups to the table.

"Just what I need." Denise brought the cup to her nose. The aroma was therapeutic.

"I can guarantee you will have a massive hangover," Madison warned.

"Don't remind me," Denise answered with her eyes closed, still taking in the aroma.

CHAPTER 3

"Please don't leave me," Bling begged as he tossed and turned in the bed. Jordonna raised her head and glanced at the time. It was 9:30 a.m.

"Don't go." Bling shook his head from side to side.

Jordonna looked over at him. His eyes were closed, and she knew he was dreaming.

"Don't ever leave me again." He turned on his stomach and threw his arm around Jordonna.

"I'm here to stay," she played along, knowing he was dreaming.

"Don't leave me please," Bling begged.

"I'll be in your life for a long time with these pictures I got. If only I had my camera rolling for this." A devious smile widened her lips.

"Promise me that you'll stay." Bling turned on his back.

"I promise," she whispered in his ear.

"I have to make things right," Bling confessed.

"I'll be the woman of your dreams." She kissed his neck and made her way to his chest, placing kisses on every inch of his sculpted abs. She slid her hand into his boxers finding his manhood.

Bling opened his eyes and tossed her aside. "Get off me! What the hell are you doing in my room?" He scurried out of the bed as if he saw a ghost. His feet landed on the floor, and he was off balance. He took a quick glance at his foot. It was still wrapped in the towel. "I'm calling the police."

"I see I'm unappreciated for my services rendered." She put her legs in her panties and covered herself.

"Are you trying to set me up? I know how you females do. Where is your damn phone?" he took her pocketbook and emptied the contents on the floor looking to confiscate her phone.

"What are you doing?" she ran over to him trying to get her pocketbook.

"Where is it? Where is the damn phone? Where is it?" he tossed the pocketbook across the room.

"You damn psycho!" she went to get her bag, then got down on her knees and gathered her belongings from the floor, grabbed her clothes, and ran to the bathroom, slamming the door behind her.

"You have five minutes before I call the front desk to report a break-in." Bling stood by the door like a security guard.

"I only need one minute so you can use the remaining four to go fuck yourself," she yelled.

Bling paced the floor counting down the seconds in his head. "Your minute is up!" He pounded the door.

"You don't have to tell me twice." Jordonna open the door and was completely dressed.

"I don't know how your crazy ass got in here, but I'm letting you out." He opened the door—and Denise was standing there. Bling slammed the door, not knowing what else to do in the moment. "This can't be happening," he muttered, bracing his back against the door.

"Bling, open this door now!" Denise pounded the door.

"What are you doing here, Denise?" he asked in a panic.

"I'm not going to speak to you through this door!" she yelled.

"Are you checking up on me?" Bling didn't know what to say or do so he turned to the unlikely source. "Please, you have to help me. It's my wife, and you have to cover for me," he whispered to Jordonna.

"I don't have to do shit—" her voice was on high. Bling quickly grabbed her and covered her mouth as she fought him.

"What's going on in there? You better open this door now!" Denise demanded.

"Nothing is going on . . . " Bling still had Jordonna in his grip.

"Open this damn door!" Denise pounded multiple times.

"Please. I beg you. Just help me out," he pleaded with Jordonna as he released her.

"Let me think. No, I just can't." Jordonna shook her head. "I have to be on my way." She reached for the doorknob.

"I'll do anything, just name it." He blocked her exit.

"Well, that's an offer I won't turn down. Since you are an artist I know you have a little change in your pocket. So my demands are as follows . . . " Jordonna retreated from the door.

"Name it," Bling eagerly stated.

"I would like my rent paid." Jordonna placed her hand on her hip.

"Fine." Bling agreed with anxiety in his voice. He extended his arm to open the door.

"—for a year," she added.

"What?" he asked in disbelief and his hand dropped to his side.

"Deal?" She stretched her hand forward for a handshake. "Or no deal?" She reached for the doorknob.

"OK, deal," Bling gave in.

"And my car note paid off," she added.

"Open this door before I break it down!" Denise demanded.

"Just a minute!" he said nervously. "And yes to your damn demands." He turned his attention back to Jordonna.

"And one other thing. Ten thousand dollars cash or else our little sex tape goes viral."

"What sex tape? You're a damn crazy bitch."

"Am I? Last night was one to remember." She raised her voice.

"Open this damn door!" Denise yelled.

"Your demands will be met," Bling hastily agreed.

"Now we're on the same page." She slithered her index finger along his jawline.

Bling took a deep breath, then opened the door. Denise stormed in pushing him out of the way.

"You must be Mrs. Mills," Jordonna spoke in a professional tone while extending her hand for a handshake.

Denise stared at Jordonna as if she was covered in shit. "Who the hell are you, and what are you doing in my husband's room?"

"Well, as my name tag states . . . " Jordonna traced her finger over her name tag. "My name is Jordonna, and your husband had a little too much to drink last night and seems to have amnesia."

"I just did a little damage, that's all." Bling walked away.

"I beg to differ. But if you could step this way." Jordonna led the way to the bathroom. "I was informed by one of my staff that the bathroom was destroyed and you can surely see that the bathroom mirror has been broken. There is also broken glass all over the floor, which obviously cut his foot."

Both ladies exited the bathroom, then Denise turned her attention to Bling who was now sitting on the bed.

"I had a little too much to drink last night." Bling tried to cover his ass.

"Well, I have to go file a complaint, and I have to inform you that this will be billed to your charge card." Jordonna remained in character.

"If that's all, you can leave." Denise dismissed her.

"He's all yours as soon as he agrees to keep his promise to pay up."

"Yes, I agree," Bling confirmed his promise.

"And on that note, it was nice doing business with you." Jordonna exited with a smirk on her face.

"So why are you here, Denise? You think you can just pop up on me like I'm a child?" Bling's tone was aggressive even though he wanted to grab her and rip her clothes off, but the fact that Jordonna had violated him made him feel dirty.

"You could have fooled me. But I . . . " She sat next to him.

Bling got up from the bed not wanting her to smell the receptionist's lingering perfume. "You dump me here, and I accept my punishment, but I'm not going to live under a microscope," he warned.

"It's understandable that you might have resentment about me letting you spend the night here, but I came to the conclusion that . . . " Denise walked over to her husband, and he evaded her.

"I'm just not in the mood for company right now. I have a lot on my mind, so maybe it was a good idea for you to dump me here." Bling hated the fact that he was hurting her feelings, but it was better to do it this way then her finding out he was in bed with another woman.

"With your damn attitude you *need* to stay here." Denise walked to the door.

"What did you expect to happen when you came here?" Bling wanted to know her feelings.

"I expected you to be on your knees pouring your heart out. A million reasons why you want this to work should be coming out of your mouth. Fight for my love the way you went to war for that bitch!"

"I wanted to go home with you and you dumped me here, so deal with it." Bling was intentionally hurting her feelings, and he intended to make up for it later, so he watched her leave with a broken heart.

The minute Denise was out the door Bling rushed to his overnight bag hoping to find his Axe body wash, and it was right on top. He made his way to the bathroom where he took extra precaution stepping, not wanting to get another glass splinter in his foot. He took the makeshift bandage from his foot, then turned the shower on. Bling removed his boxers and stepped in. The water was a little too hot so he adjusted the gauge. He glanced down at his manhood, and he felt disgusted. The thought of the receptionist having her way with him made him want to scrub his skin off it.

He lathered himself from head to toe, then he rinsed himself and lathered his body again. He was determined to get her off his body. He continued the process several more times before deciding that he was clean.

He left the bathroom in a rush to get dressed and go make up with his wife because even though she didn't say it in so many words he knew she was there to forgive him. He grabbed the duffle bag and tossed it on the bed, but as soon as he took the clothes from the bag he realized that his wife had not intended for him to leave the room.

"What the hell is this?" He was unpacking clothes that he hadn't worn in a few years, clothes he had packed in a box to donate to Goodwill. "Has she lost her damn mind?" Bling took a dingy Aéropostale graphic tee and paired it with blue jeans. A dirty Puma sneaker was at the bottom of the bag, and he knew for a fact that these items were from the donation box he had packed. Bling dressed himself, then emptied the remaining contents out of the bag. "Those I'll leave but not my Louis V. duffle bag." Bling stepped into the sneakers and laced them to his feet.

He poked the numbers hard on the hotel phone and cleared his throat as he waited for an answer. "Trey, it's Bling," he stated. "I need you to meet me at the Marriott downtown.

"Come on, Trey, the only Marriott downtown. By the way, what happened to you yesterday? You know what, save it for when you pick me up." He ended the call.

He opened the door and stepped out with his mind set on never to return because tonight he would be sleeping in his own bed. Bling got to the lobby and walked over to the desk. "I'm checking out." He left the key and was in motion for the exit.

"Excuse me!" The receptionist tried to get his attention, but Bling kept walking. "Sir, there's an envelope here for you."

"Keep it," he said without stopping.

"It seems to be important." The receptionist ran after him. "Jordonna said I should make sure you get this."

Hearing Jordonna's name Bling abruptly stopped and faced her. "Are you getting a commission for this?" he insultingly asked. He looked down at the envelope, and it was addressed with the words *Last Night* in bold letters. He grabbed the envelope. "Are you in on this?"

"Excuse me?" The receptionist furrowed her brows.

Bling kept his mouth shut and calmly walked away. He was grateful that he had beaten all charges and was set free, but it seemed as if he was being punished in other ways. The door slid open and Bling stepped outside. He had entered the hotel with his wife's ultimatum, and as he exited he was faced with blackmail. Bling took a seat on the last of the four steps in front of the hotel. He looked at the envelope in his hand, and then decided to open it. He ripped the envelope and read the note.

Last night was wonderful. I'm hoping our baby will be as handsome as his daddy. Lol. I think I should win an *award for my acting skills, don't you think? But, let's get down to business. I'm demanding $40,000. I believe I have cheapened myself for asking for this small amount, but I didn't want to be too greedy. Below you will see my account. You have until tomorrow noon to deposit half my money.*

"What's the wish of a free man?" Trey called out to Bling.

Bling was deep in thought, and he didn't see Trey pull up. He hastily stuffed the note in his back pocket and walked to the car. "This free man seems to still be in hell," Bling said as he climbed into the passenger seat.

"Will a strong drink help?" Trey put the car in motion.

"Nah." Bling put his window down as they drove off. "Just taking in this fresh air is all I need." He lay his head against the headrest.

"Fresh air? You're a free man. You should be doing it big!" Trey's voice was on high.

"Sometimes you need to enjoy the smaller things that life has to offer," Bling stated in a calm voice.

"You going soft on me, man?" Trey shook his head.

"If that's what you want to call a man wanting to be one with nature, I'll be that." Bling remained nonchalant.

"What happened to you yesterday?"

"I got a flat on the way. But in my defense, I did show up, and you were gone. But from what I saw on the news, your wife was on time." Trey cleared his throat, knowing he was being a hypocrite.

"That was all a front on her part. She dropped me off at the hotel with an overnight bag." Bling adjusted his seat.

Trey laughed. "You should be happy that she didn't skin you like a pig."

"Ycah, I know. But I'm going home to make things right. I messed up, and I am not going to lose my wife to another man."

"On a different note," Trey changed the subject, "I was on my way to Top Dot when you called me. Derrick wanted to have an emergency meeting."

"Why is Derrick having emergency meetings like he's in charge?" Bling asked.

"Where have you been?" Trey's voice was still on high. "Oh, in jail. Derrick is the man in charge. He was a silent partner, and he also knows the business."

"So what's this meeting about?" Bling asked with no enthusiasm.

"He didn't really say, but I hear talks of people wanting out of the contracts," Trey informed him.

"Yeah, I'll swing by there because I would love to hear the bullshit."

The traffic on I-95 was bumper-to-bumper, but Trey's solution was to rip the shoulder lane like it was his personal runway, flooring the gas pedal for about two exits.

"Don't you think that you should merge with the traffic? The police may be looming nearby," Bling advised.

Trey tried to bully his way back into traffic but a car cut him off, causing him to pull back into the shoulder lane. "Fuck you, asshole!" he cursed the driver. He accelerated on the gas pedal catching up with the car, only to see that it was an old woman tightly holding on to her steering wheel as if it was her lifesaver. Bling and Trey both laughed. After another ten minutes driving in stop-and-go traffic, Trey was fed up and opted for the shoulder lane again, even though his exit was in sight.

When he finally exited the highway Bling breathed a sigh of relief. "I wouldn't want to see that ticket."

Trey pulled into Top Dot Records and parked his car. "I see that everyone is already here," he acknowledged when he noticed everyone's car. He unbuckled his seat belt and opened his door. "Are you coming or not?" Trey asked.

"Go ahead. I'll be right behind you." Bling reminisced about the first time he came to Top Dot Records and signed his contract after the night he gave into temptation. "She sold me a lie even then, and I fell for it."

Getting out of the car Bling took his attention to a FedEx deliveryman who exited the lobby with boxes piled up on a Pullman hustling off to his next destination. With his eyes fixated on the multiple packages Bling wondered if he would have the patience to load and unload packages every day. He took the elevator to the third floor, and as he strolled up the hallway he could hear Derrick's voice, and it was intense.

The conference room door was left ajar, so he took a peek inside before he entered. He noticed a few new faces, and, of course, all the others that hated him for killing Hype, including Trigga. Bling procrastinated, not sure if he wanted to deal with everyone chastising him. "It's better now than later," he said quietly as he pushed the door open, and, of course, all eyes were on him.

"And the murderer walks free." Trigga clapped his hands.

Bling didn't entertain him with a reply. He sat in the seat that was obviously not for him because no one knew he was coming.

"For those who don't already know who this is, this is Bling, but I doubt it if everyone doesn't already knows who he is. So since that's out of the way, let's get back to business." Derrick ended the introduction.

"Well, the real business just showed up," Trigga jabbed again.

"What the hell is your problem, man? Let the man live," Trey defended his friend.

"So tell me, Killer B, did you cheat on your wife in jail too?" Trigga had the room laughing.

Bling was trying to keep his composure because he had expected it. But Trigga had gotten under his skin. He aggressively pushed his chair aside. "What the hell is your damn problem?"

"Calm down, Bling!" Derrick called out to him.

"Nobody was telling him to calm down when he was yapping like a bitch," Bling addressed Derrick.

"I know you are bigger than this pettiness. That's why I'm addressing you," Derrick talked back.

Bling sat back in his chair, and Derrick proceeded with the meeting, but Bling couldn't keep his focus. He pounded his fist onto the table taking out his aggression.

"Some of us at this meeting want to know what's going on with our career." Trigga expressed his frustration with Bling again.

"Your career is dead, if you ask me," Bling fired back.

"Isn't that funny, because if you ask me, the wrong man is dead," Trigga came back hard. Trigga had struck a nerve with Bling, hinting that Bling should be dead instead of Hype.

"We *could* take this outside. Action speaks louder than words," Bling taunted.

"You been acting like you run shit just 'cause you smashed boss lady. Rumor has it that—"

"Enough!" Derrick cut him off in midsentence. "You will respect the fact that Keisha—"

"Let him talk!" Bling cut Derrick off. "The man has a lot to say. 'Cause his music isn't saying shit," Bling jabbed.

"How's that pretty wife of yours? Or maybe I should ask Trey."

"What the fuck is your problem. Don't bring me in this shit." Trey got out of his chair.

"Tell me, Trey, since you his lackey—taking care of his business while he was behind bars where he should still be—did you run up in his wife?" Trigga had a smirk on his face.

"I see what you trying to do, but it's not going to work," Trey dismissed his accusation.

Bling was holding himself back from letting his fists go upside Trigga's head, even though it would be a sure way to release some stress, but this was neither the time nor the place.

"I'm just coming from jail, and I don't want to go back any time soon. So you *will* live to see another day." Bling tightened his jawbone.

"Why did they let a murderer walk free? I know you were somebody's honeybee in jail, bitch," Trigga continued to press his button.

Bling's chair was making its way to Trigga's head. The room was in chaos.

"Everybody clear the room except for Bling!" Derrick yelled.

"Let's go, pretty boy! Me and you, one-on-one." Trigga was still running his mouth.

"Get out. Everybody get out!" Derrick's attempt was unsuccessful. The room was in an uproar. It took another five minutes before everyone exited the conference room.

Derrick locked the conference room door and braced his back against it. "What the hell just happened?" he asked.

"What the hell is his problem, is the better question." Bling was pacing the room. "It seem like half the label turned their backs on me. I didn't go after Hype. He came for me. He fucking took me at gunpoint. He was going to kill me! Was I supposed to let him take my life? It was a fucked-up situation. I have to be making up for it with my wife. Now I have to deal with this at work. I would like to see them in my shoes. I feel like my world has been turned upside down." Bling walked out of the room.

***

When he got outside he looked to his left and right, making sure the coast was clear. Just in case Trigga wanted to step to him.

"Get in, man." Trey pulled up next to him. "You all right, man?"

"All I know is that Trigga is out of his damn mind to step to me like that. I didn't do anything to him."

"You did." Trey drove out of the parking lot.

"Do you know something that I don't?" Bling asked.

"The bottom line is that you were smashing boss lady, and you got special treatment," Trey rubbed it in.

"What the fuck! I'm tired of this shit. It's always coming back to Keisha."

"Let's do the math, Money B. You killed a man because of Keisha. You almost lost your freedom because of Keisha. You almost ended your marriage—"

"Yeah, yeah, because of Keisha," Bling mocked Trey.

"You need to go to the studio and let off some steam. Put it in a song." Trey slowed at the light preparing to make a stop when a hard bump from the rear sent both Trey and Bling's bodies in a forward jolt.

"What the fuck!" Bling turned his head and looked to see what happened. Trey quickly undid his seat belt and opened his door, but the black Honda with tinted windows sped off, running the red light.

"Did you see that shit? There are no plates," Bling said.

"I'm going after him!" Trey sped off without concern that the light was still red.

"Just don't do nothing stupid. I am not trying to go back to jail."

"This is no accident. Tinted windows with no plates. This was intentional." Trey was doing way over the speed limit, but the mystery car was still ahead.

"You have problems in the streets?" Bling questioned.

"I don't have any problems. But it seems as if you have acquired some."

"Why would—" Bling stopped himself.

"Don't forget that Hype's family is now your enemy. Besides, Trigga just made it clear that he's not a fan of yours." Trey blurted the exact thing Bling was thinking.

"Slow down! Slow down. Let it go. This is just too much for me right now. I've just gotten off a murder charge, and now I'm in a high-speed chase."

"He's going to get away!" Trey was amped with adrenaline.

"I'm not mentally prepared for this right now!" Bling wanted no part of the chase.

"You better be prepared because you already started it." Trey let up off the gas as he slowed for a stop sign.

"All I did was finish something that Hype started."

"Hype's family is a bunch of hotheads. You better get ready for the real war. I'm surprised they didn't snipe you when you exited the courthouse. Just watch your back. They just showed you that they're ready for war."

"If it's like that, I'll be ready too," Bling made it clear to Trey.

"Fill me in on what exactly went down that day," Trey said.

"You really want to take me back down that road, man?" Bling was in no mood to relive that horror.

"When people talking shit I just want to tell them that's not what happened," Trey clarified himself.

"You don't have to defend me, man. The courts already proved that I am not guilty," Bling spoke proudly.

"Well, the streets have their own verdict," Trey said under his breath.

"You keep talking about the streets, it starting to sound like it's you who have doubts," Bling checked him.

"Don't come at me like that, Money B. I had your back when everyone else tossed you to the wolves," Trey defended his loyalty.

"These days you never know who's who," Bling made his statement.

"Well, you know who I am." Trey tried to hide his guilt.

"Do I really know you, Trey? These days, I trust no one." Bling made a firm stand.

"Let's go have a drink on me. It'll wash your sorrows away." Trey tried to change the subject.

"It's too early for that." Bling denied the offer.

"It's never too early for a strong drink of Satan's Piss." Trey tried to lighten the mood.

"Well, you can drink all the piss you want. I want no part of it. But I do need your help. I have to come up with a creative way to win my wife back."

"I'm not a married man. I'm just a ladies' man. But in my opinion, it's always good to reenact a moment that is special to her; a moment that holds sentimental meaning for both of you. She's really distraught, Money B."

"Why the hell you speaking as if you know my wife's feelings?" Bling was caught off guard by his statement.

"Come on, Money B. Her feelings is public knowledge," Trey quickly cleared himself.

Bling reclined his seat, and there was a brief moment of silence. As Trey neared the house he was getting sweaty and wiped his face with his forearm. "Are you all right, man?" Bling asked, noticing Trey's discomfort.

"Feels like I'm having hot flashes, man." Trey put his window all the way down.

"Isn't that a woman thing?" Bling asked.

"Maybe I need to go the hospital to get checked out. Maybe my blood pressure is too high." Trey tried to find a reason to detour. It was all too soon for him to return to the house.

"Maybe you're high off something else. Are you smoking the pipe? Maybe it's the Devil's Piss." Bling laughed at his own joke.

"I just don't feel too good, that's all." Trey's voice was weak. The high-spirited man was now as meek as a church mouse.

"Let me find out you hiding from one of your side chicks on my street . . ." Bling said.

Trey wiped his forehead. "I got caught up in a situation with the wrong woman." He was visibly nervous.

"What could be so wrong about her, Trey?" Bling shook his head. "Let me guess, she got kids."

"She's a married woman. It wasn't anything planned. It just happened," he said. Unbeknownst to Bling Trey was confessing his sins.

"I got your back, man. Besides, if they live on my block I could probably defuse the situation."

"I'm sure you can," Trey said in a sarcastic tone.

Bling was one left turn away from being home. Trey made the turn and slowed his speed to a crawl.

"Stop being a punk," Bling taunted. "Speed up, man."

Trey was wiping sweat from his forehead. Even his hands were visibly shaking. "I really think I should go to the hospital. I might be having a heart attack."

"Just pull over here. I'll walk the rest of the way." Bling got out of the car and walked past two houses, then he noticed his car had a for sale sign on it so he ran to his car and pulled on the door. "She even left my door open. I have an expensive stereo system." Bling took the sign off the windshield and ripped it to pieces.

Denise's car wasn't in the driveway, but he knew where to find the spare key under the welcome mat on the step. He didn't have his key because when Hype had taken him, everything was left in his car, and his wife had possession of his belongings. The apartment was immaculate. Nothing was out of place. He was at least expecting to see a disaster like a tornado had passed through.

"My clothes!" He ran upstairs and found the bed was neatly made. He opened the closet door, and to his surprise, all his clothes were still there.

Her perfume still lingered in the air so he knew she had just left. He picked up her favorite perfume, Gucci Guilty, and brought it to his nose. A silver frame housed a wedding picture of their happier times, and he traced the outline of his wife's lips with his finger. Suddenly, he heard loud booming music and looked out the window. Trey had his music on blast. Bling went outside in haste. "Turn that shit down," Bling called out to him.

"I always told you that your music was shit." Trey stood outside bopping his head.

"That's my song." Bling ran to the car . . .

"You big time, Money B. You getting spins on the radio."

For the first time since his release Bling felt he had something to celebrate. He felt like a free man. He was in high spirits as he took in the moment.

"I'm free. I'm free!" Bling shouted doing a celebratory dance.

"You won't be free after I call the police. Get away from here with all that ruckus," an angry neighbor shouted from her doorway.

"Sorry, just enjoying life," Bling shouted back.

"I would love to enjoy my life on a beautiful beach in the Bahamas right now drinking Piña Coladas, but I'm not, so turn that music down!"

"Drinks are on me!" Bling shouted.

"It's about time you treat me to a strong drink. Let's go!"

"Go ahead, I'll take my car." Bling walked away but turned quickly on his heels. "I got it!" he shouted.

"You damn right you got it because I'm having *three* rounds on you."

"No. I got it!" Bling repeated walking back to Trey.

"What are you saying? Are you paying or not? Why are you being cheap?" Trey asked in confusion.

"Yes, but not that. I mean . . . I got it, Trey!"

"One minute it's yes, then it's no, so which is it?" Trey questioned.

"Can you shut up and let me finish. I mean I got it," Bling said with anxiety.

"You keep saying that. What is it that you've got? You got an STD?" Trey chuckled.

"The neighbor just gave it to me."

"Are you OK, Money B?" Trey put his hand on his forehead checking his temperature. "That lady gave you a piece of her mind, that's all she gave you."

He removed Trey's hand. "Think about what she said."

"OK." Trey played along. "She said she was going to call the police."

"What's the other thing she said?" Bling asked.

"Something about the beach in the Bahamas and drinking Piña Coladas." Trey shook his head. "Where is this going? Because now I *really* need a drink."

"God was trying to tell me something." Bling still didn't get to the point.

"Trying to tell you what? That you should drink Piña Coladas?" Trey opened his car door, fed up with Bling's gibberish.

"I'm going to need your credit card," Bling blurted.

"What the hell does my credit card have to do with you, God, and the old lady?" Trey was baffled.

"Remember when you said I should do something special for my wife? Something that holds a sentimental value. Well, I have to take my wife to the Bahamas and renew our vows, and I need your credit card to book the tickets." Bling finally came out with it.

"Why me?" Trey questioned.

"I want it to be a surprise. I don't want her tracing anything back to me."

"I will do you this favor because I know it's for a good cause, but your limit is $2,000." Trey got in his car.

"I'm going to need you to increase that limit." Bling leaned in close to the window.

"Those are some expensive tickets."

"I'm going to need a ticket for the pastor too," Bling added.

"Pastor for what?" Trey asked.

"I'm going to renew my vows, and I need our pastor there to make it official." Bling tried to sell him his plan.

"OK. $2,500," Trey agreed with reservations.

"I need you to still go a little higher."

"Come on, man. What now?" Trey decided to step out of the car.

"Her sister has to be there too."

"You're paying me back with interest."

"And . . . Since it seems like you're the only friend I've got, I would love for you to be my best man," Bling announced.

Trey's keys fell from his hand. Bling picked them up and gave them to him. "What's the matter, man? You never been someone's best man before?"

"I just don't think I'm qualified to be your best man." Trey declined the offer.

"Come on, Trey. You're the only friend I have aside from my family, and at this point, you're like a brother." Bling patted his shoulder.

"I have to tell you something, and it's not good." Trey spoke with his head down.

"The only news I want is good news, so I don't want to hear it. I'll meet up with you at the bar."

CHAPTER 4

Bling started his car, and the engine roared, answering to his command. The black Ferrari showed signs of neglect. He turned his windshield wipers on washing away the settled dust.

Bling drove out of the driveway, and within minutes, he was at the car wash. He was in line with a few cars behind him when he decided to get his wallet.

"Damn it!" he cursed when his wallet didn't present itself. Bling searched his pockets hoping he would find some cash. "Shit." He cursed when he came up empty. He looked behind him wanting to back up, but it would be impossible. "Yo!" He called out to the attendant.

The man walked to his window. "What's up, man?"

"I don't have my wallet on me, so I need to get out of this line."

"What's the holdup?" another attendant asked.

"I don't have my wallet on me. I need to get out of here," Bling repeated.

"Yo, it's you," the attendant pointed at him.

Here we go. Don't tell me he's another one who thinks I should rot in jail. Bling braced himself for the insult.

"That's Bling!" the attendant shouted. "I love your music, man."

"Thanks, man," Bling humbly said.

"This wash is on me, man!" The man was overjoyed.

"I owe you one, man." Bling gave him pound. "As a matter of fact, give me your number and I'll hook you up with some tickets to a show."

The man hurriedly wrote his number and rushed back to Bling. "Here you go, man." The attendant was elated.

"What's the damn holdup?" someone shouted from behind.

"Let him through," the attendant ordered.

"What's your name, man?" Bling asked.

"Big Mac," he said, rubbing his belly.

"I got you, Big Mac." Bling put his windows up and went through the car wash. In a matter of minutes his car was back to looking brand new.

Bling stopped at a red light. The smell of fried chicken from Popeye's rushed to his nostrils, and his stomach growled. He stepped on his gas pedal trying to outrun the aroma. Next, he heard sirens behind him and took a look in his rearview mirror. He was being pulled over. "What now?" He pulled to the side.

"License and registration, please," the officer asked.

"I don't have my wallet on me," Bling replied.

"Are you aware that this car is reported stolen?"

"No, sir. But this is my car."

"How are you going to prove that with no ID? Step out of the car, sir."

"You can call my wife. She'll vouch for me." Bling did as he was told.

"Put your hands on the car where I can see them and spread your legs." The officer patted him down. "Name and address."

"Anthony Mills. 2188 Stony Brook Dr.," Bling complied.

The officer walked back to his car leaving Bling in the assumed position.

"I can't believe this shit," Bling murmured. He held his head down feeling embarrassed as nosy people passing in their vehicles stared at him.

"Well, this vehicle is, in fact, registered to an Anthony Mills, but how can you prove that it is, in fact, you?" the officer asked with a straight face.

"Can you call my wife?"

"I can't do that, but you can when you get to the station cause I have to bring you in until you can prove that you are who you said you are."

"Just do what you have to do, man."

"You have the right to remain silent . . . "

Bling didn't think he would be hearing those words anytime soon. His body was overcome with emotions. He gave his car a hard kick, and the officer found it offensive and tightened the cuffs.

"Ahh!" Bling expressed his discomfort.

"So tell me, were you on your way to the chop shop?" the officer asked, pushing him forward, leading him to the cop car where the flashing red, white, and blues were still going.

"I didn't steal shit! I told you, that's my car." Bling raised his voice.

"Are you raising your voice at me, boy?"

"Call it what you want. I said I didn't steal shit!"

The cop pushed Bling hard into the backseat, and he fell on his face.

"I'll file a lawsuit on your ass," Bling threatened.

"Keep running that mouth, you might swallow a few of those teeth," the cop warned.

He swung the door, and it came hard against Bling's foot.

"You will pay for this!" He shouted in pain. The car drove off, and Bling still was mad as hell. "This is police brutality!" The car stopped suddenly and Bling was flung forward, hitting his head on the partition.

"How is *that* for brutality?" the cop laughed.

"I'll have Al Sharpton on your ass for this!" Bling shouted.

"I'm just a black officer upholding the law. That's a protest he won't be interested in." The cop laughed out loud again.

Bling reclined his head trying to ease his headache, but the cop made sure it would be a bumpy ride for him. There wasn't a pothole that he tried to miss. When they got to the station he pulled Bling out of the car like a common criminal.

"So what's the catch of the day, Officer Jackson?" The officer on desk duty inquired.

"Just another thug running a red light and resisting arrest."

"You're a damn liar. You said I was under arrest for a stolen car."

"Add verbally assaulting an officer to that," Officer Jackson added.

"I need to make my one phone call."

"The phone is right over there." Officer Jackson pushed him toward the phone.

"Are you going to free my hands?" Bling looked back at him.

"No, I'll dial the number for you though." Officer Jackson gave him another push.

"Are you going to speak for me too?"

"It all depends. Is your wife hot or not? On second thought, maybe I should just drive by the house and check her out."

"I'll fucking kill you!" Bling was heated.

"Did you just threaten an officer?" The officer had Bling in a choke hold.

"OK, Officer Jackson, let him loose," another cop ordered.

Bling gasped for air as his body hit the floor. Officer Jackson kneeled close to him and spoke.

"The judge let you walk free, but you will pay for killing my brother." His fist jabbed into Bling, knocking the wind out of him.

"Ease up, man!" another cop call out to Officer Jackson. "Are you going to book him or not?"

"Let his ass sweat for a few hours." Officer Jackson walked away, leaving Bling breathless.

Another officer helped Bling to his feet and led him to a cell. "It seems like you have more enemies than friends, but just to let you know, you have a bounty on your head, and I just might collect." He slammed the cell door hard and walked away.

"I need to make my phone call," Bling demanded. He looked at the small bed in the corner, wanting to sit, but he was turned off by the thought of bedbugs. Instead, he scooted to the floor.

Bling felt like a caged circus animal. He was fed up with everyone who thinks his life is something they can toy with.

Bling sat deep in thought. He had a lot of problems on his plate. Starting with his wife, blackmail, and now a bounty on his head. Seconds turned to minutes, and minutes turned into hours. His mind drifted to Keisha. He wished he could have stopped the bullet from penetrating her back. But at least she wasn't dealing with the repercussions of her actions. Soon, he heard footsteps coming in his direction and he stood to his feet.

"You're free to go!" the officer called out to Bling.

Bling didn't say a word because what he wanted to say he knew he couldn't. Besides, he didn't want to spend another minute with these corrupt cops. He was escorted to the front desk and given a copy of his arrest report. "You can make your phone call." The officer pointed to the phone in the corner. But once again he kept his mouth shut and walked out of the police station.

Bling walked back to his car. It was about five blocks away. When he got there, a parking ticket was waiting on him. He ripped the ticket to shreds and proceeded to stomp the tiny pieces into the ground.

"I'm not paying shit!" He jumped into his car and sped off.

Bling had to get to Mt. Grove Cemetery. Hype's family was out to get him, and he felt like he had to pay him a visit. A few minutes later, he was at his point of interest.

"We're closed!" the guard warned.

"Come on, man. I need to visit my brother's grave. I'm here on a business trip, and I would like to visit his grave before I leave." Bling was hoping that his lie would get him in.

"We'll reopen in half an hour."

"Can't you break the rules just once? I'm on my way to catch a flight to Chicago right now."

"You better get going then before you miss your flight because you will not be getting in here."

"Don't take this the wrong way, but will fifty bucks get me in?"

"Don't bribe me, boy. I'm fixing to call the cops."

"OK. I don't want any more problems." Bling headed back to his car.

"You know nothing about bribing, boy. Add another fifty to it and you get ten minutes."

"I can definitely do that." Bling's hand went to his pocket, but he remembered he didn't have his wallet. "Goddamn it!"

"Is there a problem?" the security asked.

"No, but I'm a little embarrassed to admit that I have no idea where the grave is."

"What's your brother's name?"

"Hype. I mean Marcus Jackson—" Before he could get the name out the security guard cut him off.

"That young buck is your brother? You should have said so. I love his music. He would have been one of the best. You need to put a hit on that punk that took your brother's life. For the right price I would do it," the old man laughed.

Bling adjusted his fitted hat on his head, not wanting to be recognized. "So can we cancel that bribe?"

"You can keep your money in your pocket. I'm a fan of your brother's." The guard lifted the gate, and Bling got back in his car and drove in, but before he cleared the gate he stopped.

"Can you point me in the right direction?"

"Just go straight down and make the second right. You should see it. It's the one with the microphone."

Bling departed with a nod. A dark feeling consumed his body as he got closer. The headstone with a Bible and a microphone became visible. He parked the car at a safe distance and viewed the grave with his eyes fixated on the date: 1990–2012. They were just about the same age. The name Marcus Jackson aka Hype stood out in bold letters and gave confirmation enough that he was really dead. He shook his head trying to keep the memory of him taking Hype's life from resurfacing. Finally, he gathered his courage and walked closer to the grave.

"I didn't plan to kill you. You turned it into a war. I know you felt betrayed, but Keisha was neither yours nor mine. Now your family is out for me, and why the fuck you haunting me like a bitch in my dreams? All is fair in love and war, man, and you lost. Let it go and let me be." Bling stooped to the ground. "This shit is ruining my life."

Bling thought he heard a voice as if Hype had spoken to him. He turned quickly to look behind him and fell on his ass. He quickly jumped to his feet and did a 360 view of the cemetery.

"Hey! Your time is up," the guard called out to him.

"I'm not going to let you do this shit to me!" Bling kicked dirt from a newly dug grave awaiting the body that would soon be Hype's neighbor. "Good one, Hype." Bling laughed at himself for believing a dead man had actually spoken to him.

"All right, man!" He acknowledged the guard. "You can stop yelling now!"

Trey's house was his next destination, and he couldn't care less about breaking the speed limit. *What's another ticket compared to a thousand bullets with my name on each one?* Bling drove recklessly, not caring for his life or others'.

When he got to Trey's house he pounded on the door like he was the SWAT team going after a wanted man. "Open the damn door! I know you're in there!"

Trey opened the door, and Bling pushed past him. "What the hell happened to you? You look like shit," Trey asked with a curious look on his face.

"I was in jail." Bling walked to the kitchen.

"Good one, but I'm not buying that lie." He followed behind Bling.

"I feel like I'm haunted by Hype." Bling turned on the faucet and washed his face.

"So are you trying to tell me that Hype is the reason you went to jail?"

"Bingo!" He reached for a paper towel.

"If you didn't want to go to the bar you could've just say so. No peer pressure around here. But this bullshit excuse, I'm not buying."

"You want proof? Here it is." He brought his hand to his back pocket, then came forth with a piece of paper and gave it to Trey.

"What is this?" Trey asked, taking the document.

"My proof!" Bling answered.

"Assault, resisting arrest—"

"All lies." Bling cut him off as he read the list of charges. "You were right; they are not going to stop until I'm six feet under."

"Why would the cops have a problem with you?" Trey seemed puzzled.

"Not the cops. Officer Jackson. Hype's brother."

"So what's your next move?" Trey asked.

"I won't go down without a fight, but right now, I want to fix my marriage before I die or go back to jail. I want my wife to know I love her. So are you ready to take a trip to the Bahamas or not?"

"I can't, man. I have to work on my album." Trey gave another excuse.

"Come on, Trey, it's only for a few days," Bling pressured.

"I have a deadline to finish the album, man. Besides, you guys are already married. You don't need the whole shebang."

"I want it to be official; besides, I need you there for mental support." Bling kept pushing.

"How the hell are you going to pull this secret off?"

"Believe it or not, I have to get her father involved."

"Really? I would think that her family would want to throw you to the wolves."

"Her father always treated me like his son. So, I figure if I go to him with my true intentions, he will give me his blessing again."

"Just as long as you don't add a ticket for him too."

"Well . . . "

"Come on, man!" Trey left the kitchen.

"I'm just kidding," Bling laughed. "I'm going home to wash these jail cell germs off me." Bling was out the door when Trey stopped him.

"Let me ask you a serious question. Is it over with boss lady?"

Bling's focus on mending his marriage hadn't allowed him to put a serious thought toward Keisha. But he knew he owed her the respect of visiting her in the hospital. He got in his car and drove off without giving Trey an answer. Bling considered about going home to take a shower and getting his wallet, but he decided against it and drove to the hospital.

He parked his car on the third floor of the multilevel parking lot. The ground level wasn't an option because he saw a news camera van parked outside, and dealing with the media wasn't anything he wanted to do today.

"May I help you?" the lady at the desk asked as if someone was forcing her to do her job.

"Do you mind telling me what room Keisha Burkett is in?"

"I need to see your ID." She extended her hand without looking at him.

"I don't have it on me."

"Well, I can't give you any information on that patient." She turned her back, dismissing Bling.

"I have to see her. You just don't understand."

"I guess you need to understand that without an ID or you being an immediate family member I can't give out any information." She continued doing her paperwork.

"I need to see her now!" Bling demanded, pounding his fist on the nurse's desk. Everyone in the waiting area's eyes focused on him as his voice traveled throughout the hallway of the hospital.

"Sir, I already told you that we can only give access to immediate family members." She gave a neck roll.

"I *am* her family! I am her . . . " *What am I to her?* Bling questioned himself.

"I'm waiting to hear it. You are her what, sir?"

Bling kicked the empty chair, causing it to flip over.

"Security to the nurses' station!" the angry oversized nurse yelled in the intercom. She placed her hands at her hip, making Bling aware that she wasn't going to budge.

"I suggest that you walk out of this hospital without causing anymore disturbance."

Bling turned his head to see a security guard standing several feet behind him with a can of mace pointing in his direction ready to spray.

"If I wasn't so damn pissed off I would take the time to laugh at you looking like a damn clown," Bling insulted.

"Insulting a high-ranking security guard isn't wise and don't think for one second that I won't spray your face with this mace, boy."

Bling realized that his attempt to see Keisha was futile and in that moment he knew he had to take another approach; besides, getting banned from the hospital wasn't his intention.

"OK, you win." Bling put his hands up and surrendered.

"Get out of here and go calm your damn nerves. You young bucks don't know how to control your tempers. But not on my damn watch."

Bling went back to his car and left the parking lot. He slowed to a crawl as he drove by the hospital viewing the twelve-story building, scanning the windows, wondering which could be Keisha's.

The only person Bling knew he would be able to get any updates from would be Derrick, but he didn't have his phone. Remembering that there was a Jamaican restaurant at the end of the block he pressed on the gas. A car pulled out when he got to the restaurant, and he did a parallel park. He pulled open the restaurant door, which caused a bell to ring alerting of a customer.

"How can I help you?" a lady asked with a thick accent.

"Is it possible for me to use your phone?"

"Are you buying something?" She gave him a neck roll.

"Let di man use di phone," the chef yelled at her.

"Why don't you mind your business?" she shouted at the chef.

"Here you go, my youth. Just make it quick." The chef came from around the back and gave Bling the phone.

"Respect. Mi appreciate it." Bling brought his accent to light.

Bling dialed Trey's number and waited for him to answer, but he only got voice mail. He ended the call and started to dial the number again.

"Yuh get permission fi one call, not two. Hand over the phone." The lady stopped him from dialing.

Bling didn't hesitate. He handed her the phone, and she rolled her eyes at him. He began to walk away, but the phone started to ring so he paused just in case it was Trey calling back.

"Hello, Island Cuisine," the lady answered the phone. "This is a restaurant. Why would we call you?"

"I think that's my call. Can I talk to him?"

"This phone is a business phone not for personal use," she scolded him.

"You gossip on dat phone all damn day. Give di man di phone," the chef spoke.

She extended her hand with the phone toward Bling, and he rushed to get it.

"Trey, it's Bling. I need you to hook me up with Derrick. Don't worry about that, just do it." Bling remained silent for a moment while Trey connected him. "Derrick, it's Bling. Do you have any updates on Keisha?"

CHAPTER 5

Bling stood on the patio overlooking the white sandy beach. The cool Bahamas breeze gently caressed his face. He watched as the hotel workers decorated the perfect spot in the sand where he would renew his vows. His heart was racing as doubts consumed him, not knowing if his wife would forgive him. He had managed to convince his father-in-law to entrust his daughter to him again by expressing his love and his regrets. Her father concocted a story about sending her and her sister away to the Bahamas to unwind, and Denise accepted her father's offer.

Bling also had a brilliant idea on how to get his wife to attend the ceremony without blowing his cover. He placed invitations under a few of the hotel guests' doors with an earlier time printed, and then he had a hotel worker place an invitation under his wife's door with the right starting time. The guests would show up before his wife arrived, and in that case, she would be convinced that she too was also a guest.

"I have to start from somewhere. Hopefully, when I ask her to remarry me she will know that I'm truly sorry." Bling gazed out at the ocean. It was peaceful and soothing. The waves were calm and welcoming, and he felt at peace. "Seems like today will be a good day." Bling raised his glass in a toast.

There was a knock at the door. He placed his drink on the table. "That must be the pastor." He opened the door. Pastor Blake was on time.

"I hope you didn't get dressed up for me," the pastor joked. He was a replica of T. D. Jakes. People always say everyone has a twin out there somewhere.

"Come in, Mr. Blake." Bling stepped aside for him to enter.

"It seems like you mean business. Flying me down to the beautiful Bahamas, and you know I wouldn't say no to an island vacation."

"Yeah, and now I'm way overbudget." Bling escorted him to the sitting area.

"So man to man, what the hell went wrong? Excuse my French." Pastor Blake took his seat.

"I signed my contract, and in the process, I got tempted." Bling also seated himself.

"Well, in that business, temptation comes in many forms, like drugs, alcohol, and, of course, sex. But here is the question: Are you over your mistress? Because I understand that it wasn't a one-time thing. It was ongoing." The pastor crossed his legs, getting comfortable.

"I tried to stop, but I kept going back for more. There was an instant connection." Bling too crossed his legs.

"Was it a sexual or mental connection?" Pastor Blake asked.

"A little of both," Bling answered without hesitation.

"The mental part is what keeps you going back as much as you want to think it's the sex. But before I can proceed with reconnecting you to your wife I have to know from the horse's mouth. Are you over your mistress? And I want you to take a minute to think. Search your heart and soul, because only you know the truth." Pastor Blake wanted Bling to be honest with him.

"There is no denying that I love my wife, and that's all that matters, but I can only hope this beautiful scenery will do the trick." Bling got up and walked back to the patio.

"The scenery is beautiful, but that's just the icing on the cake. Listen to me; if you don't mean business, don't jump the broom. Take some time to think about it." Pastor Blake patted him on the shoulder.

"I'm already here; there's no turning back. I only hope that her sister hasn't already convinced her to file for a divorce." Bling kept his eyes on the water.

"Her sister can't force her to do what she doesn't feel is right, but look at it from your wife's point of view. You took a man's life to protect your mistress, and that is priceless. But the diamond ring on your wife's finger has a price tag." Pastor Blake gave him some food for thought and walked away.

"What's that supposed to mean? I don't understand all that parable talk." Bling went after him.

"It's simple. In your wife's head, you gave her up. You were willing to give up your freedom to protect your mistress, so in her eyes, you already filed for a divorce. If anything, she will only put it in writing. But let's hope she finds it in her heart to forgive you." He spoke with his hand on Bling's shoulder.

"I can only hope." Bling took a seat.

"This is not how I usually work. I would like to do some counseling with your wife as well, but I'm just a man like you, so if you feel like this way is best, who am I to judge?"

There was a knock, and Pastor Blake and Bling both brought their attention to the door.

"That must be Trey." Bling went to the door.

"Money B! You ready for this, man?"

"Why wouldn't I be? I know what I want, and that's my wife."

"Are you sure about that? We're in the Bahamas and there are all ethnicities of females on vacation. We could play all day in the sun. So what do you say?" Trey tried to coerce Bling to join in his escapades.

"Stay away from the rum punch." Bling left him at the door.

"What happens on the island stays on the island." Trey came in after him.

Pastor Blake cleared his throat, making his presence known.

"Pastor Blake, this is Trey, the bad influence." Bling introduced the pastor to the devil.

"Young man, your friend is trying to do the right thing. So don't go planting any bad seeds in his head now."

"I was just testing him to see where his head is at. I meant no harm. Forgive me, Pastor, for I have sinned." Trey got down on his knees at the pastor's feet.

"Get up, boy! We all have sinned, but it's up to you to repent of those sins."

"OK, Pastor, man to man. I mean pastor to man. I mean . . . " Trey tried to address the pastor respectfully.

"Whatever is comfortable for you, son. Go ahead."

"I have a scenario. If I happen to give in to a woman in need who was also married but in that moment she needed to be loved, is my action justified?" Trey asked, trying to clear his conscience.

"In my opinion, once a woman is married she's off-limits regardless of her needs or wants," Pastor Blake spoke pointing his finger.

"You're going to hell, man." Bling patted Trey on the back.

"Who are we to judge? Leave that to the man upstairs," Pastor Blake interjected.

"You are my type of guy. I mean, you are my type of pastor, Mr. Blake." Trey still struggled with how he should address the pastor.

Pastor Blake looked at his watch. "OK, boys, it's time to go take our positions in the sand."

"OK. Trey, this is the plan," Bling spoke.

"What plan, Money B?" Trey kept walking to the door.

"When we get off the elevator I want you to scope the lobby since my wife isn't familiar with your face."

"What you really need to plan for is her not coming out of her room to celebrate a wedding when she's nursing a broken heart." Trey opened the door.

All three men headed to the elevator. Pastor Blake said a short prayer, and they all said amen. When the elevator came to a stop, Trey got off first and scoped the lobby as planned because he couldn't let on that he had met his friend's wife up close and personal.

"The coast is clear," he called, and the men came out of hiding and rushed out the door. They approached the beach, and the setup was spectacular. The scenery was breathtaking. A gazebo displayed a variety of tropical flowers marking the spot for the bride and groom to recite their vows. Two pieces of white linen draped along each side of the arch danced in the wind. Six chairs decorated with flowers sat on both sides, leaving a pathway that represented the aisle. Bling took the stroll up the aisle with the pastor by his side.

"Where did Trey disappear to?" Bling asked aloud.

"That young man is chasing everything that moves," Pastor Blake chuckled.

Bling positioned himself, and his heart pounded in his chest.

"How are you feeling, my son?" Pastor Blake patted his back.

"My heart is racing," he answered.

"I recall you giving her a scare on your wedding day when she showed up at the church and you weren't there."

Bling's mind drifted to that day. He was on the way to the church but decided to get a tattoo of his wife's name on his arm to calm his jitters despite the protest of his best man. When he finally made it to the church an hour late the entire congregation stood to their feet clapping.

"I guess we will be having a wedding after all," Pastor Blake announced with his raspy voice. *"Young man, we were starting to think that you were a runaway groom."*

"I'm here and ready to make my woman my wife," Bling remembered saying, and the church applauded again.

"You heard the man, let's get started then," Pastor Blake said gleefully.

"Your first guests have arrived," Pastor Blake informed Bling, but he was still reliving his wedding day. Pastor Blake nudged his shoulder.

"Thank you for coming," Bling greeted the couple that was already seated on the left.

Two more couples joined them, and they sat on the right side.

"Welcome," Pastor Blake acknowledged the couples.

"I could surely use a strong drink right now." Bling was getting nervous.

"Just say a prayer. That will calm your nerves."

A single female was walking toward them, and her silhouette resembled his wife's sister. Bling started to panic because his wife wasn't with her.

"Everything is ruined, everything is ruined." Bling stooped to the ground.

"What are you panicking about?" Pastor asked.

"My wife's sister, isn't that her approaching?" Bling remained close to the ground.

"Not from what I can see." Pastor Blake focused on the woman.

Bling held his head up and took a better look. It wasn't his wife's sister.

"Welcome, young lady," Pastor Blake greeted as the woman got closer.

"Thank you," the young lady answered back.

"This young man is in a panic because this is a surprise he concocted to win his wife back. So let's hope the surprise isn't ruined," Pastor Blake enlightened the guests.

"I hope we didn't miss the wedding!" a chirpy young girl with a much-older man spoke very loud with a southern accent. The gentleman sat on a chair, and the young lady sat in his lap. "We just got married, and we're on our honeymoon," the vibrant girl said, then kissed her husband on the lips.

"Here she comes," Pastor Blake announced.

"What do I do?" Bling was panicking.

"Get down on your knees. She won't see you," Pastor Blake advised.

"Is she here yet?" Bling asked, not being able to see.

"They stopped."

"Is she turning back?" Bling became concerned.

"Yes. Wait! No. They're taking their shoes off," Pastor relayed their activity.

"What is she doing now?" Bling impatiently asked.

"She's laughing."

"That's good, but is she coming or not?"

"OK. She's walking. They're getting closer and closer . . . and she's here."

"Pastor Blake, is that you?" Denise asked in an astounded tone.

"It's me in the flesh," he said with a smile.

"What are you doing here? I take that back. It's quite obvious you are officiating a wedding. It's a small world after all." She took a seat.

"Denise, can you join me, please." Pastor Blake stretched his hand forward.

"You're not going to ask me to give a speech, are you? Because I'm really bad at it."

Denise proceeded to the front, and the violinist started to play. Pastor Blake met her halfway and escorted her to the front. Bling stood to his feet, and Denise placed her hand over her heart.

"Oh, hell, no." Madison ran to her sister's side. "So you think you can win my sister back with this setup and these people that she doesn't even know?" Madison was furious.

"What's going on?" Denise asked.

"Are you blind, Denise?" Madison stepped in the middle, separating her sister from Bling. "This is your wedding. You aren't a guest. You are the *bride*."

"Your husband has something to say, and I think you should hear it, and then it's up to you where you go from there," Pastor Blake counseled.

"If it was up to me he would be castrated," Madison added.

"Well, thank God it's not up to you, Miss Madison, because what God has joined together let no man put asunder." Pastor Blake quoted the Bible.

"Denise, I know I messed up, and I want to make it right." Bling took his wife's hands into his, but Madison separated them.

"The right thing to do is to let my sister kick you in the nuts, cut your heart out, and then I can watch you bleed to death with a smile on my face," Madison said smiling.

"Miss Madison, can you please stay out of it. Go for a walk or something." Pastor Blake had enough of her chiming in.

"No. My sister stays," Denise said firmly.

"That's right, Pastor, I stay. I'm not going to let you or this parasite convince my sister to do anything." Madison did a neck roll.

"I brought you here because I would like to renew our vows." Bling got down on his knee as if he was going to propose to her again. "I gave in to temptation, and it almost cost me my life and my wife. It wasn't my intention to bring you pain. I've destroyed my marriage. I destroyed us." He covered his face and tried to compose himself.

"Let it out, son," Pastor Blake encouraged.

"As a man we all search for a woman of virtue, and I found her in you. I know I didn't make a mistake choosing you as my wife. I have the best. You are my everything." Bling spoke from his heart. Tears escaped Denise's eyes, and she let them travel down her face.

"Not on my damn watch!" Madison tried to break up their union, but Pastor Blake held her back.

"I will make it right. I promise. Let me show you I can be the man I should be. I love you. Let me take away your pain." Bling wiped her tears.

"I messed up too," Denise confessed.

"No. I'm the one that messed up. I did this to us." Bling took the blame.

"I just want my husband back," Denise spoke, looking into Bling's eyes.

"Does this mean that I can carry on with the renewing of your vows?" Pastor spoke.

"Yes," Denise answered. The guests stood to their feet clapping.

"If you won't tell him I will," Madison threatened her sister.

"Don't do this, Madison. There's nothing to tell." Denise tried to stop her from talking.

"You don't need him, Denise. Don't do this," Madison warned.

"I love my husband, and I'm accepting his apology." Denise stood facing her husband.

"Are you going to tell him you cheated?" Madison dropped the bomb, and the guests gasped.

Denise turned to her sister. "Don't you want me to be happy? Why would you want to ruin my life? Take it back! Tell him it's a lie."

"Am I lying, sis?" Madison smiled evilly.

"You just don't want me to be happy. You would do anything to ruin this for us." Denise turned to Pastor Blake. "You can proceed with the ceremony."

"Do you, Denise Mills and Anthony Mills, recommit your love for each other and forsaking all others?"

"I won't be a witness to this, and you, Pastor Blake, can go to hell." Madison bumped shoulders with Bling as she left the ceremony.

"I don't plan on it. But I can prevent you from diving in headfirst," Pastor Blake replied.

Bling embraced his wife, and they held each other tightly.

"We do," they both answered.

"You may kiss your wife."

Bling kissed his wife, and the guests cheered. The violinist played, and Bling lifted his wife off her feet, carrying her to their room.

Bling laid his wife on the carpeted floor. Piece by piece he undressed her body. Her erect nipples pointed up at him, and he didn't hesitate to greet them. His tongue ran tracks around them as he tried to ignite her body like the Olympic torch. Bling explored his wife's body, slowly making his way down to her shaven haven, placing multiple kisses all over her haven.

"Daddy's home." Bling beat his chest like a gorilla.

Denise spread her legs enticing her husband. He dived in headfirst for his feast, eating the appetizer, not leaving a crumb. Her body was calling out to him, and he was going to answer. Bling released himself from his pants and his love stick was wooden. He slowly entered his wife, and she expressed her satisfaction with her nails deep in his bare back. He fed his wife the main course, and her appetite was hungry for more. He gave her all of him.

He played her tune, and she danced to every beat. Bling was at his climax, and Denise was right there with him. Then they lay on the floor out of breath in the missionary position, holding each other as if they were conjoined twins.

His wife fell asleep in his arms, and he watched her in amazement. The way she breathed, the way she slept with a smile on her face. Her eyes were puffy, and he could tell she had been crying because of his actions. He scooped his wife's naked body off the floor and brought her to the bed.

There was a knock at the door. Bling wrapped himself with a towel and hurried to the door, using the peephole to confirm who the nuisance was because he thought for sure it would be Madison, but to his surprise, it was Trey.

"What the hell happened to you earlier?" Bling fired at him.

"I was feeling sick, so I went back to my room. So how did it go?" Trey asked out of curiosity.

"She forgave me, man, and I would rather be admiring my wife than to be looking at you right now." Bling attempted to close the door.

"I just spoke to Derrick." Trey pushed the door open.

"And . . .?" Bling was less than interested.

"Don't worry about it, man. Go be with your wife." Trey walked away.

"You wouldn't have come to the door if you didn't want to tell me what Derrick had to say, so spill it. Does this have something to do with my contract?" Bling had half his body out the door.

"Kind of, but not really. It all depends on how you look at it."

"You're starting to get under my skin. I don't have time for this." Bling brought his body back inside.

"The sleeping lioness is awake," Trey blurted.

"What the fuck is that supposed to mean?"

"Think about it, man."

Bling didn't think for long before he cracked the code. He closed the door with Trey still standing there. Quietly, he dressed himself and left the room. Bling went to the hotel bar and ordered Hennessey on the rocks. The ordeal of what they went through plagued his mind. He ordered one refill after the next, trying to drown his memory. The bar cut him off when they realize he was past his limit. Bling staggered back upstairs to his room and settled for the couch.

"I was wondering where you were hiding." Denise flipped on the light switch, invading his space. Bling shielded his face with his hand, giving his eyes time to adjust to the light. "Why are you sitting in the dark, babe?"

"Whatever you're selling I'm not buying. So you can leave me alone." He fanned her off.

"Babe, it's me." Denise kneeled in front of him.

Bling tried to focus his eyes, but all his senses by now were impaired. He had consumed way more than his body could tolerate.

"Were you drinking?" she asked when the smell raced to her nostrils.

"Bartender, give me another one." He raised his hand pointing his index finger.

"Babe, you're not at the bar. You're here with me."

"Can you call me a cab? I don't think I'm in no shape to drive home." He tried sitting up, but he fell back down.

"Babe, it's me! Look at me!" Denise took ahold of his shoulders and shook him.

"I see . . . " he pointed with his finger, "one, two, three little pigs," he said with his eyes partially closed.

"Babe, it's me." Denise grabbed his face and focused it on her.

"Is it really you?" Bling slowly brought his body to an upright position, extending his arm to touch her face, but he was seeing double and his vision was blurry.

"Who else would it be?" Denise took his hand bringing it to her face.

"It can't be. But you . . . " Bling widened his eyes trying to concentrate, but his brain wasn't communicating with his eyes. His vision was still a blur.

"You just had too much to drink, babe. It's really me."

"You came back to me." He focused his eyes on the silhouette that was before him and eagerly kissed her. "Promise you won't leave me again. I won't let you go. You just came back to me. You can't leave me again." Like a blind man he extended his arm finding her body. He gave her a tight embrace. "Promise me you won't leave me again, Keisha."

Denise's five fingers greeted his cheek hard. "What part of me looks like your damn mistress?" Denise was throwing fists to his body, and he fell to the floor. Her right and left wanted to beat him senseless.

Bling could barely defend himself. His attempts to strong-arm his wife was pitiful. She had the energy of a wild beast.

She backed away looking at him with sadness in her eyes.

"Come back here, Keisha." Bling reached for her.

"I'm not your damn whore of a mistress. I'm your wife. I'm your *wife!*" Tears flowed from her eyes.

"Are you crying, Keisha? I'm here, baby." Bling slowly raised his body. "Did I say something wrong?"

"This is wrong. *You* are wrong. I'm *not* your damn mistress, I'm your *wife!*"

She walked away from him, but her legs gave out. She scrambled backward before she got back on her feet and ran out of the room. Bling brought himself to stand and took a few steps forward, but his legs had no stability. It was more like a baby learning to walk. He fell to the floor hard, and he lay there without any attempts to get up.

"This should wake your ass up!" Denise dumped a pitcher of cold water on his face. Bling struggled to catch his breath, as if he was drowning. His breathing was short, as if he was having an asthma attack. He sat on his ass and looked deep in his wife's eyes.

"Are you trying to kill me!" he yelled at her.

"No, I'm just bringing your ass back to reality."

CHAPTER 6

"Bingo! And my name shall be Derrick." Bling exited his car. "This plan has to work," he convinced himself as he made his way to the hospital. He had caught an early flight back from the Bahamas, selling his wife a lie that Derrick had scheduled an emergency meeting to discuss his contract, and she fell for it.

"What's my damn plan?" Bling stopped on the sidewalk in front the hospital. "I'm going to pretend to be Derrick, that's the plan," he answered himself as he proceeded to the door. "But what if the same nurse is on duty? You didn't think that through, did you?" He stopped short of the door, doubting his plan. "I didn't think about that." It's like he had the angel and the devil both perched on each shoulder. He exhaled aloud. "I should just scrap this crazy idea." He departed from the hospital entrance. "But I need to let her know that I didn't abandon her."

"And people call *me* crazy," a homeless man spoke aloud for Bling to hear after he observed Bling talking to himself.

"I have to make sure she's OK. I have to do this." When the automatic door opened, Bling stepped in but swiftly moved to the corner, scoping the room. "Yes," he exclaimed when he saw a different nurse at the desk. Not wanting to jump the gun, he scoped the area again, making sure that the boisterous nurse wasn't around. Convincing himself that the coast was clear he started in pursuit to the desk.

"Don't forget that you have to train the new volunteer."

He heard the familiar voice and quickly made a U-turn. "Damn it," he said in disappointment. Bling went back to the corner and repositioned himself so he could better view the desk.

The boisterous nurse raised her head from behind the desk and spoke. "Cathy, you should take your break now because it's bound to get busy sooner than later. On second thought, I have to go up to pediatric, so you have to take your break when I get back." Her voice echoed in the room.

"Today must be my lucky day." Bling was relieved.

He followed her with his eyes, watching as the nurse got on the elevator, then he swiftly walked over to the desk and put on the charm. The young nurse was smitten and a wide smile took over her face. Her bubbly personality was much more suitable for the hospital than that of the previous nurse.

"You have a beautiful smile," Bling complimented with a smile.

"Thank you." the nurse smiled back at him.

"I know a beautiful lady like yourself gets lots of compliments all day," Bling continued with the charm.

"No. You are actually the first." She engaged the conversation.

Bling took a quick observation of the room. "Well, I guess these people are all blind."

She was thoroughly smitten, and her smile spread wide. "How may I help you?"

"In many ways, but for now I'll start with one. Do you mind telling me what room Miss Burkett is in?"

She entered the name into the computer. "I'm not sure I can," she informed him with her eyes still on the computer screen.

"Why is that?" Bling asked while trying to remain cool.

She brought her attention back to Bling. "I'm not allowed to give information on Miss Burkett unless you are on the visiting list, so can I have your name, please."

"Well, that shouldn't be a problem. I'm Derrick McDonald in the flesh. The man who also would love to take you out on a date," Bling flirted, hoping if the name didn't get him in maybe his charisma would do the trick.

A smile invaded her face once more. "OK, let's see. Yes, you are. Derrick McDonald. Her business partner, I see."

"Wow. Does it also have my Social Security Number and address too? I don't want you stalking me now," Bling joked.

"I see that you're a comedian too. But I need your ID for verification, and then you'll have the room number."

Shit. Bling wasn't expecting the hospital to enforce a security checkpoint. He started to feel his pockets as if searching for his wallet. "I seem to have left my wallet in the car. Are you going to make me go all the way back to my car to get it?" he asked with a sad puppy dog face.

"Yes, because I don't want to lose my job," she spoke with assertion.

"Who's going to know? It's not like I'm not on the visiting list." Bling was a little irate.

She was uncomfortable with his tone. "I can't."

"What about if you just turn the computer screen toward me? Technically, you didn't tell me anything." Bling kept pushing his luck.

"I'm not allowed to," she spoke with a slight quiver in her voice.

Bling was getting irritated. The information he needed was on the screen, and she wouldn't let him have it. "Listen, I'm her business partner, and I have to make a crucial decision. I just need her to confirm the go-ahead."

"How do you expect her to confirm anything when she has amnesia?"

"Amnesia?" Bling was in total shock.

"But you knew that already, right?" the nurse questioned his reaction.

Bling found an angle that he could use to his advantage. "Actually, I had no idea, which means you've just violated patient confidentiality, and I can report you for that."

"I can lose my job," the nurse panicked.

"Give me the room number and I can sweep this under the rug or you can keep wasting my time and you will, in fact, lose your job. Do I make myself clear?" he threatened.

The nurse was in a predicament that she didn't want to be in. The elevator door opened, and both Bling and the nurse looked.

"My supervisor." Cathy was panicking, and so was Bling.

"Room number—or else," Bling threatened through gritted teeth.

"Room 205," she said out of fear.

Bling darted off in the opposite direction of the approaching nurse. "Damn, that was close." He turned the corner and braced his back against the wall. "Will she even know who I am?" Bling proceeded down the hallway in the hopes of finding another elevator, and he did.

Bling was very anxious. He hadn't seen Keisha since she was placed in the ambulance and he was carted off to jail. The nights he spent in jail weren't anything he wanted to relive, but if he had to save Keisha's life again, he would. His heart was pounding fast as the elevator came to a stop and he stepped off it in pursuit of Keisha.

"*Paging Dr. Francis to room 205 stat,*" the voice came over the intercom. He quickened his steps with an urgency to get to the room. "203, 204 . . ." he said the numbers aloud as he passed by the rooms. He was footsteps away from room 205 when a doctor and a nurse ran with urgency beating him to the room.

"Sorry, sir, but you can't go in when the doctor is in there." A nurse denied him entry.

"What's going on?" Bling asked in a panic.

"Miss Burkett, I'm Doctor Francis. I know you have lots of questions, but I would rather that you relax."

"Sir, you can't be in here," the nurse bluntly stated.

"What's going on?" Bling asked again as the nurse escorted him out of the room. The only view he had of the room was through the 4-by-6-inch glass on the wooden door that allowed him limited visibility.

"Why am I in the hospital?" Keisha asked, ripping the IV and other tubes from her arm. The machine let off multiple beeps, but that didn't stopped her from trying to free herself.

"Calm down, Miss Burkett. I'm going to help you understand why you are here."

"So tell me, why am I here? Because these nurses are dodging my questions and are giving me sleeping pills to shut me up."

"They aren't allowed to answer certain questions, and I was engaged elsewhere so I will apologize for not getting to you much faster. But if you can just relax and give me a chance to do my evaluation . . ." Dr. Francis tried to calm her.

"Do what you have to so I can get out of here." She reclined on the bed.

Dr. Francis shined a small light into her eyes checking her pupils, and then listened to her heartbeat.

"We already informed your family so you should be seeing familiar faces soon."

"The only face I want to see is my husband's. Where is he?"

"Tell me the last thing that you remember, Miss Burkett." He took her hand in his checking her pulse.

"Please call me Keisha, or Mrs. Harvey will do. I'm a married woman now."

"OK, Keisha. Why don't you tell me your last memory?" He took a small notepad from his breast pocket and jotted down his notes.

"I got married a week ago at the courthouse to my husband Damien Harvey. We went to Florida for our honeymoon, and we just got back last night. So tell me why am I waking up in a damn hospital bed?"

"I see. What month is this?" Dr. Francis continued to write his notes.

"Is this supposed to be a trick question? I'm not in the mood for a questionnaire. But the answer is May." She rolled her eyes. She was growing impatient by his multiple inquires.

"Interesting." Dr. Francis jotted down more notes.

"I've had enough of your twenty-one questions, now are you going to tell me how the hell I ended up in the hospital?" She pressed on the button bringing her posture to an upright position. "Ouch!" she let out a painful sound when she felt a sharp pain in her back. She surrendered to the pain and brought her body back down.

"You came in with a gunshot wound to your back. That should explain the pain you just felt. You were also comatose for two weeks," the doctor spoke looking intently at Keisha.

"Doc, I think you need to visit the psych ward." She busted out laughing. "Two weeks in a coma? I told you I just got back from my honeymoon last night."

There was a knock at the door and both Keisha's and Dr. Francis's head turned at the same time.

"Dr. Francis, can you step out for a minute please?" Nurse Reed interrupted. Dr. Francis didn't hesitate. He headed to the door.

"What's wrong with her, Doc?" Bling impatiently asked.

"If you're a family member I'll fill you in momentarily." The doctor turned his back and walked to the nurse's station and Bling sneaked in the room.

"Who the hell are you?" Keisha asked.

Bling was astonished by her query. "It's me. It's me. Bling."

"Am I supposed to know who you are? This is getting even weirder by the minute."

"Nurse Reed, can you escort him out, please?" Doctor Francis ordered.

"I have to get out of here." Keisha made a second attempt to get off the bed.

"Calm down, Miss Burkett. I know all this isn't making sense to you, but in time it will." The doctor spoke in a tranquil tone, hoping to calm her.

"I know what you're up to. You are trying to make me think that I'm crazy." Keisha was in a panic. "You people are crazy. I need my husband!" she yelled.

"I don't have a husband on file for you, but your father was contacted so you will be with family soon," Nurse Reed tried to console her.

"Don't you dare come any closer. It all makes sense now; my father put you up to this!"

"Miss Burkett, your father didn't put us up to anything. Besides, he's been here every day to check up on you," Nurse Reed assured her.

"You people plotted with my father to kidnap me and you are holding me hostage." She ripped the remaining tubes from her arm.

"Calm down, Miss Burkett. I can guarantee you that we are not holding you hostage." Dr. Francis tried to calm her down.

"What have you done to my husband? Where is he?"

"I know this is all confusing to you, but you are experiencing amnesia. Not necessarily caused by the gunshot wound, but it can be triggered by traumatic events that occurred in a person's life," Dr. Francis explained.

"Hah! What a joke. My life is perfect except for the fact that I ran away from home as a teen. So tell me, Doc, what the hell is so traumatic about that?"

"I understand how all this can be confusing to you, but we have your best interest at heart." Dr. Francis folded his arms.

Keisha walked up to him. "Well, if you're not holding me hostage or plotting with my father, let me walk out of here."

"I'm afraid I can't do that." He shook his head. "I have to release you in the custody of an immediate family member."

"I need my husband!" She turned away from the doctor. "You can't fool me. I know my father put you up to this." Keisha pounded her fist on the window. "Help! Somebody please help me!" she called out, hoping to be rescued by the passersby on the street.

"I'm here, baby girl." Her father rushed into the room.

Keisha locked eyes with her father. "I should have known that you were in on this. You will do anything to stop me from living my life the way I want to."

"That's not true," her father defended himself.

"You are going to have me committed. You are plotting to say I'm crazy." She started banging the window again. "Help! Please help me!"

"You aren't crazy, baby girl." Her father wore a puzzled look. "What is she talking about, Doctor?"

"Is this your payback for me running away from home?" She approached her father.

"Baby girl, we are past that now. We made amends, remember?"

"How could we, when I haven't seen you since I was sixteen. But I have news for you. I'm now twenty-one years old and a married woman." She held her hand up, but there was no ring on her finger. "Where's my ring?" she hurried back to the bed, frantically searching through the sheets.

"What's wrong with my daughter? What did you do to her?" her father frantically asked.

"Your daughter is suffering from amnesia. Meaning she has gaps in her memory. She has reverted to a time in her life that was significant to her." The doctor observed Keisha's antics.

"What time was that and how do we get her back to the present?" her father asked looking at his daughter desperately searching for her ring. He had recently gotten back in her life and was looking forward to having good times. But now she had reverted to the time in her life when she despised him the most.

"The best thing for her right now is not to force her to remember, but to try to relive this part of her life with her, and from what I hear, you weren't a part of it."

Tears ran from her father's eyes. He wiped his face, but they kept coming. Dr. Francis passed him some tissue.

"The best thing for you to do is to find the young man that she was or is married to and see if he will come on board since he was present in this era of her life."

"You damn bitch! You stole my ring!" Keisha pointed her finger at Nurse Reed. "Where is it?"

"Baby girl, calm down. You need to relax. I'll help you find your ring." Her father took a few steps toward her, but she lashed out at him.

"Stay away from me!" She broke down into tears. "I need my husband!" She backed herself toward the corner trying to get away from her father. "I need my husband!" Keisha retreated into the corner.

All eyes watched her in complete silence. She appeared to be scared and confused. Bling came in the room again, and all eyes went to him.

"Who gave you permission to be here? Your name is not on the visiting list." Keisha's father took out his frustration.

"I need my husband!" she covered her ears. "I'm not going crazy. I'm not going crazy," she recited in tears.

"What have you people done to her?" Bling questioned. "I'm taking her out of here." He walked toward her but was blocked by her father.

"You aren't taking her anywhere! *You* are the reason why she's in this situation. Go home to your wife. Haven't you done enough damage?"

His words cut Bling like a knife, and he felt guilty, even though he knew he wasn't at fault.

"They're holding me hostage. They are trying to tell me that I have a gunshot wound. I have no enemies. Who the hell would want to kill me? My father is in on this, so you can't trust him. Please get me out of here."

Bling was looking at Keisha in amazement. He couldn't believe his eyes or his ears.

"You need to help me locate my husband. You need to be my witness." She wiped her tears. "They stole my wedding ring, and they won't call my husband, and as far as I know, they are probably holding him hostage in another room."

Bling wanted to touch her. He wanted her to know that they shared a bond. He extended his hand to her. She hesitated for a moment, and then she extended hers. She slowly got up off the floor keeping her eyes on him. Bling wrapped his arms around her, but she pushed him away and stepped away from him.

"What the hell are you doing? How dare you! I don't even know who you are."

Bling couldn't believe she was treating him like a stranger. This was the woman who almost ended his marriage. Bling searched her eyes for any glimmer of hope that she remembered who he was. But her eyes told no tales of ever knowing him.

"You need to leave this room now!" her father demanded.

Bling slowly walked out of the room heartbroken and disappointed. A feeling of emptiness consumed his body. He wanted to get to the elevator faster than his feet would allow. His breathing got heavy as he tried to fight back all his emotions. "Hold the door!" he called out as a man exited the elevator. The man obeyed, and he hurriedly stepped in. The door closed, and he hunched over, putting his hands on his knees, inhaling and exhaling deeply as if he was fighting to get air to his lungs.

"I can't accept this. How am I supposed to accept this? Is this supposed to be my punishment?" He pumped his fist into the elevator. "Is this my punishment for cheating on my wife? You are so unfair! She doesn't deserve this!" Bling continuously threw punches at the elevator, sobbing. "Why did you give me a heart if I am not supposed to love?" Tears ran from his eyes. "It's not fair!" He braced himself and slid to the floor. "You took her from me. You took her." He wiped his face with his forearm. The elevator door opened, and he didn't care to see who entered. He just sat there in his misery.

The elevator opened once again when it stopped to release passengers in the lobby, but he didn't exit or make any attempt to. He just remained lost in his thoughts. He rode the elevator to the fifth floor where a nurse guided a wheelchair occupied by a new mother cradling her baby into the elevator to join Bling.

"Don't mind me." Bling spoke without making eye contact.

The elevator accepted and released its occupants back to the lobby. Bling finally gathered himself and walked out of the elevator without motivation or inspiration.

He got in his car with no final destination in mind. Bling was so deep into his thought he didn't notice the light had turned red, and he kept driving. The blaring of horns still didn't get his attention. He was the middle of the intersection, and the driver in the approaching car stepped on his brake, his burning tire leaving an outline in the street. Another car coming from the right had to brake to avoid ramming Bling's car, but with all that commotion, he drove right through not realizing the chaos he left behind.

Bling drove almost unconsciously to Keisha's apartment. He remembered Keisha always would complain about her neighbors. *These sanctimonious bitches need to get a life.* Bling cracked a smile. He viewed the neighborhood, and everybody continued with their daily routine. A lady was walking her two poodles and carried a shit bag in her hand. A school bus came to a stop, and a surgically enhanced woman greeted her kids with a hug when they exited the bus. The same annoying dog kept barking next door. Everything seemed to be normal, not caring about the fact that Keisha wasn't the same.

Bling got out of the car and discreetly removed the spare key that Keisha kept by the garage door in the belly of a turtle that was strategically hidden by a flowerpot. When he opened the door, the aroma of a Glade-scented plug-in rushed to his nostrils. He paused at the door wishing this was all a dream and Keisha would come running to him. A flashback of their first escapade consumed his memory. He shook his head, bringing himself back to reality. He made his way to the bedroom and dropped his body in her king-size bed, then turned his attention to the closet that could very well be a department store on its own.

The doorbell chimed, and he ignored it. "One of the nosy neighbors probably saw me come in."

The person started to pound on the door. It sounded as if it was multiple hands so he became curious and went to the door. He squinted his right eye and looked through the peephole. "Kids." He shook his head and opened the door.

"Would you like to buy some cookies?" a little girl with ponytails asked with a forced smile.

"I have no cash on me. Sorry," he lazily spoke.

"Why don't you go get some inside?" a sassy little girl asked.

"So why did you open the door then?" The first girl rolled her neck giving him attitude.

"How about if I take all your cookies and close my door?"

"This isn't your house. The lady that lives here is dead my mother said," the feisty little girl replied doing her neck roll.

"Do you know that I eat kids for breakfast?"

"Ahhhh!" The kids ran down the steps screaming.

"Tell your mother to mind her own damn business!"

CHAPTER 7

"I am entrusting my daughter to you only because I need her to get better, but I'll be watching you like a hawk!" Keisha's father pounded his fist in his hand as he made his point to Mark aka Damien, and his voice echoed in the hospital parking lot.

Damien took on the name Mark when Keisha concocted a plan for him to seduce her roommate Nikki. Nikki was a protégé of Keisha, but she decided to further her education instead of using men for money, and Keisha took offense to her decision. Keisha knew Damien would do anything to win back her love, so she recruited Damien to carry out her plan, which was to stop at nothing to ruin Nikki's life. In return, Keisha promised Damien a second chance at their marriage that had ended years ago because he cheated. Damien jumped at the chance and took on the name Mark as his disguise. Keisha's master plan worked out in her favor. Nikki became pregnant with Mark's baby and flunked her exams, and the truth was revealed that Mark was really Damien. But when Damien professed his love for Keisha she laughed in his face, and he quickly realized she had used him to do her dirty work.

"You don't have to worry about me bringing harm to your daughter. I married her for a reason and that reason was love," Damien sarcastically stated.

"She's my only daughter, and if you even step on her toe by accident, you will answer to me." He poked Damien's chest with his index finger.

"I understand your threats loud and clear, but don't forget that I'm doing you a favor, and if you continue with your empty threats I will walk away, leaving you to deal with the wrath of your daughter. Do *I* make myself clear?" Damien asked, looking directly into his eyes.

"You think my threats are empty? Then it's obvious you don't know me at all." You could see his jaw tighten as he tried to control his anger.

"Playtime is over, old man. Let's get down to business. How will I be paid for my hard work of deceiving your daughter?" Damien leaned against his car.

"I'm not paying you to lie to my daughter. I'm paying you to relive the part of her life when she was married to scum like you. That's my baby girl, and it kills me to know that she's not herself right now." He got choked up.

"Yeah, yeah, yeah. You're putting me to sleep, old man. Enough of that crying shit. How will I be paid?" Damien had no remorse or empathy for his grief.

"It will be on a weekly basis." He cleared his throat.

"No, no, no way. What the hell do you think this is? You're not going to act like I'm working for you. I would rather collect my lump sum of $100,000 or have it in two payments like we discussed."

"I don't feel comfortable handing over that amount of cash without any work being done."

"You need me, I don't need none of this mess. Your daughter already caused a lot of stress in my life. I guess you can find my twin somewhere out there in the world because I'm walking." Damien turned to walk away.

"OK. OK. I got your damn money." He opened his car trunk and removed a duffle bag and tossed it to Damien.

"Now we're talking." He caught the bag. "How much?"

"You get half now and half later."

"Come on, don't look so down. I'm sure this is from Top Dot Records and not from your personal account." He opened the bag.

"I cleared out all her clothes from the apartment and her personal property, leaving only the basic furniture, figuring it's needed. I had a cleaning crew clean the apartment, so it should be spotless. It's evident that she will have to start over from scratch."

"I wouldn't say from scratch, but from when we were in love. I did love your daughter despite what you think, but maybe we will produce a child in our second go-round." Damien was getting under his skin.

"If you ever!" Keisha father was enraged.

"Hold your horses, old man. No offense, but she isn't worthy of my firstborn." Damien tossed the bag in his car trunk.

"That's *my* daughter you're talking about!" His voice echoed in the underground parking lot.

"You need to face the fact because as much as you love your daughter, she wasn't a saint. She was more like a devil in disguise. But on a lighter note, it was a pleasure doing business with you, pops." Damien patted his shoulder, then walked away, leaving Keisha's father looking at him sternly.

Damien left the hospital with Keisha, feeding her lies as they best suited him. A few weeks ago Keisha had reneged on her offer to give him a second chance, but now he was being paid handsomely to be a part of her life. Damien wanted nothing to do with her after he discovered that she was a heartless bitch, but the price was right, and he would get his revenge by spending her money.

"I'm so glad I'm out of that damn hospital, but I just don't understand why they would lie to me. If I fell in the shower and the faucet punctured my back, why wouldn't they just say that?" Keisha poked for answers.

"Technically, they didn't lie, they just got your chart mixed up. We already went over that." Damien stuck to his story.

"But it's still puzzling about why I don't remember falling in the shower."

"You had a bad concussion. There's a lot you don't remember. But I know you remember how to do grocery shopping because a man got to eat. And since the fire destroyed everything, you'll have to do a little clothes shopping too."

"What fire?" Keisha quickly asked.

"While you were in the hospital there was a fire at the apartment. The downstairs neighbor left a candle too close to the curtain. Everything's gone."

"Where are we going to live? Not at your mother's, I hope."

"No. I got us a condo in Connecticut." Damien kept the lies coming.

"Come on, Connecticut is for old, retired people," Keisha was less than enthusiastic.

"Stop being so judgmental. Aren't you tired of the city life? A little fresh air won't hurt."

"As long as I'm with you I can enjoy living in the wild," Keisha laughed.

Keisha had a lot of questions. Damien was pulling answers out of his ass. He also had to explain why everything seemed different. There was a nine-year gap in Keisha's memory, and he was prepared to lie to her to the best of his ability, and he didn't have a problem with that. He had been lied to by her, so this was his payback.

"You said you would take me back if I destroyed Nikki's life," Damien remembered pleading with her the day Nikki found out the truth about his true identity.

"Do you believe in Karma?" Damien asked.

"That's just something people with no backbone say to scare you from going after what you want, especially if you have to step on their toes to get it. 'Karma is gonna get you,'" she mocked in a baby voice. "But in my book, all is fair in love and war. Do you believe in Karma?" She gazed at him.

"Well, I do and she's alive and kicking, and she's gonna bite you in the ass." He poked her in the side, and she giggled.

It took another twenty minutes for Damien to get to the apartment, but Keisha was antsy like the kids from the movie, *Are We There Yet?*

"Honey, we're home!" Damien announced, pulling in the driveway.

"What part of Connecticut is this?"

"The part that my wife deserves to live in."

"We can't afford to live in this neighborhood. I hope you aren't . . ." She looked at him.

"Dealing drugs?" he said what she was thinking.

"How much is the rent?" She gazed out the window.

"Let's just say an opportunity fell into my lap. But if you don't want to live here we can go back to my momma's house." He opened the car door.

"Hell no!" she quickly opened her door and got out of the car.

"Let's do this then." Damien went to his trunk to get his money bag but noticed Bling's car parked on the opposite side of the street watching them. Damien walked back to Keisha and pulled her in to him, then kissed her in an attempt to make Bling jealous. He lifted her off her feet and carried her to the door and let her inside. "I'll be right back. I have to get my bag out of the car."

Composed, Damien walked over to Bling. "Is there something I can help you with?"

"Is there something I can help *you* with? You're the one who approached *my* car." Bling redirected the question to Damien as he reclined his seat.

Damien cracked a smile and placed his hand in his pocket. "I know how it feels to watch from a distance as the woman you love frolics around with her new man. But regardless of how bad you miss her, don't show your face around her again."

"Or else what? You gonna call the police?" Bling smirked.

"I won't get the police involved. I'll get rid of you myself," Damien smirked back.

"Is that supposed to be a threat?" Bling put his window all the way down.

"More like a gift from me to you."

"I can promise you this." Bling brought his seat back to the standard position. "Her memory will come back, trust me. But you can continue playing house . . . for now," he smiled.

"Well, until then, I'll be having her for breakfast, lunch, and dinner." Damien walked away.

"Her memory *will* come back!" Bling yelled out to him.

Damien didn't engage his taunt. He entered the condo and Keisha was captivated by the apartment. The high ceilings and spacious rooms were luxury in comparison to her old apartment.

"Baby, I'm in love," Keisha said as she continued to explore.

"You have full range to decorate from bedroom to bathroom and from the windows to the wall."

"What about pink toilet paper for the bathroom?" she asked, walking to him.

"That's where I draw the line."

"I was just kidding, babe." She kissed him on the lips.

Damien had a smirk on his face. Keisha had used him to get back at Nikki and also made it clear that he would never sleep in her bed again. But the table has turned, and he was now her knight in shining armor.

"Babe, I'm famished. What's for dinner?" she asked.

"What do you suggest?" Damien queried.

"I'm craving pizza."

"I'll go pick up a hot and ready and be right back." Damien left the house.

Keisha took her time in the luxurious kitchen, sliding her hand over the granite countertop. The doorbell rang. She hurried to the door thinking it was Damien playing games, so she quickly opened the door, and her eyes met with a stranger. "May I help you?" she said with a puzzled look.

"It's me, Tina," her old friend informed her.

"Am I supposed to know who you are?"

"If I were you I would want to forget me too. But you can cut the act."

"State your business because I have no time for unimportant conversations such as this one," Keisha said insultingly.

"I see nothing has changed. But I want to put our past behind us and try to move forward with our friendship. It took awhile for me to get over the situation, but I can honestly say I forgive you." Tina reached out to touch her, but Keisha stepped back.

"Forgive me for what? I don't know you or of what you speak."

"Cut the act, Keisha. If you're still upset at me for siding with Nikki, just say it."

"First, the man at the hospital, and now, here, you go claiming to know me. But I really don't know who any of you are."

"I'm not trying to be presumptuous, but did you lose some of your memory when you went through that terrible ordeal?" Tina questioned in a whispering tone.

"What terrible ordeal?" Keisha furrowed her brows.

Tina realized that something was off with Keisha, so she kept the conversation on a lighter note. "So how have you been?"

"Like I said, I don't know who you are, and I don't want to be rude by closing the door in your face, so I suggest you back away from my door."

"I don't know what happened to you, but we were friends once, and if you need me, I'm still here."

"Is there a psych ward close by that you people are escaping from?"

"Tina, what are you doing here?" Damien frantically asked while pulling in the driveway.

"Well, well. Hello, Mark."

"So you two *do* know each other, and why is she calling you Mark?"

"Your wife Keisha seems to have forgotten about her past."

"You better shut your damn mouth!" Damien exited the car.

"How do you know her, Damien?"

"She's someone I had a short relationship with in the past that can't get over me, so she's determined to ruin our future."

"That's a damn lie, and you know it," Tina spoke through gritted teeth.

"Tell the truth, Tina. I'm sure you're here pretending to know my wife from the past. I know you would want to destroy us, but my wife has more sense than to buy into your nonsense." His lips met with Keisha's.

"Pathetic. You two deserve each other, but if your memory does come back, find me on Facebook. Tina Marshal. I'll have an earful to tell you."

"Get this tramp away from me," Keisha ordered.

"You have some nerve. I guess you must have *really* forgotten who the tramp is. You was the one spreading your legs to everyone."

"Don't get it twisted. You're the one who wants to spread your legs for a married man."

"No, honey, that's you. Does the name Bling ring a bell? Don't get brand new with me, bitch."

"Tina, you need to leave now!" Damien instructed.

"I'll leave you two to your filth." She descended the steps.

"My husband chose me, so deal with it."

"Don't worry about her." Damien guided Keisha inside.

Damien lied about his relationship with Tina to keep her away from Keisha. He didn't want anyone jogging her memory. She was his cash cow, and he wanted it to remain that way.

"Why did she call you Mark?" Keisha took a slice of pizza.

"It's obvious that she wasn't worthy of my real name. Besides, don't worry about her. She's in the past, and that's where she's going to stay."

"I'm starting to believe in reincarnation, because these people must know me from a past life, and it seems like I was a real bitch." Keisha laughed.

"You said it, not me." Damien reached for his second slice of pizza.

"I'm going to take a shower. Do you want to join me?"

"I'll pass, but I'll be impatiently waiting for you to finish." He slapped her ass.

"Not so hard!" she rubbed her right butt cheek.

Keisha departed to the bathroom, and Damien waited until the shower was running before he went on his phone.

"I'm in the door. I'm going to get as much cash as I can before my gravy train runs dry. I hope I'm on top of her screwing her brains out when her memory comes back, because the look on her face would be priceless." He let out a loud laugh. "Hell, yes. I already collected my money. Man, I'm all set for now, but if her memory takes long to come back I'm upping the ante. My price tag for me playing house will go up plenty. Hold on. I think I hear something." He walked toward the bathroom, but the shower was still running. "The coast is clear. She's still in the shower. Maybe this house is haunted. Maybe Nikki the angry ghost is here," he chuckled. "I never believed in Karma before, but I sure believe in her now, and I'm definitely in love with her, because she's working in my favor. I'm rich, bitch!" His laugh traveled throughout the house.

"How am I supposed to dry this water from my body?" Keisha appeared in front of him with water dripping from her naked body.

Damien ended the call. "I didn't hear you leave the bathroom."

"How could you? You were laughing so hard. I had to come and see who was tickling you."

"Why don't you come over here so I can tickle you all over your body?"

"Catch me if you can," she teased.

Damien chased her, and she giggled like an adolescent. He caught her and pulled her down to the carpeted floor. "Got you." He tickled her side.

"OK. OK. I can't take it."

"Would you rather take something else?" Damien pinned her to the floor.

"But what do you mean? Are you asking me to cheat on my husband?" She role-played with a southern accent.

"I'm asking you to do what you do best. Be a little slut." He insulted without her knowing what he really meant.

"But I love my husband." She continued to role-play.

"I'll pay you. How much do you charge?" Damien took his wallet from his pocket.

"But I'm not for sale." She shook her head from side to side.

"Oh yes, you are." He took money from his wallet and made it rain on her.

CHAPTER 8

"Right on time," Bling said in excitement. The dozens of red roses he ordered to win his wife over after he had called her his mistress's name had arrive. Bling had apologized multiple times, but he knew what he did was unforgivable. Today was his wife's birthday, and he wanted to shower her with roses to let her know that he loved her. It took the deliveryman several trips back and forth to unpack the order. Bling didn't know what time his wife would be home, but he knew she would probably be home sooner than later. He transferred the bouquets from the steps to the house, making room for the deliveryman to put down the others. The apartment now resembled a rose garden. The living-room floor, center table, and side tables now held roses. He traveled to the dining-room table where he unloaded four vases. The deliveryman was still placing roses on the steps.

"I really think I overdid it." He started to line the staircase leading up to the bedroom with roses. He placed two vases on both sides of each step leading up to the bedroom, leaving a small pathway. He had a bouquet that still needed placing. So he ripped off the petals and tossed them on the bed. He made his way to the bottom of the staircase and stood back and viewed his work. "Total overkill," he admitted.

Bling left the house and drove with speed. He had planned to meet his wife for dinner, but he was running late because he had to wait for the flowers to be delivered.

Their reservation was at seven, and that was in five minutes, and he would definitely need fifteen more minutes to get to Milford.

Bling made it to the restaurant and spotted his wife's car, so he parked next to her.

"Do you have a reservation, sir?"

"I'm meeting my wife, and she's already here."

"Oh yes, she has been waiting. Right this way, sir."

He led the way, and Bling followed. Denise was sitting with her back turned to him.

"I'll take it from here," Bling declared. He sneaked up on his wife, kissing her neck, and she jumped to the touch. "Go, shorty, it's your birthday." Bling recited the words to 50 Cent's song.

"After you have me here waiting on you starving, why would you want to give me a heart attack on top of that?"

"Sorry for being late, but I'll make up for it later." He kissed her cheek.

"I'm hoping . . . with a new car." She smiled.

"In that case I'm screwed," Bling admitted.

"That's what I told you I wanted when you asked me last year."

"Well, I had something better in mind."

"Are you ready to order?" the waiter asked.

"I'll have grilled salmon, and my husband will have the same," Denise ordered.

"You can make my drink a glass of cognac," Bling added.

"Would you like me to refill your wineglass, ma'am?"

"Thank you," Denise agreed.

"I want to let you know that I'm truly sorry for what happened in the Bahamas and I—"

"I understand that you were drunk, and we'll leave it at that. Besides, you wouldn't have recommitted to me if you didn't love me. It's my birthday, and I will not be having a discussion about it." Denise dismissed the conversation.

"Fair enough. But I want you to know that I'll love you now and forever."

"Your cognac, sir." the waiter announced, and then he proceeded to refill Denise's glass and left the table.

"Do you want it now or later?" Bling asked as he brought the cognac to his mouth.

"I'll take it now," Denise answered without hesitation.

"I have to warn you that it's not too big, but it packs a mighty punch."

"I would love to see what took the place of my car." Denise eagerly rubbed her hands together.

"I know you're going to love it." Bling was taking something from his pocket.

"I can't wait." She stretched her hand forward.

"Your dinner is served," the waiter interrupted.

"I'm famished." Bling's fork was on its way to his mouth before the waiter excused himself. He was devouring his meal like a hungry hyena. Denise also skipped the salad and went for the entrée. They had no complaints about the meal. It was to their satisfaction. Bling rested his fork and drank his liquor.

"So can I get my present now?" Denise also rested her fork.

"Yes, you may." Bling went in his pocket and brought forth a small gift wrapped box. "Good things come in small packages." Denise reached for the box, and he slapped her hand. "Not so fast."

"OK. OK." She pulled back.

"Babe, I love you, and I want to give you everything your heart desires, so I'm starting with the most important of all. So as your husband, my job is to make you the happiest woman on earth, and the one thing I know you want more than anything I wrapped it in this pretty little box. So, Happy Birthday, my love." He handed the box to her.

"I'm so excited." Denise gently opened her neatly wrapped gift. Upon opening it, she was less than happy but more surprised. "A pregnancy test? Is this a joke?" She made a frown.

Bling raised his hand in acknowledgment of someone, and Denise turned her head to see Trey walking to their table. She didn't know what to think. Right now, Denise didn't know if she should confess or run out of the restaurant. "Why is he here?" she asked in a panic.

"You know my wife. I'm sure of that." Bling shook hands with Trey.

"Mrs. Mills." Trey gave a slight nod.

"Why would you do this on my birthday?" Denise asked in a panic.

"Happy birthday? If I had known I wouldn't have interrupted. I'll catch up with you later. I'm going back to my date." Trey left.

"So he wasn't . . ." Denise stopped herself because she now knew that her secret was still safe.

"No, he wasn't going to join us." Bling finished her sentence with what he thought she was going to say.

"But I still don't understand why you would give me a pregnancy test for a present." She questioned his motive.

"Think about it, babe. What's the one thing you want more than anything?" Bling reached for her hand.

"Not a pregnancy test," she answered.

"I know, but you always wanted a baby."

"Yes, but I'm not pregnant," she pointed out, and still remained skeptical.

"Think a little deeper. The pregnancy test signifies us starting our family. I know I've been putting it off, but I think I'm finally ready to make you the mother of my child. Let's go half on a baby."

Bling's words were exactly what she wanted to hear. She'd been put off so many times by him, but finally they were on the same page.

Denise walked over to her husband and sensually kissed his lips. "I couldn't ask for a better present."

"I think I know what's for dessert," Bling said with lust in his eyes.

"A slice of my apple pie, I hope," Denise flirted back.

"Are you ready to order dessert?" the waiter queried.

"What I have in mind isn't on this menu so I'll take the check," Bling informed the waiter.

"I'll be back with the check." The waiter cleared the table.

Bling paid the bill, and they walked out of the restaurant arm in arm.

"I love you, baby." He kissed her cheek.

"I love you more," Denise reassured.

"How about if we take a drive down the highway and stop wherever our mind takes us?" Bling suggested.

"I didn't plan for that," Denise procrastinated.

"Come on, Denise, live a little. It's your birthday, for God's sake." Bling was annoyed by her lack of spontaneity.

"OK. OK. I'll go along for the ride. But what about my car?"

"What the hell? Let them tow it."

They got in Bling's car, and he merged onto I-95. He put the pedal to the metal, and Denise begged him to slow down. He passed through Stamford, and he still headed south. He passed the Bronx and kept going. He went toward the George Washington Bridge, and hit the Jersey Turnpike. Bling followed the sign to Atlantic City.

"Let the chips fall where they may, right?" Bling looked at his wife.

"Let the chips fall where they may," Denise cosigned.

They headed for the casino, and Bling went to the blackjack table. Denise was his cheerleader. Surprisingly, Denise was having the time of her life. Bling was on a winning streak. Denise ventured off to another table, and she was also on a winning streak. They played until the wee hours of the night, and luck was still on their side.

"I'm Laura!" a free-spirited young lady introduced herself to Denise, and Denise did the same.

"You come here often?" the lady asked.

"No! This is my first time!" Denise divulged.

"Me too!" Laura said excited.

"It's my birthday!" both ladies said in unison.

"What are you drinking?" Laura asked.

"No, thank you," Denise declined.

"Come on, you only live once!" Laura pressured.

"OK. Cîroc with pineapple juice." Denise let her guard down.

"Coming right up!" Laura was in good spirits. She appeared to have already found her buzz.

Denise continued at her game, and the crowd cheered her on.

"It's my birthday!" she shouted, informing the people at the table.

"Turn down for what?" Laura returned with Denise's drink.

Denise finished her drink faster than usual. Laura was cheering her on. They became best friends in an instant.

"I have to find my husband." Denise took her winnings and left the table, and Laura followed her. Bling was still in the same spot. His chips had doubled.

"Babe! Look at all this!" Denise took Bling's attention from the game.

"Hi, I'm Laura!" she introduced herself with a handshake.

"Aren't you turned up on something strong?" Bling acknowledged.

"Turned down for what?" Laura reiterated what seemed to be her favorite phrase. "I want to hit up a nightclub, how about you?"

"We're here to have a good time, so I'll take you up on that offer." Bling left the table, and they cashed out their chips. They got to the club, and the line was long. Bling figured he could use his celebrity status to get in, and it worked. It was packed inside. He found a spot at the bar allowing the ladies to do their thing. Bling was enjoying seeing his wife let loose. He ordered another Hennessey on the rocks, and his mind was at easy. He knew his wife was back in love with him, and he too was in love with his new wife.

"Hey, meet my husband. Charles. I found him in the crowd." Laura brought him over to Bling.

"Your wife seems to have a good effect on my wife!"

"Yeah, she has a free spirit!" Charles noted.

"Come on, babe, let's dance the night away!" Laura pulled him back to the dance floor.

Denise was doing her thing on the dance floor. Bling kept his eyes on her, watching her every move. After another few minutes, Denise came over to Bling grinding on him. Bling was being turned on by her antics, so he didn't try to stop her.

"A drink for you." Charles approached giving Bling the glass.

"And a drink for my bestie." Laura also gave Denise a glass. "Cheers to new memories." Laura tossed with Denise.

"I'll drink to that," both Bling and Charles agreed.

"I think we're gonna head out!" Bling was ready to end the night.

"We are too," Charles cosigned.

Both couples headed out of the club, and the men held on to their ladies.

"What hotel are you staying at?" Charles questioned.

"Thanks for reminding me. We have to get one for the night." Bling hugged his wife.

"We're staying at the Hilton. Why don't you check to see if there's any availability?"

"Sounds like a plan," Denise spoke.

The hotel was a skip away, and Bling was fortunate to get a room. "Good night, folks," Bling said when he got his key.

"How about if we end the night with one last shot from the hotel bar?" Laura was still in party mode.

"I don't know about that. I'm turning in," Bling declined.

"Don't disappoint the lady, man. Come on, one last drink won't hurt," Charles pressured.

"OK. But only one because I can't keep up with you guys."

"Babe, I'm going up to the room. I think I overexhausted myself." Denise took one of the keys and left.

"On that note, maybe I should be a lady and leave the men to end the night with one last shot." Laura also left.

Bling and Charles did their shot. And another, then on the third they both agreed that they had passed their limit. Both men got to the elevator and braced themselves because they couldn't keep their balance. Bling looked at his key card and pressed the third-floor button and staggered to his room. The bathroom light gave him enough light for him to make it to the bed without bumping into anything. He dropped his body on the bed and felt for his wife's body. "Wake up time for dessert." He pulled the sheet from her body.

Bling stripped himself and snuggled up to her. He massaged her breasts, then his mouth found her nipples. His hand found her cat, and she spread her legs and moved her body to his touch. He inserted his finger, and she answered.

"Yes," she whispered and spread her legs wide. The combination had her moist. She rolled Bling on his back, and his wood was hard. She held him in her hand

and elongated her tongue, licking him like ice cream on a cone. Bling lost his mind when she took him in her mouth, not leaving an inch. She slowly freed him, then repeated her action again.

Bling grabbed on to the bed for extra strength to endure the pleasure that he felt.

"Where did you learn to do that?" Bling was impressed by his wife.

She let up off his pistol and climbed on top of him, riding him like a stallion.

"I wish I had known you're a bedroom bully in the dark," Bling complimented her.

They were really going at it. Bling wanted to be in control, so he changed positions and backed her ass up on him. Bling was holding his own, even though he was drunk.

The sheets were now off the bed because their romping had escalated into a sex war, and she wasn't backing down. She pinned him on the bed and got back on top. She was the jockey, and she proved to him that she was a rider. She grabbed his neck with a firm grip as she neared her climax, and he moaned like a beast and exploded like a busted pipe. Finally, she collapsed on his chest, and they both were exhausted from the workout.

It wasn't until morning when Bling open his eyes and turn to his wife. "Laura?" Bling was in shock.

"Good morning!" Laura had a smile on her face.

"Don't tell me . . . " Bling was at a loss for words.

"Yes, we did, and you didn't disappoint." She reached for him. Bling jumped off the bed. "This can't be happening again."

"Don't act like you didn't know it was me."

"I was drunk. This can't be." Bling found his clothes on the floor and dressed in a haste.

"How the hell did this happen?"

"You see, Bling, I caught up with Denise and both our key cards fell, and I switched hers with mine."

"I have to find my wife."

"Don't worry, he won't touch her. He's impotent. And I'm tired of these damn toys, so I was on a mission to end my night right."

"You are fucking crazy."

"I just wanted to have some fun. Come on, Bling. You were enjoying the ride."

"What's the room number?" Bling asked, buttoning his shirt.

"Room number 325. They're in for a surprise," Laura laughed.

Bling dashed out of the room and ran down the hallway. He was pounding on the door hard enough to break it down.

Charles opened the door, and Bling pushed past him. "Did he hurt you?" Bling rushed to his wife.

"No. Why is he in our room?" Denise was terrified.

"Come on. Let's get out of here. It's a long story."

"What the hell is going on?" Charles asked.

"Ask your wife." Bling and his wife left the room.

"I don't understand why he was in our room." Denise tried making sense of it all.

"Let's forget about it. That girl Laura is trouble."

"I understand that she's on the wild side, but it's not fair to judge her."

"Just trust me. I know trouble when I see it." Bling was going to spare his wife the details once again. First Jordonna, and now Laura. But even though neither was his fault, he was going to spare his wife the details.

Two hours later Bling and Denise were home, and he rushed inside to take a piss. Denise came in after him. "What's all this?" Denise paused.

"I did it yesterday," Bing shouted from the bathroom.

"I'm in the middle of a rose garden." She walked over and smelled a bouquet. "It's beautiful." She took one of the long-stemmed roses and walked with it to the kitchen.

"What the hell is that smell?" she said when an atrocious odor rushed to her nostrils. She pulled out the garbage, and it reeked. She hurriedly tied the bag and brought it outside. But she froze when she saw Trey. "What are you doing here?"

"What's with the attitude? I'm here to see your husband."

"Why?" she hurried toward him.

"Don't worry, your secret is safe with me."

"You better lower your damn voice." She looked to the door, making sure Bling wasn't there.

"We have to tell him." Trey walked past her.

She grabbed him by his shirt. "We will *not* be telling him anything."

"I can't pretend that this didn't happened."

"Yes, you will. You see, Trey, I let my emotions get the best of me. I was hurt, and I felt betrayed. I was feeling empty, and I wanted to fill the void. I made a terrible mistake by looking for a quick fix and locked lips with you. I'm shamefully living with regrets every moment that I breathe. I love my husband, and I've forgiven his infidelities, knowing that I have deceived him also. But I'll be damned if I'm going to let you rip my husband from me after I gave him a second chance after he publicly humiliated me."

"How do you suggest that I set my conscience free?"

"By the mere fact that if you open your damn mouth I will find a way to cut your dick off and stuff it down your damn throat. Not to mention that I will deny that anything ever happened between us. That should set your conscience free."

"The truth is—" Trey tried to speak.

"Nothing happened. *That's* the truth." Denise shut him up.

"What truth?" Bling probed, standing at the door.

Denise and Trey both looked at each other, not knowing if Bling heard their entire conversation.

"The truth is that it's too hot for my black ass to be standing in this heat."

"Well, bring your black ass inside." Bling went back inside.

Denise rolled her eyes at Trey and walk past him. Trey gave her some lead way, then followed behind her. Bling led the way to the living room, and Denise went upstairs to the bedroom.

"Have a seat," Bling instructed.

Trey was having flashbacks of him having his way with Bling's wife. His manhood pulsated in his shorts, and in that moment, he knew he wanted more of his friend's wife.

"My life seems to be getting weirder by the minute," Bling confessed.

"What do you mean by that?"

"I ended up in Atlantic City last night, and the worst thing happened to me."

"Let's get one thing straight. I have no money to lend or give."

"Can you just listen and keep your mouth shut? When I woke up this morning I was in bed with a woman who wasn't my wife." Bling checked the hallway for his wife.

"Don't tell me you pick up a tranny?"

"No, she was a real woman." Bling returned to sit.

"So where was Denise during all of this?"

"She was in the room with the husband."

"What the hell? I didn't know you and your wife get down like that."

"No, we don't. Laura set the whole thing up."

"Who is Laura, 'cause I would love to meet her?" Trey rubbed his palms together.

"Laura is the wife of the husband."

"You mean the chick that was in your bed? I got it." Trey shook his head, dismissing the thought.

"Yes. But my wife doesn't know what really went down." He checked the hallway again.

"What you mean she doesn't know?"

"Laura switched keys, giving my wife her key, so she went to Laura's room and fell asleep, and I'm guessing he fell asleep too because they were still dressed when I went to the room like a madman."

"So the question is . . . Did you?"

"I did!" Bling led the way to the kitchen.

"Nooo." Trey went after him. "How could you not know the difference?"

"I was drunk, and it was dark."

"Good one, but you have to have noticed some differences. Like the ass. Was it bigger or smaller? The grip and the level of excitement? As a matter of fact, the entire ride. You should have known something was different." Trey was fascinated by the tale.

"I just thought my wife was extra turned up on her birthday."

"You got the treat. It wasn't even your damn birthday. So, are you gonna tell her?"

"Are you out of your mind?" Bling's answer was quick.

"What happened in Atlantic City stays in Atlantic City. I guess two wrongs will make a right."

"What's that supposed to mean?" Bling asked.

"I'm just saying, first you cheated with Keisha, and now Laura the stripper." Trey was amused.

"She wasn't a stripper. I don't think." Bling too was unsure.

CHAPTER 9

"You have an hour, Keisha, because I have things to do." Damien parked his car at the Macy's entrance at the mall and took money from his wallet.

"I'm going to need more than an hour," Keisha whined.

"Well, in that case . . ." He took back two hundred-dollar bills from the money in her hand. "With only two hundred dollars, it will take you less than an hour."

"Oh no, you don't." She wrestled with him and took the money back. "Two hours." She kissed his cheek and exited the car.

The shoe section was her first stop. She was drawn to a pair of Michael Kors pink pumps with gold metallic heels. It had a price tag of $150. "A girl has to treat herself."

"Would you like to try those on?" the salesclerk asked.

"No. but I'll take them in a size eight to go." Keisha paid for her shoes and strolled over to dresses and browsed through a few before she came across a low cut dark blue knee-length dress by Body Con.

"Perfect." She headed to the fitting room and got undressed, and for the first time she viewed her wound in the mirror. "I can't believe I almost destroyed my perfect body. But I'm glad that it wasn't my beautiful face."

Keisha wiggled her body into the dress, and it hugged her like a glove. She perked her breasts. "Did you grow overnight? Not to mention my hips. Girl, you look damn good." She placed both feet into the six-inch pumps and stepped out of the fitting room to the hallway mirror and the door adjacent to hers was also open.

"I guess great minds think alike." Keisha acknowledged the person wearing the same dress.

Denise was face-to-face with Keisha, and Denise froze in place.

"I wouldn't do basic black shoes, though. It's a little too safe," Keisha said, looking down at Denise's shoes.

"You have some damn nerve to be speaking to me," Denise spoke with her hands akimbo.

"I didn't mean to insult your shoes, but you do look beautiful in the dress. Just don't show up to the same event as me." Keisha paraded herself in front of the mirror.

"Are you *seriously* going to act like you don't know who I am?" Denise's voice was loud.

"I would be lying if I said I did. Do you mind refreshing my memory?" She walked up to Denise.

Denise slapped her hard across the face, and Keisha stumbled backward and lost her balance and fell to the floor. "Did *that* refresh you damn memory? Now, do you remember fucking my husband?"

"I'm not the one. You're mistaken."

"I know a whore when I see one." Denise charged at her.

"Break it up! Break it up!" security separated them.

"I want to press charges. She attacked me for no reason," Keisha yelled.

"Spreading your legs for my husband is reason enough for me to scratch your eyes out."

"Let's go, ladies." The security guard escorted both Keisha and Denise to the security office. "You ladies are banned from the mall for six months. If you attempt to enter this mall, you will be escorted out. Are we clear, ladies? I need you ladies to read this carefully, then sign at the bottom."

"All security to the food court!" a voice yelled on the walkie-talkie.

"Wait right here," the guard ordered the ladies, then ran out the door.

"I don't have time for this." Keisha headed for the door.

Denise grabbed her arm. "We aren't done yet."

Keisha pulled her arm away with force. "If your psycho ass ever crosses me again, I promise I won't be this friendly next time." Then Keisha stormed out of the room.

She was bare foot walking out of the mall. She tried walking fast, but the dress restricted her movement. When she finally exited, Damien was sitting on the hood of his car, and she screamed at him. "Take me home now."

"What the hell happened to you?" he asked, seeing her rumpled appearance.

"I just got in a fight with a woman claiming I slept with her husband." She sat in the car.

"Did you really?" Damien asked, while laughing.

"I'm glad you find it amusing." She folded her arms.

"Did you at least get a few punches in?"

"And why is everyone claiming to know me?"

"You probably have a twin out there that's a husband stealer." Damien still had a smile on his face.

"Really, Damien? Are you listening to yourself?"

"Maybe you will have better luck shopping tomorrow." He drove off.

"I'm banned from the mall."

"Well, there are plenty of other malls. You have Milford, Stamford, Danbury, and you have the option of all the malls in New York . . . Unless your twin has been there too." Damien laughed while poking her side. "Lighten up."

"This just doesn't make sense. First, there was the man at the hospital, now this crazy woman."

"What man at the hospital?"

"I think his name was Bling. He barged in the room acting as if he was someone I'm supposed to know."

"I see." Damien dismissed his smile.

"But on a different note, I've been thinking about getting a job. Just so I can feel more independent."

"No! I told you I would take care of you, and that's what I'll do."

"Why are you trying to control my life? You won't let me drive, you won't even let me go anywhere by myself."

"Is it such a bad idea to want to spend every minute of the day with my woman?"

"I'm starting to think you don't trust me. Is that it, Damien? You think that I'm gonna run off with the first person that says hi to me?"

"I trust you, baby. But I'm a little selfish when it come to my woman."

"You call it a little? More like a control freak."

"I'll make you a deal. I have a plan that I'm working on, but if it doesn't pan out, you can go find a job."

Damien brought her back to the house, and Keisha, upsettingly, got out of the car.

"Put on something sexy for when I get back. I have to go take care of business." Damien drove out of the driveway.

Keisha watched him leave, and then hurried in the house changing into her little black dress and her black pumps. She let down her wavy Malaysian hair weave from a bun to letting it lay on her back. She straightened her center part and freshened her makeup.

"You will not keep me trapped in this house. There's nothing wrong with me wanting some independence." Keisha walked to the door and made a sudden stop. "I don't have a ride or a damn phone to call a cab." She descended the steps and went to her neighbor's house. She rang the doorbell, and the dog by the window started to bark. "What you need to do is shut up."

"Look what the cat dragged to my door," the neighbor said, placing her hand at her hip.

"Excuse me?" Keisha said with a frown.

"I've been your neighbor for years, and you never said as much as a hello, but I'm not going to hold it against you. What can I do for a damsel in distress?"

"You must be confusing me with another person, but I don't have a phone, and I need to call a cab."

"You—calling a cab? Ha! What happened to your car? I notice I haven't seen it parked in your driveway."

"You seemed to be getting me confused. But I just moved here with my husband, and I don't know who you are."

"And my boobs are real. Child, please." She fanned her off. "You aren't fooling me."

"Can I use your phone or not?"

"I'm going to mind my own business." The lady walked away from the door.

"Why is everyone claiming to know me? I'm starting to believe I really *have* a twin."

The neighbor came back with the phone, and she called the cab. "Thank you." Keisha went back to her apartment and took a seat on the step. A man next door watering his lawn kept looking at her, making her feel uncomfortable, so she decided go inside and wait. But the cab came as soon as she got up. "Saved by the horn," she said when the cab honked. She was starting to become annoyed by everyone claiming to know her. "Bridgeport train station, please."

The metro north express train took her to Port Chester in less than half an hour.

Salmon & Clayton Law Firm. The sign stood out in bold black-and-white letters. She entered the building, and a receptionist looking to be in her forties gave her a smile.

"How may I help you?" the receptionist greeted still wearing a smile.

"My business is with Mr. Salmon. Is he in?" Keisha's tone was rather unpleasant.

The receptionist was no longer displaying a friendly attitude. "Do you have an appointment?"

"No, but he'll be more than happy to see me." Keisha cracked a fake smile.

"And your name is?" The receptionist was annoyed by Keisha's attitude.

"I would like to surprise him, if you don't mind." Keisha gave another fake smile and a wink.

"Mr. Salmon, there's a lady here to see you. But she refrained from giving her name, sir."

Keisha didn't wait for confirmation. She went right in the office, and Mr. Salmon almost had a heart attack. He reached for his asthma pump, sticking it into his mouth.

"Hello to you too." Keisha seated herself.

"I paid you off already. What more do you want? I'm a changed man. I was a . . . "

"Pervert." Keisha finished his sentence.

"I hope you're not here to start trouble."

"I knew you had a thing for younger girls, so at sixteen, I blackmailed you, but don't worry, I'm not here to cause any problem for you or your family, if you can honestly say that you're a changed man."

"I am. I've change my life, and I pray to the Lord for forgiveness because I know I've done wrong." He pleaded his case with remorse in his voice.

"That's good to hear, and with all that said, I need a favor." She leaned back in her chair.

"Just name it." Mr. Salmon also reclined, folding his arms across his chest.

"I need a job," Keisha said with a straight face.

He furrowed his brow, astounded by her simple request. "I have no job openings right now, but if something comes up, just leave your information with the receptionist, and I'll give you a call."

Keisha brought her body forward. "There is a position, but you just have to make it available."

"I can't think of any openings."

"I hear you're looking for a receptionist." Keisha crossed her legs.

"No." Mr. Salmon got out of his chair. "I can't. Karen has been with me for years."

"I'm afraid you don't have a choice."

"I will not. You don't walk in here thinking you can make demands," Mr. Salmon addressed her sternly, and then sat in his chair.

"Are you sure about that?" Keisha stood with her arms leaning on the desk and her body bracing toward him. "I'm sure you don't want your happy family to be unhappy."

"Leave my family out of this!" he reached for his asthma pump again.

Keisha placed her ass back in the chair, crossing her legs. "I would suggest you call her in and break the bad news. She's about that age for retirement anyway."

"I just can't. Let me right you a check." He took out his checkbook from the drawer. "How about $5,000?"

"No, thank you. I would prefer to take her job." She inspected her nails. "Her tone was very unprofessional when she greeted me. You have five seconds to choose between your family and the receptionist. 5, 4, 3 . . . "

Mr. Salmon pressed the button for the receptionist and called Karen to the office.

"Yes, sir." Karen entered the office.

"This is very hard for me to do. I want you to know that." He turned away, not having the courage to face her.

"What he's trying to say is that your service is no longer needed," Keisha unsympathetically informed her.

"Is this true, Mr. Salmon?" Karen started to cry. "I need this job. I'm the sole provider for my family."

"I'm sorry, but I will give you your regular pay for six months."

"I'm sorry to hear your story, but you seem to be a feisty lady. You'll figure something out." Keisha tapped her nails on the desk.

"Please, I beg you." Karen was on her knees. "My husband relies on my medical insurance. You *know* he has cancer!"

"That disease is a killer. But when life gives you lemons, make lemonade." Keisha shook her head.

"You're a killer! *You* are cancer!" Karen faced Keisha with tears running from her eyes. Mr. Salmon walked to her, trying to console her and help her off the floor, but she held on to his legs and cried. "Lord, I leave it in your hands. Lord, I leave it in your hands."

Keisha took a deep breath. "Overly dramatic, wouldn't you say? So, what time am I supposed to report to work in the morning?"

Karen got up from the floor and left the office. "The Lord will make a way for me."

"I need a minute to digest all this." Mr. Salmon went back to his chair.

"Well, I don't want to take up anymore of your time, so I'll see you 9:00 a.m. sharp." She left the room with a smile spread across her face. When she got to the receptionist's desk, Karen was still clearing her belongings.

"Father, forgive her for she knows not what she has done." The receptionist shook her head.

"I'm sorry for your stress, but I have to eat too." Keisha left and walked the full block back to the train station, hoping a train would be coming soon because she wanted to make it home before Damien.

"Excuse me, do you know what time the train should be here?"

"I think there's a delay. Should've been here already," the man spoke while looking in the direction the train should be coming.

"Just my luck." Keisha shared the bench with the man.

"In life, everything happens for a reason. That's how I look at it. That train is delayed for a reason unknown to man."

"And women too, I see," Keisha replied.

After a few minutes an inaudible message broadcasted over the intercom, and Keisha's patience grew thin.

"I see it coming." The man got up.

Keisha finally made it home and was surprised to see Damien sitting on the step outside. He angrily walked to the cab, and before she could put her feet on the ground, he grabbed her by the arm. "Where have you been? I told you to stay your ass in the house." He pulled her like a stubborn animal.

"You're hurting my arm!" she called out to him.

"Take your ass inside." He released his grip and walked back to the cab. "This is the last time you will ever do a pickup or a drop-off at this address. Do I make myself clear?" Damien's temper boiled. The cab drove off without giving him confirmation. He stormed in the house and found Keisha standing in front the bedroom mirror putting her hair up. He grabbed her arm again, and she fought back. His hand smacked her across the face, and she fell to the floor. "Don't ever disobey me again!" he stooped down on his knee and spoke. "I need to know your whereabouts at all times. I'm your husband, and I said I need to know your *every* move. If you think you're going to be sleeping around and make me look like a fool, you have another think coming."

"What has gotten into you?" Keisha shouted at him.

"Did you meet up with him?" He hovered over her.

"I didn't go meet up with anyone. I went to find a job." She tried to get up off the floor, but he pushed her back down.

"You're not lying to me, right, Keisha?" his eyes were evil. "If I find out you've lied to me, you *will* be sorry." He retreated. "You have to know that I'm just a little overprotective of my wife."

"I think we should spend some time apart." Keisha stood to her feet.

Those weren't the words he wanted to hear. He certainly didn't want to drive his cash cow into another man's arms. "I'm so sorry." He embraced Keisha with a tight hug. "I just don't know how I would live without you." He kissed her forehead. "Let me make it up to you." He kissed her lips. "You love me, don't you?"

Keisha nodded her head in agreement to his question, and he smiled. "I know you do, and if we're going to make this work, you have to trust me. I have a few enemies out there, and they will hurt you to get to me. That's why I'm protecting you." He slid his finger down her cheek.

"Since when do you have enemies?"

"There's a lot that you don't know, and I would like to keep it that way. I don't want you going anywhere unless I'm taking you. I just don't want anything to happen to you. That's all I'm asking of you. Is that too much to ask?" He looked her directly in her eyes.

"No. I trust you. I know you have my best interest at heart." She rested her head on his shoulder.

The doorbell rang, and Damien stepped back. "Wait here." He kissed her forehead.

Damien swiftly sauntered to the door. Keisha's father's face wasn't one he was glad to see. "I told you to never show up here," Damien whispered. "I told you where to meet me with the money." He stepped outside.

"I want to make sure my daughter is OK before I give you another penny." He made his stand with his thunderous voice.

"I'm sure your daughter doesn't want to see you. Besides, she's a little upset right now because I had to rough her up a little."

"If you hurt one hair on her I will—" he stepped to Damien.

"Calm down, she's fine. But I see the bitch in her wants to come out. She's sneaking off without my approval."

"She's free to go wherever she wants to. She's not a damn prisoner!" He raised his voice.

"That she's not, but she's *my* wife, and she will abide by *my* rules. Now since you made the trip here, give me my money." Damien extended his arm.

"Since when did food shopping cost $10,000?"

"Since the price of food keeps going up." Damien cracked a smile.

He tossed the bag to him, and Damien opened the bag, sniffing the money.

"Keisha!" Her father called out her name.

Damien grabbed him by his shirt. "You're not running shit. *I* am!"

"Get your hands off me. I want to see my daughter!" he demanded.

"Not today you won't." Damien went inside and closed the door in his face.

"Who was at the door?" Keisha queried.

"That's was my business partner telling me my investment paid off." He took money from the bag and threw it at her.

"Oh my God! This is a lot of money."

CHAPTER 10

Bling wrote his thoughts on paper, but he kept balling the paper up and starting over. He thought he would be able to free his mind from Keisha at the studio, but she was all he could think about.

"I was told I could find you here." Keisha's father spoke, frightening Bling out of his seat.

"What the hell do you want?" Bling was furious.

"I think I made a mistake by letting her go with him," Mr. Burkett said, shaking his head.

"Is something wrong with Keisha?" Bling probed with an inquisitive look.

"I think he's abusing my daughter." Mr. Burkett attempted to sit but decided against it and paced the floor.

"No, don't tell me that shit!" Bling balled his fist.

"I don't want any trouble." He walked closer to Bling. "I just thought you might be able to do something." Keisha's father looked him in the eyes. "If you know what I mean."

"What are you expecting me to do? She doesn't even remember who I am," Bling spoke with anger in his voice, swiping his hand, knocking a carton of cigars from the table.

"Maybe I should've gone to the police." Keisha's father was uncertain of what action to take.

"No. He'll just come up with a lie to cover his ass. I'll check on her."

Bling left the studio like a man on a mission. The thought of Damien putting his hands on Keisha fueled his anger. "I'll break his damn neck." Bling had been trying to subdue his true feelings, but the truth was hard to conceal. It kept popping up like corn in a hot pot. He pulled up at the apartment. Damien's car wasn't in the driveway, so he used the spare key to let himself in, but as soon as he opened the door, the sound of passion filled the house. Disappointment and disgust were written on his face. *Is she screwing another man?* was the thought that plagued him. He positioned his feet to leave, but he changed his mind and followed the sounds to the bedroom.

Keisha's naked back was facing the door, and Bling could see her scar. She rode in a steady motion, and her skin was moistened from perspiring. Keisha released her hair from the bun, and it cascaded to her back. The person cupped her bouncing breasts with both hands. Bling tightened his jaws and doubled his fist as his anger boiled.

"I love you." Keisha's sensual voice raced to Bling's ears.

Bling couldn't get himself to move. He watched Keisha giving her body to someone other than him, and he became green with envy. They changed into the doggy position, revealing the person was, in fact, Damien. Damien released his inner beast, pounding into her. Their bare skin slapped against each other, and Keisha's moans got louder. Bling wanted to pound his fist into Damien, but instead, he punched the wall, making his presence known.

Keisha screamed out of fear seeing Bling standing in the doorway. Damien quickly jumped to his feet, pulling up his boxers, and Bling rushed to him. They went blow for blow. Bling fought hard, but Damien was holding his own. Both men fell to the ground, and Bling managed to get the upper hand.

"Tell her the truth!" Bling demanded, holding Damien in a choke hold.

"You're hurting him!" Keisha said frantically.

"Tell her she's in love with me, not you." Bling tightened his grip.

"You're hurting my husband!" Keisha tried to peel Bling away.

"Stop calling him your damn husband! You have amnesia. And he's using it to his advantage. The year is 2014." He stepped toward her, leaving Damien on the floor gasping for air.

With each step he took, Keisha backed away from him. "Please don't hurt me," Keisha begged.

"I would never harm a hair on your body." He took his shirt off and gave it to her.

She grabbed the shirt and covered her body, realizing that she was still naked.

"You suffered a gunshot wound to your back, and you were in a coma for two weeks. Your uncle Patrick also got killed."

"He's lying." Damien could barely speak.

"We were having an affair, and you had a jealous lover whose name was Hype. He wanted to kill both of us. That's why you were in the hospital with a gunshot wound to your back."

"Get away from me. You are crazy! I don't believe you."

"I'm not crazy!" Bling saw the fear in her eyes. "Do your research, Keisha, you'll find the truth." He didn't want her to fear him. The last thing he wanted to do was to see her hurt, so he slowly backed away and left the house. Keisha ran to Damien, kneeling to his level.

"Tell me you don't believe him." Damien clasped Keisha's face with both his hands. "They're all working with your father to ruin what we've got."

"I don't believe him. I know you're my husband, and I love no one but you." She sealed her love with a kiss.

"He has to be stopped." Damien elevated his body from the floor.

"Don't do anything stupid," Keisha pleaded as they both dressed.

"I'm just gonna handle some business." He led the way out of the bedroom, and Keisha trailed behind him.

"Be careful!" she spoke in a worried tone.

"Stay inside," Damien regulated before he marched outside.

Keisha locked the door behind Damien and went to the bedroom where she fell across the bed. Even though she believed her husband, her curiosity got the best of her as Bling's words replayed in her head. "Uncle Patrick. He said he was dead." She promptly sat up. "Can he really be dead?"

Her thoughts were disrupted by a loud knocking. She tiptoed out of the bedroom looking toward the front door, but the knocking sounded again and she redirected her attention to the kitchen.

"It's your next-door neighbor," the voice called out from the patio door.

"What do you want?" she questioned without opening the door.

"If you need anything let me know. I know you're going through a lot."

"I'm fine. I trust no one but my husband. Leave my premises now," Keisha shouted.

"Suit yourself, but I'm on your side." The woman walked away.

"One crazy person after another." Keisha was fed up. "My father will pay for this." She was overwhelmed with everything that had transpired. She went to the bathroom knowing that a bubble bath would calm her nerves. She filled the tub halfway, then poured in her favorite peppermint body wash and watched the bubbles form. Then she immersed her body in the water and closed her eyes, letting the aroma calm her nerves while slowly drifting off into serenity.

"No!" Keisha brought herself to a sitting position, and the suds slid off her body. "It can't be. You can't be dead." The memory of her holding her uncle's lifeless body as he lay on the floor, dead, came back to her memory. "My mind is playing tricks on me. I'm not going to believe anything he said." She relaxed her body once more, and this time, the memory of the bullet piercing her back surfaced. Keisha sat up as if she was awakened from a nightmare. She felt her back, and the scar marked the spot. "I'm not falling for this."

She stood to her feet, and a few suds clung to her body. She stepped out of the tub, and water dripped from her body to the floor as she braced herself looking in the mirror. "Do you *really* have amnesia? Could these people be telling the truth, and my husband is the one that's lying?" she asked, reaching for a towel. She wrapped it around her wet skin. "No, I'm not going to let them brainwash me into thinking my husband is a liar." She exited the bathroom.

Keisha dressed herself and decided to go make a bowl of salad. But she couldn't keep her mind from drifting back to the memory of her uncle Patrick lying in her arms covered in blood. "I need to get to a phone." She opened the door intending to go bother her neighbor, but a muscular man posted on the top step made eye contact with her. She hurriedly closed the door, locking all the locks and even using the chain. She watched through the peephole and the man still stood there. *If he's here to kidnap me, why would he be standing in public view?* She tried to calm herself. She cracked the door and spoke with the chain still on. "Who are you, and what do you want?"

"I'm your bodyguard, and you can call me Max." The man kept his eyes toward to street.

"Who hired you? I don't need a bodyguard."

"You have to take that up with your husband. I'm just doing my job."

Keisha opened the door and went outside, but the man stopped her before she could descend the steps.

"You have to go back inside, ma'am." The man spoke with a firm voice. "I was instructed not to let you leave the house."

"What did you just say?"

"I'm just following instructions, and you're not to leave the house, so take it up with you husband."

"Well, I'm just going next door. That should be no problem." Keisha made a step, but he blocked her.

"Sorry. I can't let you leave the house."

Keisha went inside and slammed the door. She was upset that Damien had her on house arrest. But she brushed it off as it was in her best interest. She patiently waited for Damien to get home, but after several hours, she gave into sleep. It was almost 8:00 p.m. when she was awaken by a knock on the door. She didn't make a move to get it, and Max announced himself. She lazily went to the door.

"What is it, Max?" she answered with irritation in her voice.

"Your husband won't be coming home tonight due to business, so he wants me to stay here with you."

Keisha opened the door with her full body in view. "What business is that? Why can't he come home? I can stay by myself, Max. I don't need a babysitter."

"Sorry, I can't do that."

"What orders were given to you by my husband, Max?"

"I was told to never let you leave the house without permission from Damien, and wherever you go, I shall follow."

"Are you here for my protection, or is it to protect his lies?"

"I was hired to do a job, and I just told you what it entailed."

"I need to speak to my husband. Can you call him back?"

Max dialed the number and waited for Damien to answer. "The Mrs. would like—" Before he could finish his sentence Keisha took the phone.

"Why aren't you coming home?" Keisha waited for him to speak. "What business? You better not hang up this phone. Damien, you better not!" Keisha threatened, but he hung up anyway.

The next morning Keisha exited her bedroom. She tiptoed to the living room to see if Max was still asleep so she could sneak out, but to her surprise, the blanket that she had given him was folded neatly without any sign of him. She went to the door spying through the peephole, and Max was back at his post.

"I need to go to the store." Keisha opened the door and spoke in a demanding tone.

"I have to confirm with your husband." Max took his phone from his pocket and walked away.

"Yeah, yeah, the usual routine." Keisha waited for confirmation.

"The answer is no," Max informed her, walking back.

Keisha slammed the door and pounded her fist into it a few times. "I have to get out of this damn house." She opened the door again.

"Yes?" Max answered without looking at her.

"I really need to get some feminine products from the store." Keisha pleaded her case.

"Your husband already said no."

"How will he know if you take me to the store? I don't think he's coming home anytime soon."

"I'm gonna do you this favor, but if you breathe a word of it, I will lose my job," Max warned.

"OK. I won't." She went to get her pocketbook.

Max led the way to the car, and Keisha ran down the steps and into the car. "Take me to Walgreens." She was ecstatic.

"Understand that I'm not taking you to another store, so don't ask."

"I won't." She snapped her seat belt.

Max made a right turn on Park Ave, then a left on North Ave. Within minutes they were pulling into Walgreens parking lot. They both exited the car, and Keisha walked ahead of him into the store. She was drawn to the array of vibrant colors of nail polish so she paused in the first aisle.

Max shook his head. "I thought you said feminine care."

"It is. Nail polish is feminine." Pink, turquoise, and lavender were the chosen colors, then she moved on to aisle two, picking up a Dove powder fresh deodorant. Aisle three was next, and she picked up a face wash. *On second thought, I think I should switch to another brand.* She brought it back to the shelf. "Which do I chose?"

"Come on, Keisha, we have to wrap this up." Max spoke with assertion.

"OK. OK. But I need razors, Nair, body wash." She walked from aisle to aisle, tossing whatever she needed in the basket.

"You have five minutes," Max announced, walking a few steps behind.

"OK. I'm done. I'll go to check out. But not before I get a bag of potato chips." She grab a big bag, knowing it would have to serve for a while. Then she strolled to the cash register.

"Do you have a Walgreens card?" the cashier asked.

"No, I'll be paying cash." Keisha took money from her purse.

The cashier giggled. "It's not a charge card."

"What the hell is so funny? I could care less what it is! And your face isn't a face. It's a monkey's ass. You shouldn't even be allowed to be showing your face in public," she insulted, and the cashier didn't say another word except to tell her the total cost of her purchase. Keisha paid her tab and left the store.

"The nerve of some people!" She was obviously still annoyed when she got home. "Why the hell does everyone keep acting like I have stupid stamped on my forehead?" She searched in her bag for her potato chips, but it wasn't there. She looked at the receipt and scrolled the list of items, and she was, in fact, charged for it. "That little troll probably kept it for herself." She was about to put away the receipt, but something caught her eyes. "*2014.* Am I living on another planet? This isn't making sense . . . The train ticket." She dug through her pocketbook coming up with her receipt from the train station, and the date also matched.

"Max!" Keisha ran to the door. "Max!" she hollered getting his attention.

He blew the smoke from his mouth, then faced her. "What now?"

"What I'm about to ask might seem strange, but I need to know what year we are in."

"It's 2009." He took a pull from his cigarette.

"That's what I thought." She closed the door. "Something just isn't adding up. The woman at the mall accused me of sleeping with her husband, and Bling professing his love. But Bling mentioned that the year was 2014. Somebody is lying, and I have to find out who is."

Keisha needed answers. She remembered that her neighbor came knocking at her door. Now it was her turn to pay her a visit. Knowing she couldn't go through the front door, she exited through the patio. She went down the three wooden steps, then turned to her right, making her way to her neighbor's. Keisha knocked on the door hard enough to be heard, but not to have her neighbor call 911 or shoot and ask questions later.

"I've got a gun!" the neighbor alerted while the dog barked.

Keisha stepped to the side protecting herself, just in case she was crazy enough to shoot. "Whatever you do, don't shoot. It's Keisha."

"Why are you at the back door?"

"The same reason that you were at mine." Keisha could see her clearly through the glass patio door, and she did, in fact, have gun. She slid the door on its hinges, and the dog jumped on Keisha.

"I see he's very friendly." Keisha gave a forced smile.

"Get back in here, boy." The lady snapped her fingers, and the dog obeyed. "You wouldn't be at my back door of all places if you didn't need something."

"Do you have a computer that I can use for a few minutes?"

"You're not using it to do anything illegal, are you?" The lady walked back into the house.

"I just have to do some quick research," Keisha nervously answered, looking toward her porch.

"Don't just stand there, come on in." She looked back at Keisha. "And by the way, my name is Tammy."

Keisha entered through the kitchen and saw a fruit basket on the table with a variety of fresh fruits. There was also a burning candle on the marble countertop. She approached the living room. The furniture was of good quality. You could tell they weren't from Bobs or the Rent-A-Center.

"Here you go." The neighbor handed her an iPad.

"What's this?" Keisha asked, unfamiliar with the gadget.

"It's called an iPad. The year is 2014. Technology has come a long way."

"Who paid you to say that?" Keisha raised her voice.

"Just tap the screen. The information you seek is right there. I knew one day you would come." Tammy walked away from her.

Keisha tapped the screen, and the headline caught her attention.

Husband stealer caught in a deadly shoot-out with her lover Bling aka Anthony Mills.

Heartless Keisha left her friend for dead after she took the bullets that were meant for her.

After being shot in the back, Keisha awoke from a coma with amnesia.

"Is this true?" Keisha took her eyes from the iPad, calling out to Tammy for answers.

"Yes, it's all true," Tammy answered while nodding her head.

"Is that the real reason why I was in the hospital?"

"Yes, you got shot by your jealous lover, and your friend Nikki was gunned down on your steps. I witnessed it with my two eyes."

"Why don't I remember any of this? Did someone pay you to set this up?"

"You came knocking on my door, remember?"

"This isn't true. Can't be," she recited as she read the headlines again. "Maybe this is all a dream. There's one way to prove that my husband isn't lying, but I have to get to my old apartment."

"What old apartment? You've been living here for years. But you wouldn't know that if you have amnesia."

"I need you to do me a favor. I need your help to prove that you're not lying to me."

"Name it."

"I need you to take me to the Bronx."

"The Bronx? Honey, I don't do the Bronx."

"You're my only hope of getting there and away from my bodyguard."

"And how will you do that? If you haven't noticed, there's nothing but woods in the back."

"You'll distract him so I can get to your car." Keisha revealed her plan.

"How will I do that? The man is like a stone wall. He has no emotions."

"Every man has a weakness for sex, so, be seductive. You didn't buy those boobs for nothing."

"You have a valid point." Tammy jiggled her breasts.

"I'm going back to my apartment to do my part, and I'll be back shortly."

Keisha went back to her apartment pacing the rooms. She knew when she uncovered the truth she would find out who's the true deceiver. But with all the signs pointing to her husband, she was having cold feet about seeking the truth. "She could have gotten that iPad, as she called it, from China. They're always years ahead on technology. She seems to have the money to purchase whatever she wants." Keisha tried to find reasons to abort her plan. She left the kitchen heading to the living room where she sat placing her feet on the coffee table.

"Was I really the other woman?" her mind wondered. She needed answers. "Am I really suffering from amnesia?" Her curiosity wouldn't set her free. "I have to get to the bottom of this."

Damien's fitted hat was on the adjacent couch, and she fixed it on her head. She kicked her sandals off and fetched her white Nike sneakers. "I'll just tell Max I'm going for a run. Which I know the answer will be no. Then I'll tell him I'm going to take a nap so he won't feel the need to check up on me. Then I'll sneak back to Tammy's apartment." Keisha checked the time. It was 2:00 p.m. She opened the door. Max was sitting on the steps.

"Yes?" he answered, being aware of her presence.

"I'm going for a jog."

"OK, let's go. I feel like taking a walk myself."

She was startled by his answer. "You didn't even check with my husband."

"Well, he wouldn't object to you trying to stay in shape. Beside, I need to stretch my legs."

"On second thought, the sun is still a little too hot. Maybe a little later."

"Suit yourself." Max took a pack of cigarettes from his pocket.

"I'll settle for a nap instead. Would you like to use the bathroom or have something to drink before I fall asleep?"

"No. I'm good."

Keisha closed the door and watched through the peep-hole. Seeing Max light his cigarette, she felt confident that he had bought her lie so she escaped out the back.

"I was starting to believe you changed your mind. So what's the master plan to distract Mr. Muscle Man?" Tammy looked out the window at Max.

"First of all, you need to reveal those D cups and walk outside and get him away from the front door. Tell him your dog is being attacked by squirrels in the back."

"*That's* what you came up with?" Tammy stared at her.

"You have something better?" Keisha gave a neck roll.

"Let's just say, he'll be giving me mouth-to-mouth resuscitation. Let's get this show rolling." Tammy undid a few buttons, causing her bra to expose. "Here comes trouble." She went outside, and Keisha watched from the window. Tammy cut across the lawn, and Max went into defense mode. He stood up quickly and descended the steps. Keisha could see them exchanging words, but she couldn't hear their conversation. Tammy stretched her hand for a handshake, but Max folded his arms on his chest with a firm stand. Tammy reached out and squeezed his biceps, but he didn't budge.

"Come on, Max. Don't tell me you're gay," Keisha spoke in a low tone.

Tammy seductively let her index finger travel up and down his muscular arm, then she walked her finger over to his chest, and he grabbed her arm.

"This isn't good." Keisha moved from the window, and the dog took her place and started to bark. "After all, dogs are man's best friend. Come here, boy." She opened the door just enough for the dog to get out. "Go save the day."

The dog ran outside barking but not for what Keisha's intended purpose. It ran out to the sidewalk barking at another dog. The other dog charged at him, pinning him to the ground. Tammy and Max both ran to save the dog.

Keisha saw her golden opportunity to escape and darted to the car where she lay her body in the backseat. She couldn't see anything, but she could hear Tammy telling someone that her dog was OK. After a few more minutes of both neighbors apologizing to each other, Tammy got in the car.

"You owe me big time," Tammy spoke.

"More like I owe the dog big time because your boobs wasn't doing the trick."

***

They merged unto the I-95 and the traffic was flowing until they approached Greenwich where traffic slowed bumper-to-bumper. It was already forty-five minutes into the trip, and it would be another twenty before they got to Exit Thirteen. Tammy tapped on her brake, and Keisha lunged forward.

"What the hell is that for?" Keisha asked in a frightened tone.

"You're alive. For a minute I thought you checked out on me."

"It's just a little overwhelming," Keisha admitted.

Tammy looked at Keisha but brought her attention back to the road. "I can only imagine. But the truth will reveal itself in due time."

The traffic let up when they were two exits away from exiting, and Keisha prepared herself to prove her husband right.

The GPS brought them to Barnes Ave. "Stop! Pull over," Keisha said in a panic.

"There are cars behind me, and there's nowhere to park."

"Put on your hazard lights and double-park. If I find out my husband is lying, I don't know what I'll do." Keisha turned facing Tammy.

"Yes, you do." Tammy patted her hand. "A woman always knows how to punish a man for lying."

"Why are you helping me?" Keisha asked.

"Get one thing straight. You were one of my least favorite people, but no one deserves to be lied to, even if the truth hurts. So can we go now?"

"Yes." Keisha closed her eyes and took a deep breath, then exhaled aloud. She observed a few kids drawing art on the sidewalk. There was a man teaching his son how to ride his bike. Keisha focused her eyes on them. Then she turned her head, watching them even when the car had passed. *Destination is on your right,* the GPS confirmed.

"No way" were the words that escaped Keisha's lips. "He said it was destroyed by fire."

"Well, it's here still standing." Tammy spoke with gratification.

Keisha got out of the car and approached the house. There was an old lady sitting on the porch sleeping, and Keisha called out to her, waking her from her slumber. "Excuse me! I'm sorry to bother you." She opened the gate.

"But you did it anyways." The lady straightened her posture.

"Was there ever a fire at this house?" She walked onto the porch.

"Not that I know of." The old lady got up and walked to the door.

"How long have you been living here?"

"Over five years, but you sure asking a lot of questions, and I ain't seeing no cash."

"I'm sorry to have disturbed you." She walked back to the car. "Can you please take me home?" She slammed the car door.

"With that attitude, I'm guessing that there wasn't a fire."

"He lied to me!" Keisha wiped her falling tears.

Within an hour she was back home. Max was sleeping on the steps with his head strategically resting on the door. She climbed the stairs and opened the door, and Max was ready to attack. She passed him and went inside slamming the door behind her. Her husband had been lying to her, and she wanted to know why. She decided to take a warm shower to calm her nerves. But even though she was faced with all the information, her memory still hadn't return. However, she was going to confront her husband about his lies.

She went to the kitchen where she decided her comfort food would be ice cream. She took two scoops into her bowl and brought the spoon to her mouth. Her taste buds were satisfied by the taste of pistachio, and she closed her eyes and freed her mind.

"Keisha!" Damien called out to her.

"I'm in the kitchen," she shouted back.

Damien stormed in the kitchen like a madman. "I just told Max to take off. Where did you go?" He tossed his keys on the counter.

"So he really called and tattle taled. His pay must be really good, but you should fire him for sleeping on the job." She brought another spoon of ice cream to her mouth.

"Answer the question! Where did you go?" Damien was in her face.

"Calm down." She stepped back, placing the bowl on the counter. "I went for a walk around the block. I needed to burn some calories."

"I'm going to fire his ass. He's supposed to be with you at all times." Damien stormed off.

"What are you hiding, Damien?" Keisha taunted.

Damien rapidly turned to face her. "What did you say?"

"Why do I need a bodyguard? What are you hiding?"

Damien walked back to her. "I told you I have enemies out to get me. What is it, Keisha? Don't you trust me?"

"I do trust my husband. Why don't you come have a seat?" She pulled up a chair.

"What are you up to?"

"I just figure my husband deserves to be treated like a king when he comes home to his queen." Keisha encouraged him to sit on the chair.

"I have a few phone calls to make." He tried to get up.

Keisha pulled him back down to sit. She danced seductively around him. "What could be more important than spending time with your woman?"

Damien closed his eyes, not wanting to see her antics. "I'll let you have your fun, but just know my dick won't be playing along."

"I just hope you can handle it like a man when I put it on you, because this grown woman is ready to put it down," she said with confidence.

Her talk was intriguing to Damien's ears. He suddenly put a smile on his face. Keisha unbuttoned his shirt and slowly caressed his chest. She got down on her knees in front of him and undid his belt. She wiggled her body up from the floor, then glided her hand across his chest, slowly making her way behind him. She took his arms, tying both together behind him with the belt.

"What you got in store for me, girl?" he asked anxiously. "Any other time I would be worried, but I know I'm in for a treat."

"Yeah, baby, this treat will be so sweet, you're going to have to see the dentist afterward." She removed the string from her robe and tied both his feet.

"Bring it *on!*" he said in glee.

Keisha gyrate her ass on his lap. "Is *this* what you want?"

"Yeah, baby!" he approved in excitement. "Make daddy proud." Damien closed his eyes, and reclined his head.

Keisha's five fingers slapped his face so hard she almost knocked him unconscious.

"How you like that?" Damien's head swung to the left. "So you like telling lies, I see."

"You fucking bitch!" The words flew from his mouth with the look of *I'd kill you if my hands weren't tied.*

"I thought you were having fun," she mocked with a baby voice.

"You think this is funny?" he tried untying his hands.

"Was I in a coma?" she grabbed his face, positioning him to look at her.

"So that's what this is about? You believing his lies?"

"Question number two: Was I shot in the back?" She took a chair and placed it directly in front of him and sat down.

"No! And I'm done with this. Untie me now!"

"Or you . . .?" She extended her legs, dropping them hard on his lap.

"Oh shit!" Damien bellowed out in pain. His baby maker was crushed. He tightened his jawbones trying to endure the pain.

"So are you *really* going to keep lying?"

Damien shuffled in the chair. "You better have the police on speed dial because I'm gonna kill you!"

"What would make you want to kill your wife? And, here, I was thinking that nothing could separate us."

"Don't forget until death do us part." Damien tried desperately to untie his hands.

"Did our apartment burn to the ground?" Keisha stood behind him rubbing his head.

"Yes!"

"And another lie!" Keisha slapped his face again. "That should refresh your damn memory!"

"You damn crazy bitch!" Damien shouted in pain.

"I need the truth, Damien!" she spoke directly to his face.

"Calm down, Keisha! I'm going to tell you the truth."

"Already? And I was just starting to enjoy the foreplay." Her hand traveled down his pants.

"No! No! No! Don't do it, Keisha!"

"You don't want me to show you my special skills?"

Keisha released his dick and sat in his lap, but unbeknownst to her, Damien had freed his arm and put her in a choke hold.

"You want the truth? The truth is that you're a damn bitch. And even with amnesia, you're still a bitch. I see the way you looked at Bling. You stood there naked and let him look at you." Damien freed his legs and stood to his feet, shoving Keisha against the wall with his hand still tight around her neck, not allowing her to breathe. Keisha held firmly to his arm with bulging eyes silently begging him to free her.

"You're holding on to the little air that's in your lungs. You want me to let you live? Have mercy on you? Hell no! You're the reason my child is dead, so why shouldn't I end your pathetic life right now?" He tightened his grip. "Did you want to say something? You don't know what child I'm talking about? I forgot, your damn brain is fried."

Keisha gathered strength and reached for his balls, squeezing with all her might. He released her. Both of them fell to the floor and lay there like fish out of water. Keisha knew she had to get out of there. She slowly stood to her feet and grabbed the keys from the counter. Damien went after her, but she had a lead way. She hurriedly opened the door and ran to the car locking herself inside. Damien pleaded with her to open the door, but she stepped on the gas. His foot was under the wheel. Damien screamed out to her, but she put the car in park.

"My foot, get the car off my foot!" Damien was hollering like a baby.

Keisha let the window down. "Why?" She revved the engine.

"I take back everything I just said to you!" He banged on the car.

Keisha got out of the car and slowly walked as if she were in a trance, stopping at the steps.

"She was lying right here with bullets in her body that were meant for me." Her voice was calm. "I remember walking past her, not caring if she was dead or alive.

And you . . . " She brought her attention back to Damien. "You helped me do it. She was pregnant with your child. I remember everything. You have been lying to me."

Damien was weeping and moaning, but Keisha didn't care about his pain. In fact, at this point, she wanted to torture him. And she was filled with anger and rage. "You and my father both lied to me. So tell me! What was your plan?"

"I wanted you to pay for what you did! I loved you, and you lied to me. You promised me you would give us a second chance, but you laughed in my face like I was a fool. You will pay for taking my child from me. It's because of you that my child is dead. My child's blood is on your hands."

CHAPTER 11

Bling pulled into the Planet Fitness parking lot and parked close to the entrance. Ever since Hype took him at gunpoint, he made a mental note to always park up front where he could be seen.

"I knew I would find you here." Bling walked over to Trey, who was loading dumbbells, getting ready to do some weight lifting.

"What up, Money B? You're never at the gym this time of day." Trey extended his hand, and they did their hand greeting.

"I would rather do my workout in the mornings. But I just need to clear my head and let off some steam." He took to the punching bag.

"What happen to your face, man?" Trey noticed a bruise and became curious.

"I had a run-in with Damien." Bling kept punching.

"Who the hell is he? Don't answer that. It's always something with you. Well, while you're here, you can spot me." Trey positioned himself by lying on his back, ready to lift.

Bling was still punching the bag as if it was Damien standing in front of him. He connected with the left, then the right. You could see the anger in his face with every punch.

"Money B! Can you come back to planet Earth?" Trey was lying on his back with the 100-pound weight in the air.

Bling gave the bag one last punch, then he went to assist Trey. Trey brought the dumbbell up and down a few times, then he started to feel the burn. "Help me set this down," he spoke, but Bling didn't attempt to help because his mind was far away. "Money B!" Trey called out to him with his arms visibly shaking. Trey struggled with the 100-pound weight, trying to get it back on the rack.

"Sorry, man." Bling brought his focus back to Trey just in time before his arms gave out.

"Are you trying to kill me?" Trey said while trying to catch his breath.

"I'm just out of it, man." Bling walked away.

"What's going on, Money B?"

"I just can't stop thinking about her." Bling was on the floor doing sit-ups.

"Her? Meaning, your wife?" Trey asked, still trying to catch his breath. He was crunched over with his hands on his knees.

"Not really," Bling replied on his way up after exhaling.

"Then who the hell or what got your head so messed up that you almost killed me?"

"The *her* is Keisha, and stop being so damn dramatic." He continued with his sit-ups.

"I should've known that." Trey walked away from him.

Bling got up from the floor and followed after him. "I need to get her alone. I need to talk to her. Maybe I can say the right things, and her memory will come back. I hated seeing Damien's hands all over her. It makes me sick to my damn stomach."

"Who is this Damien character? Other than the dude that gave you that black eye." Trey laughed as he reached for thc jump rope.

"Her damn husband." Bling's fist connected with the punching bag.

"Wait, wait. Boss lady is married?"

"No, she's not." Bling continued throwing fists to the bag.

"But you just said . . . " Trey was confused.

"I know what I said." Bling punched the bag hard.

"Calm down, man."

"I'm someone who she has no memory of. But she remembered being married to him. I'm the one she loves. I'm the one that makes her laugh. Why can't she remember me?"

"Can I ask you a question?" Trey asked.

"I have no answers for any questions because nothing makes sense to me right now." Bling shook his head.

"What about your wife, Money B? Didn't you just ask her to marry you again?"

"I think about Keisha more than I think about my wife. I look at my wife, and I wish she was Keisha. I touch my wife, and I reminisce about Keisha." Bling's eyes wandered far, as if Keisha were walking toward him from a distance.

"How could you not love that lovely woman? Have you taken a *good look* at your wife lately?" Trey took a shot at the punching bag.

"I should have known you would be no help." Bling walked away from Trey, leaving the gym.

He sat in his car and blasted his music and sped out of the parking lot. After a few minutes of driving, Bling pulled off the road and marinated in his thoughts. There was a light tapping on his glass. He lowered his window. "How can I help you, Officer? Let me guess, you have a bullet with my name on it too?"

"Do you mind telling me why you are parked in a no parking zone?"

"Good one. Now are you going to call for backup and tell them I'm resisting arrest? I know all you cops are on

Hype's family's payroll and want to make my life hell. Where is the no parking sign, because I don't see it?"

The officer pointed to the sign behind him.

Bling turned his head. The sign was, in fact, there. He glanced at the officer's name badge and addressed him by his name. "Officer Redding, I honestly didn't notice the no parking sign."

"Can you move your car before I write you a ticket?"

"Yes, sir." Bling drove away with a strong drink on his mind.

When he got to the bar it was packed, but he managed to squeeze himself into a standing spot by the bar. The bartender recognized him and came over to him, ignoring everyone else's order.

"What will it be?" she yelled out to him gleefully while bracing her chest for him to see her exposed breasts.

"Give me a shot of Obama!" Bling yelled so his voice could be heard above the cussing and fussing.

"A shot of Hennessey coming right up!" The bartender poured him a shot of Hennessey, and he raised the glass to his mouth and motioned his index finger for another. "Keep them coming!"

"So your workout at the gym didn't help to cure your stress?" the waitress poured his shot.

"How did you know that I was at the gym?" Bling's voice was stern.

"Let's see . . . maybe your gym shorts and sneakers."

"My money isn't good enough around here?" a voice called out to the bartender.

"Money B?" Trey called out when he saw Bling. Trey parted his way through the crowd making his way over to Bling.

"Another shot of Hennesscy coming up! But don't you think you should slow down?" the bartender asked while pouring Bling another. "Your life must be really messed up if you're throwing back shots like water! Maybe I could help you release your stress!" the bartender leaned in and spoke in his ear.

"What you drinking, Trey?" Bling called out with a straight face ignoring her gesture.

"So I'm finally gonna get that drink! You cheap bastard," Trey replied.

"I need you to tell me why you set me up." Bling pointed his finger at Trey, but he couldn't keep his or his balance. Bling was going down to the ground, and Trey broke his fall, bringing him back to his feet.

"What the hell are you talking about? How did I set you up?" Trey escorted him to a vacant table he spotted in the corner.

Bling took a seat, then lay his head on the table. "You came to my room with the information about Keisha, knowing I was reconciling with my wife. It seemed like you had ulterior motives, Trey."

"I just thought you wanted to know," Trey stated in his defense.

Bling raised his head. "There's a time and place for everything, and that was neither."

"Seems to me like you are looking to place the blame on me for you running out on your wife in the Bahamas."

Bling pounded the table with his fist. "I love my wife!"

"Let me ask you this question, and I need an honest answer. But not because you owe me one, but because I think you owe yourself one. If Keisha had woke up before you recommitted to your wife, would you have gone through with it? Seeing how fast you ran out of there."

The question hit Bling hard, and it felt like a ton of bricks fell on his heart. His breathing got heavy. "I love my wife, I love my wife." He recited the line over and over in a whisper.

"You all right, man?" Trey asked with concern in his voice.

"I love my wife! I don't need you or anyone questioning my love for my wife!" But Keisha constantly plague my mind.

"You need to face the facts because you are in denial."

"Man to man, do you think I love my wife?"

"That's none of my business, man. But the way you hightailed it out of the Bahamas would make anyone question your love for your wife. Seems like Keisha got a hold on you."

"Can you stop saying that shit? I'm just concerned for a friend."

"She's more than a damn friend. Who are you kidding?" Trey laughed.

"She has amnesia; she didn't even know who I am."

"Damn, boss lady has amnesia? I need another drink to digest this one."

"Get me another shot of Obama!" Bling rested his head on the table.

"No, Money B. You're tapped out." Trey departed from the table.

"I didn't expect to see my future baby daddy here," Jordonna said, walking up to Bling.

Bling quickly raised his head. "Are you stalking me?"

"I was expecting to get a call from you." She sat on the available chair.

"I'll get you the damn money, but I can't guarantee it won't be that $40,000 you're demanding."

"A promise is a promise, and you will deliver . . . or else," Jordonna threatened.

"Or else *what?*" Bling's tone was rough.

Jordonna dipped her hand into her purse and came up with a picture and slammed it on the table like a Jamaican playing dominoes. "This picture will hit social media so fast, not to mention a personal delivery to your wife."

"Leave my wife out of this." Bling was on his feet.

"Did I hit a nerve?" Jordonna was also on her feet.

"You need to leave or else, and *that's* a threat," Bling warned, bringing his butt back in the chair.

"Let me tell you this, asshole." Jordonna walked around to his side of the table. "You're not calling the shots. By tomorrow morning I need to see a deposit of $20,000 in my account or you will regret making love to me. That *you* can consider a threat." She winked at him, then turned to walk away, and Bling grabbed her arm.

"Get it right, in order to make love, I would have to love you, and I can't love a whore."

"You might want to take that back. Does the name Keisha ring a bell?" Jordonna laughed in his face.

"I'll make you wish you had stayed your ass behind that hotel desk and never crossed me."

"Your threats don't scare me. I have your nuts in my hand, and you know it."

Trey came back to the table with two shots of Hennessy, gently placing them on the table, not wanting to spill them. "Who is this beautiful friend of yours?" he asked, checking her out.

"She's no friend of mine. She's just a groupie trying to get a handout." Bling took a seat.

"Your friend here doesn't like to keep his word. But I'm here to remind him that his fans can make him . . . and break him." She patted his back.

"This is a feisty one. You better give her your autograph before she turns into your enemy," Trey spoke, admiring Jordonna.

"I'm already his enemy." Jordonna took one of the shots and brought it to her lips, then slammed the empty glass on the table and walked away.

Bling reached for the other shot glass, and Trey quickly intercepted, spilling most of its contents.

"What the hell is wrong with you, man? You're going to pay for that," Trey scolded.

"I might as well finish it then; bottoms up!" Bling drained the glass.

"Let's go. I'll take you home," Trey volunteered.

"Sounds like a plan! You can take my car, and you can leave your piece a shit of a car here."

"You're running that mouth a little too much now. Get your ass up." He went to assist Bling out of the chair, but Trey's phone started to vibrate in his pocket. He stopped to get his phone and his smile spread wide. "On second thought, it's best if you call a cab because I have an important stop to make."

"I don't want to leave my car here, man." Bling objected to the cab.

"Nobody is gonna steal your prize possession. But I have to go handle business."

"Go ahead, Trey, I'm a grown-ass man. I'll find my way home."

"I'll meet up with you tomorrow at the studio." Trey left the bar.

Bling took his phone from his pocket and called his wife. He had to repeat himself multiple times before she could comprehend his words.

Bling staggered to the bathroom where he took a piss. Jordonna came in the bathroom and watched until he was done. Bling turned his body and stumbled.

"Are you always a pissy drunk?" Jordonna laughed.

"There is no limit with you." Bling started washing his hands.

"I'll go to the pits of hell to get what I want." She stepped to him.

"Well, start digging." He sidestepped past her.

"I have an offer for you." Jordonna stopped him. "Let's go at it one more time and you could consider your debt paid in full."

"I'm not falling for that."

"Your wife will never know about us, and I'll abort our love child."

Bling laughed and reached for the doorknob. "Love child? I won't fall for that."

"Exactly three weeks." She circled her belly.

Bling braced his back against the door. The thought of his firstborn birthed by a stranger was unacceptable. His body temperature went up, causing him to wipe his face. He became flustered by the information, and his decision was made.

Jordonna braced her body on to him and massaged his dead wood. Bling took charge and bent her over the sink and lifted her dress, ready to give her what she wanted. He raised his head and the mirror in front of him captured a person that didn't represent him.

"Sue me for child support." He backed away from her.

"What?" She was in disbelief.

"You heard me." He left the bathroom and guided his steps back to his seat.

"I've been searching for you." Denise walked over to him.

"Looky here, looky here." Jordonna's arms were akimbo.

Denise studied the unfamiliar face. "Can I help you?"

"Don't pay her no mind, Denise. She's just a groupie. Let's go." Bling got up, but he got dizzy and sat back down.

"My business is really with your husband, but since you don't remember who I am, let's catch up. I was in his hotel room when you popped up on your husband."

"You! Now I remember. So, what business do you have with my husband other than a broken mirror? But if you need me to pay for it, I can give you cash." She was going through her purse. "How about a fifty, or maybe a hundred should cover it?"

"Keep your loose change. It will take more than that to keep our affair a secret."

"Excuse me?" Denise did a neck roll.

"I tried to excuse you, but your husband wouldn't pay up." She placed a picture on the table. "And there is a sex tape that comes along with that."

Denise was speechless. She kept her eyes on the picture that was, in fact, her husband in bed with the woman that stood in front of her. "You must be out of your damn mind!"

"I need to get paid, and since he's not living up to his end of the bargain, I figure you might want to pay his debt, and if I were you, I'd pay up to avoid another humiliation. Don't you think?" Jordonna winked at her.

It was as if Denise had bionic powers. Her hands reached for a half-empty glass next to her and tossed it in Jordonna's face. "You bitches just aren't loyal."

Jordonna jumped back when the drink hit her face. "You ruined my damn dress."

"You dumb chicks always spread your legs, and when you can't control the man with your threats, you run to the wife, hoping she will be so embarrassed and pay the shut-up money. But not this bitch. Run to the media, honey, 'cause that's the only place you're gonna get a dollar."

"I'm calling your bluff, Mrs. I will indeed forgive everything. That was your exact words the day he was released from jail, right? I know you will protect your husband's character to save face. So have a seat and listen to my demands." Jordonna leaned into her face.

"Keep pushing your luck. Get out of my face before I wrap my hand in that horse hair and drag your ass outside and beat you to a pulp." Denise leaned in, almost bumping her face.

Jordonna stepped back, seeing that Denise wasn't a coward. "Get your drunken ass up." Denise pulled Bling by his arm. She wanted to holler and scream at her husband, but for now, she would just save face until she gets home. She roughly pulled Bling's arm, helping him up.

"My information is on the back of that picture. Make the first deposit of $20,000 to my account before 3:00 p.m. or else the sex tape goes viral, and I'll become a star."

"More like a porn star." Denise stated.

"Well, Mimi got paid, and so will I." Jordonna walked away.

Denise put Bling into her car and walked around to the driver's side and turned the key in the ignition. She looked back at Bling, and he was knocked out sleeping. Her eyes zoomed in on Jordonna exiting the bar and her blood boiled. She watched as she entered her car, and then Denise reversed like a race car driver. Jordonna exited the parking lot and made a right turn, and Denise did the same. She tailed Jordonna with the intention to beat her ass as soon as she got out of the car. Denise's phone rang in her purse, but she didn't bother to look at it because she knew it had to be her sister. Denise was getting more agitated by the minute thinking about her husband betraying her again.

Jordonna made a left turn onto I-95 and Denise followed. She checked her gas gauge. She had about half a tank. "You have to pull over sometime." Another few minutes into the drive Jordonna indicated her exit. She made a left turn, then a right, and another five minutes she made another right. "Where the hell is she going?" Denise asked herself. They ended up on a small winding road with a huge mansion occupying acres of land. "Since you won't stop I'll stop you." Denise glanced in her rearview mirror. There were no cars behind her so she accelerated on her gas pedal and hit Jordonna's car hard in the back. Denise wasn't prepared for what came next.

Jordonna lost control of her car turning the curve and went off the road heading down a steep ditch, causing the car to flip. Denise stepped on her brakes, not knowing what to do, but came back to her senses and sped off.

Denise made it home and struggled with Bling into the living room. She hurriedly switched on the TV on wanting to see if there was any news report of the incident. She was visibly shaking, causing the remote to fall out of her hand while flipping the channels hoping to see a news flash but found no reports of what happened. So she paced the living room back and forth as she tried to control her nerves.

"I killed her! I can't believe I killed her!" She was still pacing.

Her scream woke Bling from his sleep. "Can you keep your voice down?"

"I killed her." She sat next to Bling.

"What are you ranting about, and who did you kill?"

A breaking news report flashed across the screen. *"A car was pulled from a ditch on Duck Pond Road a few minutes ago reportedly belonging to the driver Jordonna Robinson. Sadly, we have to report that the driver died after what appeared to be a hit and run."*

"I'm a murderer." Denise was in tears.

Bling couldn't believe his ears or his eyes. "What did you just say?" he questioned.

"I followed her because I wanted to beat her ass, but she kept driving, and I just wanted to bump her car hard enough for her to stop, but she went off the road. I didn't mean to kill her!" she broke down in his arms.

"Did anybody see you?"

"No. I don't think so."

"Don't repeat a word of this! Not even to your family. Do you hear me?"

Denise nodded her head. "But she's out of our life now. We don't have to worry about her anymore."

"Yes, she's out of our lives now." Bling hugged his wife. "I got you. I'm here with you." He rocked her back and forth in his arms until she fell asleep.

Bling's phone was going off nonstop, but he kept ignoring it. He wasn't in the mood to talk to anyone. It's because of him his wife was now a murderer. The phone kept ringing. Finally, he took it from his pocket. He didn't recognize the number so he hesitated to answer, and he missed the call.

Please answer the phone. It's Keisha. A text message lit up his phone screen. He called the number back and a frantic Keisha was on the other end. "OK, I'll be there." Bling spoke.

Bling checked on his wife. She was sleeping soundly on the couch. He hastily went to the door and went outside. "Shit, my damn car is at the bar." Bling called a cab and impatiently waited for five minutes for the cab to arrive. "Take me to M. White Lounge." Bling stated his destination. It took twenty minutes to get there, but he breathed a sigh of relief when he laid eyes on his car.

"Keep the change." He gave the driver a fifty-dollar bill. He was in too much of a hurry to get to Keisha to care for a few bucks back.

Bling revved his engine and drove out of the parking lot, making a left turn on Fairfield Ave., and a red, white, and blue light signaled him to pull over. "Here we go with the bullshit." Bling prepared himself.

Two policemen approached him on opposite sides of his car.

"You seem to be in a rush," one officer stated.

"You and I know that's bullshit," Bling answered looking straight-ahead.

"Word on the street is that there's a bounty out for a rap star. Could it be you?" the other officer said with a smirk.

"You already know who wants me dead, don't you, Officer Jackson?" Bling looked to his right.

"Oh, so the police are psychics now?" both officers laughed.

"You damn well know your family is out to kill me."

"I'm a trained shooter. So you should know I won't miss my target," Officer Jackson talked back.

"Can I go about my business now?" Bling sat up in his seat.

"Yes, you can, but you might get pulled over on the next block," the officers laughed.

Bling made it into Top Dot Records's parking lot and parked next to Keisha's car. He went inside the building calling out her name. "Keisha!" he called going from door to door. He finally opened her office door and found her curled up on the floor.

"He died in this very spot. Uncle Patrick died because of me."

Bling ran over to her. "I'm sure Patrick doesn't blame you for his death." He helped her to sit up, and they embraced for a long time without speaking.

"You have to understand that I didn't remember any-thing." Keisha broke the silence.

"All is forgiven. Just don't lose your memory again." He squeezed her hard.

"You might want to loosen your grip." Keisha tried to breathe.

"I see you're tired of me already," Bling pouted.

"How can I be tired of you when I love you so much? And I know you love me too. Let's start our lives together, Bling, because I don't want to go another day without you."

Bling elevated himself from the floor. "We can't."

"Why not? Why can't we?"

"I'm a married man, Keisha."

"So what are you saying?" She slowly stood up.

"I just can't leave my wife for you. I broke her heart before, and I just can't break it again. She loves me."

"Do you love her?" Keisha held on to him.

"She's my wife." Bling stepped away.

"What about our child? Do you love our child?"

He gave her his full attention. "What did you say?"

"I'm pregnant with your child. We're having a baby." She wiped her falling tears and smiled. She brought his hand to her belly. "We can be a happy family, Bling."

"How do you . . .?" Bling furrowed his brows in confusion.

"How do I know it's yours? Are you *seriously* asking that question?"

"I'm sorry, but I've patched things up with my wife. This is too much right now. I just can't." Bling shook his head as he walked away from her.

CHAPTER 12

A few days had passed, and Denise was back to her normal self. The fact that she had killed Jordonna made her depressed. But after convincing herself that she did it to save her marriage she found solace. "I bought your favorite. Can you smell the aroma?" Denise called out to Bling as she entered the house. "Spicy buffalo wings, Caesar salad, and mac & cheese."

Bling trampled down the stairs to the kitchen, kissing Denise on her lips. "You just made my day."

"You don't run this fast when I cook."

"For some hot wings and mac and cheese, I'll walk on water."

Denise laughed at his humor. She went to the fridge and came back with a Heineken, but she retracted the offer. "On second thought, I don't want you to get drunk and I have to pick you up off the floor."

"You better give me that. A single beer won't hurt, but if you offer me something else, I might have to refuse."

"Boy, you better not play with me. What the hell you think I'm feeding you this food for?"

"I know, all this was for a reason."

"Boy, shut up." She placed two plates on the table, then poured herself a glass of red wine and took her seat.

"I didn't know red wine was your thing." Bling played it cool, hiding the reason for his inquiry. Red wine was Keisha's favorite, but unbeknownst to his wife, she just brought his memory to the person he was trying not to think about.

"It was a peace offering from my sister, so what better time to drink it than now? Well, let's toast. Here's to making our love prevail."

"I'll drink to that." He raised the bottle to his mouth.

Denise reached for the salad and Bling went for the Buffalo wings. She took a few bites, and then slowly sipped her wine and watched as her husband devoured the meal.

"What if I slip into something really sexy, and we do a little role play? I'll be your nurse, and you're the wounded soldier."

"And that I am, a wounded man, and I can really use some TLC."

Denise departed from the table, and Bling sipped his beer and patiently waited for his wife to reemerge. *What about our child? Do you love our child?* Keisha's words replayed in his head. "How can I give to her what I promised to my wife? My firstborn child." He brought the beer to his mouth, draining it to the last drop. He gazed at the glass of red wine with his wife's lipstick stain on the rim. But his mind drifted back to Keisha. Bling reached for the unfinished glass and twirled it. "Red wine is her favorite." The words escaped his lips. Bling shook his head, dismissing Keisha from his mind because right now, his wife deserves to be happy, and he was going to give her happiness.

Bling's phone started to ring in the living room, and he went to get it. "What's up, Derrick? OK, I'll be at the meeting."

"Do you like?" Denise appeared naked in front of him.

Bling released the phone from his grip. She instructed him to sit as she sashayed to him and proceeded to give him a lap dance. She grinded on him until his third leg became rock-hard. She spread her legs and bent over holding on to her ankles, exposing her love nest from the back. Bling dropped his pants and penetrated his wife. His pace was slow as he enjoyed every inch of her. *"I love you."* Keisha's words replayed in his head. *"Do you love her?"* Keisha's question was distressing him.

"Stick your ass out," he ordered his wife in a harsh tone as he slammed into her hard.

"What are you doing?" She tried rising up, but he pushed her back down.

"You know you like it when I play rough." He slammed her without compassion. He stroked hard as Keisha's voice tormented him, and he thrust into his wife like a wild bull.

"What's gotten into you? I want to make love." She tried to stop him, but he pushed her back down.

"We are making love. You love this dick, right?" Bling went in deeper, harder, and faster.

She was expecting to be caressed, licked, and sucked like their usual lovemaking session, but Bling was pounding her hard. "Stop!" She didn't want to continue. "You're acting like an animal!" She pulled away from him.

"You want to change position?" he asked, unfazed.

She was looking at her husband as if he were a stranger. Denise was confused and startled by his behavior. "Do you love her?" Denise let out a roar like a lioness ready to attack.

"What are you talking about?" Bling asked, unsure of what to say. "Have you lost your mind?"

"Do you love her?" Denise screamed.

Bling heard his wife's voice, and it made him tremble. *Yes, no, maybe so. How do I answer this question?*

"Do-you-love-her?" Denise counted her words as she walked closer to him.

That wasn't a question he expected to hear from his wife. Not in a million years, but it seemed as if he had time traveled and he wasn't familiar with this world anymore because everything seemed to be out of sequence.

"No. I love you. You are my wife."

"What about *her?* What happened to your feelings for her?"

"I'm concerned for her as friend."

"A friend." She laughed out loud as if she heard the funniest joke. "So your damn whore of a mistress is now your friend? The type of friends that fuck each other?"

"She went through a lot, Denise, and I am human."

"What about me? Haven't I been through a lot? What about your concern for me? Instead, you're justifying your concern for that bitch as if I'm supposed to care whether she lives or dies. Honestly, I hoped she had died in that damn coma." She walked away.

"Don't you dare talk about her like that!" Bling shouted at his wife, making his stance clear.

Denise spun quickly. "What did you say?"

"That came out wrong." Bling tried to defuse the bomb he just set off.

"You must be out of your fucking mind." She walked back to him.

"I . . . I didn't mean . . . What I meant to say was . . . " Bling couldn't find the words.

"You want to stand up and honor your mistress under my roof? You must have lost your damn mind. I suggest you leave before you end up in a damn coma too. I see. I'm not your first priority anymore." Denise stepped backward walking away from her husband.

My wife is beautiful. She is perfection. How could my heart betray me? I have what every man wants, but my heart isn't satisfied.

She hurried out of the room, but Bling didn't go after his wife; instead, he dressed himself and left the house.

"It's nice of you to grace us with your presence. Did your wife have to approve your permission slip?" Keisha attacked sarcastically.

Bling sat in the seat that was obviously awaiting him. "Can we keep this business and not personal, please?" he retorted.

"*Now* you want to talk about business when your ass is an hour late?" Keisha snapped back.

It was evident to everyone that this was much deeper than business.

"Do you want to talk in private, Keisha?" Bling tried to defuse the situation.

"You will address me as Miss Burkett while you are in this business meeting." She stood up and scolded him like a child.

"Sounds more like love and war to me." Trigga made light of the situation.

"Trigga, if I needed your input, I would have opened the floor to you. But since I didn't, why don't you find a clinic to get rid of your itch." She cut him down to size.

"You need to realize that when I step into this building it's business. If I wanted to listen to a woman bitching, I would have stayed home with my damn wife who has a good reason for being bitchy, unlike you," Bling addressed Keisha.

"You will respect me as your boss!" Keisha scolded.

"I'll give respect when respect is due," Bling shot back.

Keisha gazed intently at him, but he tried not to make eye contact with her. He could feel her eyes cutting him like a knife. Keisha didn't speak another word. She allowed Derrick to take over the meeting.

Feeling disrespected, Keisha got up from her seat, and her fashion sense was on point. She wore a tight-fitted, white, knee-length dress that she paired with an orange blazer and matching orange pumps with silver tips at the front. She walked over to Bling and whispered in his ear. "Meet me at my house in ten minutes or your wife will know about our love child. I will not be disrespected, and my child won't be ignored."

Keisha arrived home and was seething with anger. She aggressively turned the key in the door and broke a nail. "Shit!" She flashed her hand and kicked her shoes off. One shoe landed on the lawn, and the other one landed on the bottom step. Her finger went into her mouth, which soothed the pain a little. Keisha pushed the door open with her body and went inside. She removed her finger from her mouth and blew on it. "Ugh!" Then she dropped herself on the bed.

"Keisha!" Bling called out to her.

Keisha got off the bed and went to him. "What is it, Bling?"

"You better leave my wife out of this!"

"I *better?* That's a strong demand. But I can tell you this much. My child will not be a secret."

"So you're planning to destroy my marriage?"

"Your marriage is already destroyed. I guess you forgot that I am the *other* woman."

"Was. Past tense."

"So why were you at the hospital when I came out of the coma?" Keisha's voice was on high.

"Are you seriously asking that question? I was concerned about you." Bling kept his voice low.

"So why did you barge in my apartment pounding on Damien?"

"Your father asked me to check up on you." He walked away.

Keisha grabbed him by the arm. "You're lying! I saw the look in your eyes. The way you were looking at me. You were begging me to come back to you."

"I was begging you to come back to your senses, not to me." Bling attempted to walk away again, but she pulled him back.

"I don't believe you. You can't even look me in the eyes."

"You want me to look you in the eyes, Keisha? You want the truth, Keisha? Well, I hope you can handle the truth. I renewed my vows with my wife. We are planning our family. My wife loves me, and I will stay with her. Now *that's* the truth, handle it." Bling was at war with his feelings. He was fighting the fact that he had fallen in love with his mistress.

"You can keep lying to her if you want, but you will be with us."

"I will be there for my child, Keisha, but until then, it's strictly business." He left the house, but Keisha chased after him.

"So that's it? After all we've been through?"

"I'm a married man. Am I supposed to end my marriage to make you happy?"

"You need to end that marriage because I know you're not happy. Isn't that the reason why you strayed in the first place?"

"And it was a big mistake." He got into his car.

"I'm carrying your firstborn, and if you don't want a family with me, there will be none. I will schedule the appointment." She walked away from him.

Bling got out of his car in a flash, grabbing her with a firm grip. "That child in your stomach will be my firstborn, and if you abort my child, you can also drop me from the label because I will never have anything to do with you again."

"I was just pushing your buttons. I didn't mean it. I love you," she professed.

"Then love my child enough not to kill it!" He went back to his car.

"You *will* come home to me!" she screamed. "Your wife will find out the truth that I'm the one you love." She went on a rant. "I will purposely name my child after you. I'll give him your first, middle, and last name. I will make her green with envy knowing I gave birth to your firstborn. I hope I'm having twins, a boy and a girl. That will put the icing on the cake. I will get her out of your life, Bling. I will."

"You've lost your damn mind." He sped off.

Raindrops sprinkled on Bling's windshield, and his wiper blades were in motion. A huge cross stood tall, reaching up to the sky as a landmark for the church. Bling swung in the parking lot, taking up two spaces. Pastor Blake's white Bentley was the only car in the lot. He ran to the door, and raindrops dampened his clothes. He pulled on the door, but it was locked.

"Pastor Blake!" He pounded. "Open the door!" He kept pounding. "I know you're in there. Open the door!"

The door opened, and Pastor Blake stood in the center of the doorway. "You missed service, but you're still welcome."

Bling dropped to his knees and wept. "Make it stop!"

"Of what do you speak, my child?" Pastor Blake rested his hand on his shoulder.

"Tell Him to make it stop!"

"I'm afraid I don't understand."

"God is punishing me. He's giving me burdens that I can't carry."

"You've got it all wrong, my son. I can't tell the man upstairs to stop doing anything."

"Aren't you a pastor? He hears you when you speak."

"My child, God hears all of us when we speak. So whatever is going on with you, take it to Him in prayer. Ask for forgiveness. He's a forgiving God."

Bling was on his knees crawling to the altar. "This is too much for me. You keep piling on more. What will it be next? I took Hype's life in self-defense. You know that! But still you punish me."

"God doesn't punish my child, He forgives," Pastor Blake interjected.

"How do you explain the turn of events in my life, Pastor? How do you explain my broken marriage, Keisha pregnant with my child, Hype's brother coming for me? My wife ki— . . . " he stopped himself from telling that his wife murdered Jordonna.

"Those mishaps are a chain reaction caused by your action. You can't prevent the inevitable." Pastor Blake spoke in a calm tone.

"But He can prevent it. He's supposed to prevent it if He's so forgiving."

"I think He lets us fall sometimes so we can see where we went wrong, and it's up to you to try to right your wrongs. Sometimes you need to humble yourself and take responsibility. Have you taken any responsibility for Hype's death? Have you apologized to the family? You are pointing out what has been done to you. Start with where you went wrong in these situations," Pastor Blake said.

"I never thought about it that way. I came here upset at God, but I'm the one who set the runaway train in motion."

"You see, my child, we are the ones who create the havoc in our life, then we want Him to work miracles when it's no longer fun. Then we curse His name when you have to suffer the consequences. He's here to forgive our sin, not to fight your battles." Pastor Blake patted him on the shoulder. Bling rose from his knees and gave Pastor Blake a handshake. They walked to the door, and by now, the rain was pouring down.

"I hope this is a shower of blessing and not Him crying tears for me," Bling joked.

"He cries not only for you but for the entire world."

Bling descended the steps running to his car. The sound of gunshots echoed, penetrating Bling's body, and he fell on the sidewalk. Pastor Blake ran to his aid, resting his head in his lap.

"Am I going to die?" Bling asked with his eyes closed. His body was soaked in blood as the rain poured down on him. He trembled, and Pastor Blake cradled him.

"I think He was really crying for me," Bling spoke.

"Hush, my child." Pastor Blake removed his suit jacket and covered his body.

CHAPTER 13

Keisha settled for the spa because she needed some pampering after the episode she had with Bling.

The warm mud bath worked wonders on her tense body. She closed her eyes and inhaled, then exhaled, letting her stress go. A sudden presence of someone entering the room overcame her.

"How's your mud bath, Miss Burkett?" the gentle but subtle voice of a woman asked.

"Less interruption would make it much better. I'm paying for relaxation not interruption," she answered harshly.

"Just relax, Miss Burkett," the voice said reassuringly.

The voice was now really close. Feeling uncomfortable Keisha raised her arm in an attempt to remove the cucumber from her eyes when all of a sudden her face was being smothered with a towel.

"So you're expecting to relax while you have ruined other people's lives? How do you sleep at night? And you have the nerve to wanna bring a bastard child into this world. Well, I'm going to solve this problem. Any spawn of yours is a spawn of the devil."

Keisha tried to get ahold of the person's arm, but the slippery mud prevented her from getting a good grip. "My baby, my baby," she said worriedly. Keisha fought with all her might, but the heavy mud held her legs down; besides, lying on her back made it more difficult.

"You're living the high life, huh? You deserve to die! And the pleasure is all mine," the female voice whispered in her ear.

"Mmhh! Mmhh!" Keisha tried to speak, but her words were muffled by the towel. *Oh, God, please protect me and my unborn child.*

God had come through for her the first time she had prayed that prayer, and this time she was hoping He would hear her again. Her energy was getting low, and she didn't have much fight left in her. Besides, she wasn't getting oxygen, and she was drifting out of consciousness when she heard her mother's voice.

He's beautiful, Keisha.

Mother? She saw her dead mother in a distance. *Why are you here?*

My grandson is so handsome. I'm here to take him with me.

No, no. You will not take him.

I'll take care of him, baby. The same way I took care of you. She was now cradling a baby, and she turned away to leave.

Stop! I will not let you take my baby.

Fight, Keisha. Don't give up. Her uncle spoke to her.

Uncle Patrick! she called out to her uncle.

Yes, it's me. But it's about you right now. Don't give up. He turned and walked away from her.

Uncle Patrick, I need you. Don't leave me again.

A baby was crying, and Keisha could see her mother comforting the baby.

What's wrong with him? Bring him back to me. He needs me! I will not let you take my baby.

Keisha was fighting to save her baby, but she couldn't get a grip on the person who was trying to kill her.

"What's going on in here?" the spa attendant called out.

The person ran out of the room, and Keisha struggled to breathe. "I can't lose my baby," she tried to speak.

"Call an ambulance," the attendant yelled.

Once again Keisha was back in the hospital. This was the second attempt of someone trying to end her life. "My baby, is my baby OK?" Keisha frantically asked.

"Your baby is doing just fine," the nurse assured her. "There's an officer waiting to ask you some questions, but only if you're up for it."

"Yes, because I would like to know who tried to kill me." Keisha rubbed her stomach in a circular motion. "My baby is fine," she consoled herself.

A tall policeman entered the room. "Miss Burkett, I have a few questions for you, but I'm going to try not to upset you."

"Who did this to me?" Keisha fired the first question.

"That's what I'm here to find out," he retorted.

"All I remember is someone trying to suffocate me."

"Did the person say anything that might give us some clue?"

"She just wanted to get rid of me and my baby. Like she wanted revenge." Keisha wiped her watery eyes.

"You said she. So we now know it's a female." He wrote on his notepad. "Anyone you might be able to think of?"

"Not right now."

"What about Mr. Mills? Can you shed some light on who tried to kill him?"

"What?" She was flabbergasted.

"I guess you didn't know someone tried to kill him too. Well, here is my card. Call me if you can think of anyone." He handed his card to her and exited.

Keisha also made her way to the door. She brought herself to the nurse's station where she acquired Bling's room number. She scurried to room #555 where he was lying on his back with his eyes closed. Keisha stretched her arm around him. "You better not scare me like that again." She raised her head, but Bling remained asleep.

"Only one visitor at a time," Keisha heard the nurse informing someone.

"Well, that's my husband, and I'm first priority."

She recognized Denise's voice and dashed behind the curtain that served as a partition. She didn't have the energy for more drama.

"I could've sworn there was someone in here." The nurse was baffled.

"Thank you, God, for saving my husband." Denise prayed when she entered the room.

Keisha spied from behind the curtain and could see the nurse taking Bling's chart from the holder on the wall and jotted a few notes as she walked closer to his bedside. She did her routine checkup and wrote more notes.

"Any changes?" Denise questioned.

"Your husband is doing as best as we expect him to. It's just a matter of time before he wakes up. But you should take a break and go take care of yourself because there's nothing you can do for him." The nurse returned the chart to the holder.

"He needs me." She groomed his eyebrows with her finger. She felt her phone vibrating in her pocket and slowly retrieved it without taking her gaze off her husband.

The word sister appeared on the screen. She had been ignoring her ever since she killed Jordonna out of fear she would let the cat out of the bag.

You better call me. I want to know what's going on the text message appeared on the screen. Denise knew she had to call her sister, but she wasn't ready to explain anything. Right now, she was in a state of mind where nothing else mattered to her but her husband.

"How is he?" Trey asked.

Denise was startled because she didn't hear the door open. "He's stable."

"Who did this?" he inquired.

"I should be asking you that question."

"What happened to you, man?" Trey stood looking down at Bling.

"I got a call from Pastor Blake telling me he had been shot." Denise spoke with her eyes on Bling.

"Pastor Blake? How is he involved in this?"

"He said Bling came to see him, and they gunned him down at the church."

"I know Hype's family wanted revenge, and I told him to watch his back." Trey stepped away.

"You have to go to the police." Denise stood up.

"You know what that can do to my reputation? I'm no snitch." Trey fanned her off.

"But Bling is your friend who almost died." Denise raised her voice.

"That he is, but he also knows the road code that we have to live by."

"But they can't get away with this!" Denise was furious.

"They won't because if they really did this, we have to take matters in our own hands."

"No. The police will handle this. I don't want my husband going back to jail."

"Not when Hype has family and friends in the police department."

"I don't want my husband involved in this!" Denise warned.

"He's already involved. This is his war, remember?"

"I can't lose my husband. I just can't!" she broke down crying. Trey wrapped his arms around her, and she sobbed in his arms.

"You will lose him to me," Keisha smiled.

"I'm here for you. I'll keep you safe. Let me take you home so you can get some rest."

"I'm not leaving my husband," Denise yelled at Trey and pushed him away.

"How are you helping? Besides, you're going to need your energy for when he comes home. He'll be bedridden for days. You'll be running back and forth like a maid."

"OK. OK. I get your point." Denise kissed Bling's face and stepped back, slowing leaving the room with Trey in tow.

Keisha came out of hiding and went to the door making sure the coast was clear.

"Keisha." Bling spoke.

Keisha glanced toward him, and his eyes were looking at her. "You're awake," she gleefully stated.

"What are you wearing?" Bling noticed the hospital robe.

"Whoever tried to kill you came for me too." She sat on the bed.

"Is my baby OK?" Bling coughed and his facial expression indicated that he was feeling pain.

"Your baby? You mean our baby," Keisha corrected.

"You know what I mean. What happened?"

"Well, I was at the spa, and a woman came in the room and tried to suffocate me."

"Hype's family is coming for me, and now I know they're coming for you too, and I won't let them hurt my child."

"How will you protect us when you have to go home to your wife?"

"I'll figure something out."

"You need to cut the act and move in with us. She isn't the one in danger, your child is. Think about it, Bling., Wouldn't it be wise to protect your unborn child?" Keisha preyed on his conscience.

"I said I'll figure something out." Bling coughed again.

"I know I've made lots of bad decisions, but my child deserves to live. Why can't you love the mother of your child enough to protect us?" Keisha pleaded with him. "I deserve to be loved too." She put on the waterworks.

"I love you! I love you, Keisha, and I won't let anyone harm our baby." Bling confessed his love.

Keisha's eyes widened looking at Bling. She didn't expect to hear him say those words. She knew he was hiding his feelings for her, but hearing him admit his love had taken her by surprise.

CHAPTER 14

After a few days staying in the hospital Trey was on time to take Bling home. Bling decided he would go home to his wife and put on a front to spare her the grief. "I'll be at the gym if you want to exercise your muscles," Trey joked.

"Not for a few weeks." He exited the car.

"I'll wait here till you go inside. Just in case bullet starts to fly and I have to take you back to the hospital." Trey poked his head out the window, laughing.

"Don't joke with my life, Trey." He took a deep breath as he fidgeted with his keys at the door.

"Honey, I'm home!" he called out to his wife in a sham, trying to cover his betrayal yet once again.

"I'm in the bathroom. I'll be out in a minute." Her voice traveled from upstairs.

Bling made his way to the kitchen and got himself a beer to calm his nerves because his heart was pounding even though he was told not to consume alcohol.

"Hi, honey." You could hear the excitement in Denise's voice.

"Hey, yourself." Bling admired the beautiful woman walking to him. Her hair was pulled to the left side of her head, and wavy curls dangled to her breast. The light from the kitchen window glared on her, exposing her cheek, and her smile created a perfect picture.

"I'm so excited," she exclaimed happily with her arms tightened around him.

"My chest, you're squeezing a little too hard."

"Did I hurt you?" She released her grip and stepped back.

"Thanks for the warm welcome." He took a seat.

"I'm glad you're home, but I'm excited about something else." She also seated herself.

"Excited about what?" Bling's curiosity was running wild.

"Baby, I love you so much," she proclaimed, not knowing that her husband's heart was elsewhere.

"Are you going to tell me what all this excitement is about?" He took a sip of his beer, hoping the news didn't include a lie detector test.

"Baby, I have good news!"

"So are you going to tell me or what? The anticipation is killing me."

She reached for his hand, but he purposefully reached for his beer, taking another sip.

"I think I might be pregnant!" Denise clapped being her own cheerleader.

Bling almost choked on his beer. His eyes bulged out of his head.

"Are you OK?" She got up from the chair and patted his back.

"What did you just say?" he asked in disbelief.

"Are you OK?" Denise repeated.

"No, before that," Bling spoke as he coughed.

"I think I might be pregnant. Aren't you glad? I finally put my birthday present to good use. I just took a test, and in about a minute, I should have the results. We might finally have the family I always wanted. Aren't you happy?" She searched his face for his joy, but it was stoic.

"This can't be happening. I can't do this." He proceeded to leave the kitchen.

"Do what?" she stopped him. "I understand you might not want to get your hopes up, but just think about it. You might finally get to be a dad." She kissed his cheek. "But I don't want to get ahead of myself. I still have to check the results." She hastily ran to the bathroom.

Bling took the opportunity to grab Denise's car key and exit the house. He couldn't stay there waiting to know if she really was pregnant. This was too much for him to handle. He turned the key in the ignition and backed out of the driveway.

Bling drove for a few minutes with no destination in mind. Then he pulled off the road and pounded his fists on the steering wheel. "She can't be pregnant. Please don't let it be positive." He raised his head to the sky.

"Are you going to do this to me? I think you know what's best for her, and that is to not let her be pregnant because either way, I'm still leaving. You hear me?"

Bling started driving again, and Trey was his go-to man. He ended up at the gym, and Trey was beating the punching bag hard. "What you doing here, man? Why aren't you home in bed?" Trey kept punching.

"I need your help, and if you want me to pay you, just name the price." He walked to Trey like a madman.

"Hold the fuck up!" he turned his attention to Bling but keep bobbing and weaving as the punching bag swayed back and forth. "How did I get into this again? And pay me to do what? You still didn't pay me for your trip to the Bahamas yet." He was breathing hard and dripping in sweat.

"I want you to seduce my wife," Bling said with a straight face.

"*What* did you just say?" Trey paused from ducking when he heard the words, but he didn't trust his ears. The bag came back and knocked him in the head. He sat on the floor.

"You heard me." Bling looked him in the eye.

"I *don't* think I heard you correctly."

"I want you to seduce my wife. You heard me," Bling repeated looking down at Trey.

"Seduce your wife? Have you gone nuts?" Trey didn't know if this was just an act on Bling's part. He was trying to keep his composure, not knowing if Bling had found out about his previous encounter with his wife.

"I can't make her happy anymore; my heart isn't with my wife. I'm in love with Keisha." Bling braced his back on the wall.

"Let me break this down." Trey jumped to his feet. "You're not in love with her anymore, and now you want to pay me to seduce her? You can't just toss your wife to the homie!" Trey was putting on a front because getting the go-ahead to seduce Bling's wife was every man's fantasy.

"How much will it cost me?" Bling asked with a poker face.

"You can't be serious. You *seriously* would leave your wife for Keisha who, from what I heard, has been around the block a couple times, and back?" Trey insulted.

"Don't you fucking disrespect my woman like that!" he said, pointing his finger at Trey.

"Calm down. You're gonna have people thinking that this is a lover's quarrel."

They both scouted the room with their eyes, and, in fact, a few eyes were focused in their direction.

"Do you think this is easy for me? But my heart wants what it wants! But if you don't want to help me out, it's cool. I'll just have to find someone who will take her off my hands." He was heading for the exit.

"Hell no, you are *not* going to take back that offer."
Trey was more than interested in the offer, but he didn't
want to seem too excited. "Hold on, Money B. I totally
agree with what you're saying. You have to follow your
heart, man. I just wanted to make sure that you were
thinking with a clear head and not just because you're
feeling guilty for what happened to boss lady."

"That has a lot to do with it, but I'm in love with her
too."

"Well, if it's like that, I'll help you out." Trey playfully
punched his arm.

"How much will it cost me?" Bling asked without
shame.

"This one is on me. You just have to pay for the basics."
*'Cause if you don't want that beautiful wife of yours, I'll
take her off your hands since you want to turn a ho into
a housewife.* Trey didn't dare say his inner thoughts to
him. "You'll have to front the cash for dining, trips, and
hotels." *I will take your money and treat your wife to the
life she deserves.* "And last but not least, what's my limit,
because I don't want to overstep my boundaries."

"You have full range of her mind, body, and soul."
Bling left the gym.

"Where are you going, man?" Trey followed behind
him. "That woman doesn't deserve this."

Bling stopped and faced his friend. "I'm giving you the
opportunity to fuck my wife. You should take it."

Bling walked to his car, and he could hear his phone
ringing. When he checked it, he had missed ten calls from
his wife. He didn't return her call; instead, he silenced the
ringer. He drove to Keisha's apartment feeling the urge to
be with her. He kept his finger on the doorbell because he
had lost the spare key. She opened the door with a smile
on her face.

"Daddy's home!" She opened her arms and welcomed him.

"It does sounds good. But you're squeezing too tight."

Bling kissed her, and she kissed him with passion. He grabbed her face and stared into her eyes. "I love you," he confirmed.

"I love you too." Her voice trembled.

She led the way to the living room, and he took a seat. She climbed into his lap and lifted her dress over her head. Her perky breasts pointed at him. He caressed them both, then opened his mouth and took in the right nipple. Then he went from left to right, enjoying both breasts. Keisha raised her body enough for him to enter her with his hardened wood. She held on to the headrest behind him and took him, inch by inch.

"Are you OK?" Bling was concerned for the baby.

"I'm fine." Keisha went in a steady riding motion, pleasing him and herself.

Bling clasped his hand around her back, bringing her closer to him, closing the gap as if they were conjoined.

Bling's moans were animalistic as he pumped more of him into her. Keisha grabbed ahold of the couch, giving her support as she worked him, giving him plenty of reasons why he should stay. Bling let his inner beast out and howled like a wolf. He kept howling as he exploded in her heaven. The session ended, and they remained in position holding each other.

"I love you." Bling kissed her cheek.

"I love you more." Keisha kissed him back.

"No. I love you more." Bling kissed her twice.

"Yeah, you do." Keisha got up and dressed herself.

"How about you get your baby daddy something to drink?"

"That, I can do. And you can find a movie on Netflix for us to watch." She went to the kitchen.

Bling settled for *Ride Along* because he knew Kevin Hart was a funny character.

"What's taking you so long?" Bling yelled out to Keisha. "I'm starting without you."

"I'm getting ice cream!" she answered, yelling from the kitchen.

"You don't need ice cream. You're already fat." Bling laughed. "Just joking, baby, you look sexy to me."

He removed the phone from his pocket, and the ten missed calls had doubled in number. He placed the phone on the coffee table.

"You're just trying to make me feel good." Keisha came out with a bowl of ice cream in one hand and a beer in the other.

"I feel like a pig, and you are not making me feel better." She passed the beer to Bling, and he reached up and touched her face. "You know I love you, girl." A sudden burst of gunshots blasted in the speaker, and Keisha jumped, almost dropping the ice-cream bowl out of her hand. Bling quickly reached for the remote and turned the volume down. Keisha was still traumatized from the gun battle she was in the middle of when Hype tried to kill her.

"I can't have my child hearing gunshots."

"But I can't have him watching these cry-me-a-river movies. Like a sissy."

"I can already tell what kind of father you're going to be." She lifted the spoon to her mouth.

"A damn good one." He took a sip from his beer. "Cheers to my boy!" He raised the bottle.

"He's moving!" The words escaped her lips with excitement.

"Am I *really* going to be a father?" he placed his hand on top of hers as she circled her belly gently.

"You know you have to change your ways when we have this baby, right?" She pointed the spoon at him.

"What are you talking about change my ways?"

"We have to do this fifty-fifty." Keisha poked him with the spoon.

"I'll be there for my boy more than you would ever imagine. My boy is going to be just like his daddy." The beer went to his mouth.

"Definitely not an alcoholic like his daddy."

The phone kept lighting up like a flashlight. Bling reached for his phone, and the name wife was on the screen in bold letters.

"I have to go. But I'll be back soon." He was on his feet.

"Is that her? When are you going to tell her about us? We are having a baby together. Don't you think it's time for her to be out of the picture?"

"It's not that easy to tell her." He walked away, and she was right behind him.

"But you can't keep stringing her along."

"And I can't break her heart either." He kept walking.

"I'll tell you this, you have to tell her before this child is born, because I can't have you going back and forth. I'm going to need you here full time."

"I have to wait until the time is right." He stopped and faced her.

"And when is that?"

"I don't know. Just not now." He started walking again.

"It's either you are going to tell her, or I will." She raised her voice.

"You seem to be forgetting that she is not just anybody. She's my wife." He spoke with anger.

"You seem to be forgetting that I'm carrying your child."

"Like I said, I have to go." He walked out the door.

***

Bling Braced himself for an all-out war when he got home and opened the door, but he didn't have to duck from pots and pans coming at his head. He hastened to the bathroom wanting to take a piss. He lifted the lid and released. He finished his business and shook his friend, letting the last drop fall in the bowl. Turning his head in the direction of the sink his eyes made contact with the pregnancy test. His heart started to pound in his chest. Bling took a minute to compose himself, then lifted his eyes slowly. He had no idea what the sign on the test meant. His eyes instinctively went to the trash can and the instructions were, in fact, right there. Without hesitation, his hand reached for the paper. (+) pregnant (-) not. Bling took his eyes back to the test and breathed a sigh of relief.

"I guess you know what's best for her after all," he said looking up to God. He stepped out of the bathroom, and Denise confronted him in the hallway.

"You went to her, didn't you?" Denise's arms were folded on her chest.

"I went for a drive. I had to think," Bling lied.

"You said you wanted us to start a family."

"That was before I got shot. How can I plan to have a child when there's a possibility I might not be around to raise my child?" He walked past her.

Bling's phone started to ring in his pocket. He retrieved the phone. "What's up, Trey?" he answered. But Trey didn't speak back "Trey!" Bling called his name but Trey was busy carrying on a conversation with Trigga in the background. The conversation was pertaining to him so he listened. He came to the realization that Trey had butt dialed him.

"Can you give me some respect and get off the phone?" Denise was pissed that he was ignoring her.

"Not now." Bling had the phone glued to his ear.

CHAPTER 15

"It's time to put operation seduction into motion." Bling spoke while reclining his car seat.

"You summoned me here, so what's the plan?" Trey was anxious without making it obvious.

"I'm going to get my wife in the mood, but instead of me going in the bed, it's gonna be you." Bling puffed on a cigarette.

"Hold on! What?" Trey shook his head. "So she's blind and can't tell the difference between me and you?"

"Shut up and listen," Bling instructed.

"OK. Go ahead, it's your crazy world, and I'm just living in it," he chuckled.

"The lights will be off so she won't know that it's not me." Bling opened a small bottle of Hennessey.

"I'm built like a damn stallion. She will know it's not you," Trey counteracted.

"A stallion should be able to bench press more than 100 pounds," Bling insulted.

"More like 150 pounds." Trey showed his muscle.

"Since when?" Bling looked over at Trey in the passenger seat. "I spotted you the last time, remember?"

"Get back to your crazy plan and hop off me." Trey reclined his seat.

"Since you can't get the concept, let me run through the plan so you can understand."

"I'm all ears." Trey folded his arms on his chest.

"My wife is in the house waiting for me to make love to her." Bling took a pull from his cigarette.

"Wife? Man, you are banned from saying that word." Trey raised his voice and shook his head.

"Will you shut up and listen?" Bling was getting frustrated with Trey.

"Go ahead, playboy." Trey backed down.

"I'm going to tell her I want to make up for the way I've been acting. Then I'm going to get her in the mood by doing a little foreplay. I'm going to turn all the lights off, and that's where you come in and we switch. I'll let you do your thing, and after a few minutes, I'll turn the light on and catch you in the act."

"Are you listening to yourself? This is sounding more ridiculous by the minute. I don't know about this." Trey shook his head.

"You backing out?" Bling asked.

"What's the rush, Money B? Why don't you let me ease into it? The plan was for me to wine and dine her and get her to fall for me. Why all of a sudden you want to do this tonight?"

"Change of plans. I know you have a sweet tooth, so why not have you enjoy the pie? So are you in or out?"

"I'll go through with it. I'll please your wife and fulfill her needs."

"OK. I'm going in. I'll leave the door open, and after twenty minutes you can come inside."

Bling checked the time on the dashboard. It was 9:30 p.m. As soon as he opened the door Denise ran down the stairs and embraced her husband.

"I was worried about you. Where were you?" She lay her head on his chest.

"I'm here now." Bling gave her a phony smile. Denise went for a kiss, but he gave her a peck and walked away.

"I'm ecstatic that you changed your mind about starting our family. I'm the happiest woman alive. I'm glad that I have my husband back." Denise followed him.

"You deserve happiness, and tonight is your night." Bling poured her a glass from the bottle of Hennessey he was sipping on.

"You came prepared. I like."

"Cheers to love." Bling clinked his bottle with his wife's glass, and they both drank.

"Wow." Denise made a face expressing her dislike.

"Stop being a punk. Bottoms up," Bling coached.

They both downed the drink. Bling challenged his wife into taking a few shots with him. When she was wasted enough, he lifted her up the stairs, letting her down on her feet when they entered the bedroom.

"Tonight, I'm going to reward you for being a loyal wife. We can do all the things you like. You tell me how you want it, and I'll comply." Bling removed her lingerie, and the white silk fabric slid off her body, softly falling to the floor.

Denise kissed her husband, and he kissed her back. Unbeknownst to Denise, this was her good-bye kiss from her husband. Bling lifted his wife to the bed and proceeded kissing her. He became overwhelmed, and tears fell from his eyes onto her face.

"Why are you crying, babe?" she asked.

"Because we're about to start a new life." Bling abruptly sat up and paced the room.

"You still want us to have a baby, don't you?" Denise didn't know what to think of his reaction.

Bling spotted Trey on the staircase, and they made eye contact. "Let's get this show on the road." He pulled his shirt over his head, and Trey did the same. "Let's turn this light off so you can let the freak out in the dark." Bling hit the light switch, and Trey made the switch.

Trey found Denise's body on the bed, and his intention was to please her. He buried his head between her legs, and her moans gave confirmation to Bling. He sat on the staircase and quietly cried, listening to his wife being pleasured by another man.

"Yes, baby, yes!" Denise's moans filled the house.

Bling went to the kitchen and emptied the bottle. Then he went to the coat closet and removed his .45 pistol from his leather coat pocket and marched upstairs. Denise and Trey were at their climax. He flipped the light on looking at his wife and the person he thought was his friend.

"Was it what you expected it to be, Trey?" Bling pointed the gun at him.

"Oh my God!" Denise was revolted.

"Shut up, Denise!" Bling kept the gun on Trey. "So when were you going to tell me you fucked my wife?"

"I don't know what you're talking about, Bling! This was *your* plan." Trey was in a panic.

"Babe! What's going on?"

"Shut up, Denise! I'll get to you."

"I'm doing your dirty work, and *I'm* in the wrong?" Trey shouted.

"How long have you been fucking my wife, Trey?"

"I never touched your wife." Trey's voice was on high.

"You might want to rethink that because that's not what you were telling Trigga when your phone butt dialed me yesterday."

"I can explain," Denise pleaded.

"I keep telling you to shut up!" He pointed the gun at Denise, then back at Trey.

"The signs were all there. That day you were nervous to bring me home. You didn't show up at the ceremony, and then Trigga took a jab at the meeting, but I couldn't imagine my wholesome wife being a whore."

"Let me explain!" Denise was petrified.

"And you . . . " he turned to his wife. "Your sister tried to tell me, but I thought she just wanted to keep us apart. And even at the restaurant you were in such a panic when he came to our table. The look on your face was priceless."

"I can't believe you set me up." The words slowly left Trey's mouth.

"Get your ass up!" Bling walked up to Trey, pointing the gun at his forehead.

"So what you gonna do, Money B, kill me?" Trey slowly back out of the bedroom.

"I should, shouldn't I? But I'm not, but I will do this!" He gun butted Trey, and he fell down the stairs. "You better leave before I put one in your ass." Bling pointed the gun at Trey, and he ran out of the house, leaving his shirt behind.

"Don't do this. You don't want to go back to jail. Think about us."

"There is no us, Denise. We are done."

"No, we're not. We can work it out like we did before."

"Before, I felt like I owed you that much to try to fix it. Before, I thought you deserved my love. But you betrayed me with my friend."

"What about us having a family like we planned?"

"I am going to have a family, just not with you. Keisha is pregnant!"

"Why do you keep mentioning her damn name? What does that have to do with us? I feel sorry for the man who fathered her bastard child."

"*I am the father!*" Bling shouted at the top of his lungs.

"What did you just say?"

"Keisha is pregnant with *my* child."

"That is a mean joke, and I don't find it funny." Denise was in disbelief.

"It's not a joke, so deal with it."

"This can't be real, this can't be real." Denise tried to convince herself that those words didn't escape her husband's mouth.

"It *is* real," Bling reinstated.

"It's not a bad thing. We can adopt the baby. I'm sure that she won't want the baby after it's born. See, God made it happen like this. She's carrying our child. Everything worked out fine. We are going to have a family after all. We should use the spare bedroom for a nursery. If it's a girl we could call her Joy, because she is going to bring such joy to our life. But if it's a boy, we'll name him after you. Baby . . ." She walked up to him and gave him a hug. "This is going to work out fine."

Bling pushed her away. "No, it won't."

"It's OK, babe. I'm not upset. I know you probably was scared to tell me, thinking I might want a divorce, but since I can't seem to give you a child, she's carrying our baby." She was still in denial of her husband's words.

Bling placed his hands on both her shoulders. "Keisha is going to keep our child."

"She can't do that. That child belongs to us."

"There is no more us! Can't you tell by the way that I'm never home?"

"Because you are in the studio a lot." Tears ran from her eyes.

"That's just what I told you so you would stop asking questions because you keep on nagging me about spending time with you."

"You can't talk to me like that! I'm your *wife!*" She wiped her falling tears.

"I'm sorry. I didn't mean to hurt you. Things happen sometimes, and we have no control over them."

"Shut up! Shut up! I don't want to hear it. You are a sorry excuse for a man who knows nothing about the value of a woman, especially his wife. Get out! Get out of my house!"

"I fell in love with her. I had no control over that."

In a state of denial, shock, and confusion, she tried to convince herself that this was a dream. "Is this really happening? I'm dreaming, right? Are you really leaving me for Keisha? No, you're not. I'm going to wake up, and this will all be a bad dream."

"It's not a dream. I'm moving out tonight."

"You are not leaving me! You're *not* leaving!" she hugged her husband.

"Don't make this harder for yourself. If I stay I'll just be living a lie."

"We can be happy again. I can make you happy."

"You need to make yourself happy. And there is someone out there that can make you happy." Bling opened the closet door and retrieved his Louis Vuitton suitcase. Laying it on the bed he unzipped it.

"What are you doing?" Denise tried to stop him.

"I'm packing." He removed a bunch of his shirts and tossed them in the suitcase.

"You aren't going anywhere!" She took his shirts and brought them back to the closet.

"Don't do this, Denise!" He piled in another bundle of clothes.

Denise took the suitcase and threw it off the bed. "You bastard! I will *not* let you leave."

"It's not up to you, Denise. I've made up my mind." Bling gathered his belongings from off the floor.

"Are you moving in with her?"

Bling didn't answer the question. He continued packing. Denise paced back and forth from the doorway to the bed and back. "Why did you fly me to the Bahamas to renew our vows if you had planned on leaving me? I know she's the reason why you left the Bahamas sooner than planned."

Bling zipped his suitcase. "I love you, Denise." He looked over at his wife.

"So why are you doing this?" She walked over to her husband and kneeled at his feet.

"I'm just not in love with you. I'm in love with her." He lifted his suitcase taking it with him. "You can have the house, and I'll make sure you live comfortably until you get on your feet."

Denise shouted from the top of the stairs. "You will *not* disrespect me like I was the bitch for hire. *She* was. But she gets to fuck my husband and enjoy the life I deserve!"

"I thought we would be together forever too, but some relationships are only fillers until your soul mate comes along. You will find that special person, Denise." Bling hurried down the steps.

"So I was just a *filler* until your mistress whore came her way to you." She ran down the stairs behind him.

"I'll be respectful and let you file for the divorce. I'm sorry for your pain." He opened the door.

"You *are* sorry." Denise lifted the heavy vase and hit it on his head. Bling fell to the floor, knocked out cold. She dragged him by his feet away from the door and closed it. "Look who decided to stay with his wife after all." She took him by his arms. It was a struggle, but she dragged him up the stairs and took him to the guestroom.

She hurried to the basement and returned with an office chair with wheels on it. She struggled with his body, trying to place him on the chair. She wanted him to sit in an upright position, but he kept sliding off the chair.

"What did I do?" She started to panic. "I need to get him on the chair before he wakes up. Think, Denise, think." She paced for a few seconds, then a lightbulb went off in her head. "Bingo!"

She rolled him onto his stomach, then lay the chair on the floor and rolled him over onto it. Afterward, she duct taped his arms behind him, then she taped his legs together. She ran to the kitchen and returned with some rope and strategically tied him to the chair. Finally, she brought the chair to an upright position.

"I thought you were leaving, honey." She sat in his lap. "What changed your mind? I did." She kissed his lips. "What was that, honey? You want me to put your luggage away? My pleasure." She took the suitcase and tossed it in the basement. Denise sat watching her husband until he awoke.

"My head." Bling opened his eyes.

"Hi, honey." Denise smiled at him.

"Why am I tied up to this chair?" Bling asked when he couldn't move his hands or feet.

"You see, you were about to leave me for that bitch. But I love you so much, I can't allow you to leave me."

"You're crazy!"

"You haven't seen crazy yet."

Denise walked out of the room like a madwoman. Bling desperately tried to untie his arms. He could hear Denise rummaging with some utensils in the kitchen.

"It's always one lie after the other!" she yelled out in rage as she came back in the room with a butcher knife.

"Calm down, Denise! I made a mistake. I won't leave you if you untie me."

Denise let out a big wicked laugh at his futile attempt to get loose.

"Do you think I'm that stupid?" She stabbed the wall with the knife, then turned, pointing it in his face. Bling stared down at the knife, seeing the white residue from the Sheetrock clinging to it. He was now in a panic thinking that might soon be his blood on it.

"On second thought, maybe I am stupid for believing that you loved me."

"I do love you. You're my wife."

"S-t-o-p lying to me!" She slapped his face.

Bling tightened his jawbone easing the pain. "I'm not lying." He spoke after the pain subsided. "I was making a terrible mistake wanting to leave. You have to believe me," he pleaded.

Bling's phone started to vibrate in his pocket. Knowing it might be Keisha he didn't want Denise to hear it, knowing it would push her over the edge and his life would be over. So his idea was to try to distract her.

"I'm ready to tell the truth," he blurted out, temporarily blocking the vibrating sound.

"Already? And I was just starting to enjoy slapping the piss out of you."

"Can I at least have some water before I go into my confession?"

"Why would I want to give you that satisfaction?" She walked closer to him.

Bling's heart started to pound out his chest. *Stop vibrating* he commanded the phone with his inner voice.

"So you love her." She pulled up a chair and sat in front of him.

The phone had stopped vibrating, and Bling took a deep breath. "The truth is I think you are going crazy! And I can get you help. But you need to untie me now!"

"Crazy?" She jumped up off the chair. "No, I'm not crazy. I'm mad as hell but not crazy. If I was crazy, your dick would be in the pot cooking right now. The dick you have been screwing that bitch with. The same dick you wanted to put in my mouth." She took his limp manhood out of his pants.

"No! No! No! Don't do it, Denise!"

"You changed your mind. Now you don't want me to do it inch by inch by inch?" She circled his dick with the knife, and tears ran down his face.

"Do you even know what today is?" She got up and left the room.

"Denise, don't do anything crazy. I love you!" His attempts of untying himself were futile. Denise returned with a small cake in one hand and champagne in the other.

"It's our anniversary!" she pounded the cake in his face.

"Cheers to five years of nothing but happiness." She drank from the champagne bottle. "Too bad you can't have a drink. You're hands are tied." She laughed out loud. "Don't worry, I'll feed it to you." She poured it into his lap.

"We can go to a therapist and work it out."

"This is my therapy, seeing you beg like a baby the way I used to beg you to stay home with me."

"I promise I'll stay with you and work on having a baby. That's what you want, right? Just untie me . . ."

CHAPTER 16

Bright and early Tuesday morning Keisha was out shopping for a crib set when a white solid wood set caught her eyes. She strolled over and fell in love instantly. "Excuse me!" she called out to the salesclerk. "How soon can I have this delivered?"

"As early as tomorrow," the clerk replied.

"My baby will enjoy the finer things in life." She traced her hand over the surface. "I'll take it." Keisha continued with her shopping, sitting in the matching rocking chair. "Fit for mommy and her king. I'll take this too." She continued browsing, picking up a few more items that would complete the nursery. On her way to the checkout Keisha heard a woman inquiring about delivery. She turned to see if they had similar taste, and they did. The woman stood with her back facing her so she couldn't estimate how far along she was in her pregnancy.

"Can you toss in that rocking chair too?" The woman was making the purchase.

Keisha became angered because the thought of her baby room been replicated irritated her, but she made the purchase anyway. Keisha left the store and checked her phone. Bling hadn't called or texted, so she dialed his number. The phone rang and went to voice mail. She called him again, and it was the same outcome.

"I should just show up at their house and tell that bitch that her husband loves me, not her." She opened her trunk and unloaded her cart. Keisha kept checking her phone to see if she had missed any calls, even though her phone ringer was on high. "Maybe he's at the studio. I should do a drive-by." Instead of going home, Keisha detoured to the studio, but she didn't see his car. She dialed his number again, but Bling didn't answer. Keisha parked her vehicle and went into the building. Trigga and Trey were in deep conversation, but turned in a flash when the door opened.

"Was Bling here today?" Keisha asked, braking at the doorway.

"Hello to you too, boss lady." Trigga stood and greeted Keisha.

"Just answer the question," she stated being annoyed.

"No offense, boss lady, but he's a married man. He might be home with his wife."

"How much do you value your career, Trigga?" Keisha didn't take his comment lightly.

"My career is my life," he replied.

"Well, come out of your mouth like that again and I will cut your lifeline." She turned to walk away, but first, she returned her attention to Trey. "What happen to your face?"

"Domestic violence," he answered.

"Don't play with my money, Trey. You have a deadline for your album." Keisha left the studio and went back to her car and drove home.

Hours turned into a full day, and Bling didn't return any of her calls. In fact, the phone had stopped ringing and started going straight to voice mail.

It was now Friday, and Bling being missing in action was puzzling to her. It has been four days now, and she found it quite strange. Keisha reached for her cell phone that was resting on the couch next to her. Dragging her finger across her touch screen phone she decided to call Bling again for the hundredth time. Placing the phone at her ear she patiently waited for him to answer, but his voice mail picked up. Keisha held her composure and proceeded to call Derrick. He picked up on the first ring.

"Hey, Keish!" Derrick's masculine voice answered.

"Have you heard from Bling?" she questioned without hesitation.

"No, I haven't."

"I've been trying to reach him, but his phone is going straight to voice mail."

"Do you think Hype's family came through on their threat?" he asked in a concerned tone.

"I don't think so, because they would come after me too." She shrugged the thought.

"Didn't they? The incident at the spa was all their doing," Derrick reminded her.

"I get your point, but for some strange reason, I don't think they're holding him." Keisha dismissed his theory.

"So how do you explain Bling disappearing?"

"I think his wife has something to do with it," she instigated.

"What reasons does she have to hurt Bling?" He was befuddled.

"Reason being, he's leaving her to be with me and my child." Keisha made her position in his life clear to Derrick.

"Come on, Keisha. Are you going down that road again?" he asked sounding disappointed.

"Well, just do me a favor and ask the guys if anyone heard from Bling and call me back." She ended the call.

She remembered the detective had given her his card, so she hurried to the bedroom to her pocketbook, grabbing it quickly, showing no love for the brand name Berkin that she worshipped. Her cell phone started to ring, so she quickly ran back to the living room thinking it was Bling calling. She looked at the phone. It was Derrick. "Ugh!" she said in disappointment.

"Any news?" she asked.

"No one seems to know where he is," Derrick informed her.

"OK. I'll talk to you later."

Keisha took the card out of her pocketbook and dialed Detective McFarlane. The phone rang several times before he answered.

"Detective McFarlane speaking."

"Hello, Detective, this is Keisha Burkett. Is there any lead in my case?"

"I was hoping that you were calling with information to give me a lead because so far, it's a cold case."

"Well, I have a suspect," Keisha spoke with confidence.

"I'm listening." Detective McFarlane's voice was firm.

"My suspect is Denise Mills."

"That name sounds familiar. As a matter of fact, she was here this morning reporting her husband was missing."

"That bitch!" Keisha didn't hold her tongue.

"Is there a problem, Mrs. Burkett?"

"There *is* a damn problem." Keisha raised her voice. "First, she tried to kill me, and now her husband is missing. I think we have a case."

"What's the connection here? Why would you think she had something to do with your attempted murder case?"

"Because I'm fucking her husband!" She hung up the phone.

"The fact that she had reported Bling missing says a lot. I know she's covering her tracks. I have to do my own investigation, but how am I going to get close to her?" Keisha paced back and forth in the living room twiddling her thumbs. "Perfect." She picked up her phone and dialed Trey. She cleared her throat as she waited for him to answer.

"Yeah!" he answered.

"You're close with Bling, right?"

"Not anymore, but what is this about?" he curiously asked.

"He's missing in action, and I think his wife might have something to do with it. I just want you to stop by his house and do some investigating."

"No, can't do it." Trey wanted no part of it.

"How fast do you want to release your album?" She knew exactly what string to pull.

"I see where you're going with this. But I'm still not doing it."

"Maybe you don't know me well enough, so let me tell you this." She was livid. "I will drop your ass from this label so fast and drag you through the gutter so *no one* will ever sign you again. So again, I need you to go check on Bling."

"When you put it like that, I guess I have no choice." He hung up the phone.

We're interrupting this program to inform you about a missing person report. Anthony Mills aka Bling was reported missing this morning by his wife Denise Mills. His ongoing feud with the family of the deceased rapper Hype seems to be the main lead.

"I haven't seen my husband in almost a week! I don't know if you are listening, honey, but be strong, and I'm praying that you're safe." Denise spoke with her shades on standing in front of the police station.

"Ma'am! Ma'am," the reporter got her attention. "Didn't your husband kill a man for sleeping with his mistress?

How are you so sure that your husband didn't run off with a groupie?"

"No, he didn't!" Keisha screamed at the TV.

"My husband loves me, and he's living every day, making up for his infidelities." Denise pulled her shades halfway down. "But you just never know with these artists and their groupie mistresses."

Keisha was furious as she watched Denise on the screen. "I've seen enough of this charade." She ran out of the house to her car, speeding to the police station.

"Miss Burkett! Come in and have a seat," Detective McFarlane greeted.

"I don't want to have a seat. I need answers."

"I can see that you're a little upset."

"Is *this* what my taxes pay for? For you to relax in your AC instead of you trying to get a search warrant and go search the house and make an arrest? Didn't I give you the name of a suspect?"

Detective McFarlane chuckled. "You are quite a character."

"So you think this is a damn joke?"

"Let me get this right. You want me to arrest the man's wife just because you said so?"

"No, because it's your damn job!"

"Where do you get off barking orders in my place of work? As far as I'm concerned, you're just making false accusations against that innocent woman. You are the one having an affair with her husband, right? I think you just want her out of the picture so you can have her husband all to yourself." He cracked his knuckles all at once.

"He is already mine." She walked out of the office.

"Miss Burkett!" He called out to Keisha, but she kept walking. "I will do my job, but I hope you're not the one I'll be arresting!"

Keisha stepped outside into the hot air. Luckily, she had found parking close to the police station so she could quickly get into the comfort of her AC. Keisha hiked up her dress as she positioned herself to sit in the car, giving comfort to her growing belly. She needed to figure out what her next move would be because Detective McFarlane wasn't moving fast enough.

The car in front of her was parked too close, so she put her car in reverse and looked over her shoulder to back out of the tight spot, but the idiot behind her was also too close to her bumper.

"If I have to back into this damn car to get out that's exactly what I'm going to do."

Her car bumped into the Nissan Altima. She pulled forward and hit the car in front also, then put her car in reverse again, ready to back up, but two simultaneous beeps of the car in front of her got her attention.

The man unlocked his car as he walked across the street but stopped short of his car talking on his phone.

Keisha rolled her window down. "Excuse me, Mr. Asshole! I know you see me waiting for you to let me out, so move your damn car." The man ignored her and proceeded with his conversation.

"You want to ignore me, OK. Let's see if you can ignore this."

Forgetting that her car was still in reverse she stepped on her gas with the intention if hitting the man's car, but instead, she put another dent in the car behind her. Quickly, she put her car in drive and rammed into the man's car.

"Are you crazy?" he yelled.

"You haven't seen crazy yet!" She hit his car again.

"Hey, Officer! This crazy woman is damaging my car." The man got the attention of the policeman, who walked over in a hurry.

"Lady, put your car in park and turn off your ignition!" the policeman ordered.

Keisha did as she was told. The man viewed the back of his car and seeing the damage he became enraged.

"You psycho bitch!"

"Get out of the car! Get out of the car now!" the officer yelled at her.

"Gladly," she said opening the door.

"I would like to press charges!" the man barked at the police.

"Step back, sir," the officer ordered. "Is this a lover's quarrel?"

"Don't insult me by sizing me up with this jackass. My standards are much higher," Keisha said, rolling her eyes at the man.

"I don't know this crazy woman!" the man reassured the police.

"I simply asked this scum of the earth to move his car and let me out of the tight space they sandwiched me into, and he told me to go to hell."

"She's a damn liar! I was on a business call, and she interrupted me with her foul mouth. I want to press charges."

The policeman led Keisha across the street back to the police station.

Detective McFarlane was standing at the front desk when she was led in, and he let out a big laugh. "What did you get yourself into, Miss Burkett?"

"Nothing that I can't get out of," she snapped at him.

"Well, she did a good job on his bumper trying to get out of a tight spot," the policeman informed him.

"Tell your little policeman friend and this object next to him that I can buy him a new car without even missing the petty cash from my account."

"Let your money talk then," the man said hastily.

"Do you still want to press charges?" the officer asked.

"I just need my car fixed," the man replied.

"Well, you don't have to worry about that," Keisha agreed.

"Just get an estimate and bring it by the station, and we will make sure that Miss Burkett writes you that check. Go with this officer and he'll take your information."

"Well, I guess it's settled." She turned to walk away. She was hoping that the owner of the car behind her wasn't outside waiting because she wasn't in the mood to deal with any more nonsense. She pushed the door open and once again she was emerged into the hot sun. She noticed that the car that was parked behind her was gone. She hastily walked to her car just wanting to get away from the scene.

"Oh, hell, no!" She quickened her steps and saw some words were inscribed in bold letters on her car.

Dead or Alive!

"What the fuck is that supposed to mean?" she shouted in anger.

She did a 360 scan of the street for any sign of who could have done it. But there was no one to blame.

"You damn coward!" she yelled.

CHAPTER 17

Denise stood on the lot viewing all the different models of BMWs "I will make myself happy! Say hello to mama." She locked her eyes on a white X6.

"Would you like to go for a test drive?" the salesman inquired walking toward her.

"I do you one better. I want to pay for it cash."

"Well, walk this way." He escorted her inside.

Denise sat on the chair facing his desk and emptied her pocketbook that contained all hundreds wrapped in 5,000 stacks.

The salesman's eyes widened, impressed by the money. He took in the aroma for a few seconds, then brought his eyes back to Denise. "You know I have to report all cash sales over a certain amount."

"It's clean. Courtesy of my husband. Let's call it spousal support." She winked at him. She signed on the dotted lines and drove off the lot. Denise then drove to the mall and walked into a jewelry store, trading her wedding ring for a diamond bracelet. Next, she went on a shopping spree with Bling's credit card, not looking at price tags as she paraded through the stores. She left the mall after getting a new wardrobe, and now, she was pondering what damage she could do next. Baby Depot was coming up on her right, and she decided to stop. Denise was infatuated with the baby booties. She picked up several pairs and willed herself away. She browsed through the newborn onesies and also picked out a few. Denise slowly browsed the store, stocking items as she went.

"Would you like a basket?" the clerk asked.

"I think I do," she said, realizing her hands were full with bottles, teething rings, blankets, and more.

"Here you go." The clerk returned with a shopping cart.

"I just love this crib. This is just perfect for my little angel." Denise traced her fingers over the crib.

"You're the third person to fall in love with this crib today. If you want, we can have it delivered tomorrow."

"It's just perfect. I'll take the rocking chair too."

"Are you expecting?" the clerk questioned.

"No, I'm adopting." Denise circled her belly as if there was a bun in the oven.

"Good luck." The clerk gazed at Denise seeing her antics. "Just go to customer service and they will take your information."

When Denise got home she made a few trips back and forth to her car bringing her shopping bags inside the house. Then she brought the bags to the spare bedroom placing them on the floor.

"Honey, I'm home." She opened the closet door revealing her husband still tied up in the chair. "Aren't you happy to see me?" Denise pulled the chair forward, leaving him in the middle of the room. "I went shopping today." She went through her bags taking out the baby booties. "Do you like them? I fell in love when I saw them. This will be perfect for our little boy or girl, won't it? How can you give me an answer with your mouth taped up?" She ripped the tape from his mouth.

"You are psycho. You need help."

"I'm as sane as can be. But I am going to need some help to move this furniture. I need to make room for the baby furniture." The doorbell chimed, and she froze for a few seconds.

"Help!" Bling yelled, hoping to be rescued.

"Oh no, you don't." She taped his mouth again, capturing his screams. Then she wheeled him back to the closet, tossing the bags in with him. "Don't do anything stupid," she warned him as she closed the closet door.

Denise raced down the stairs and spied through the peephole. "You have some nerve," she spoke when she saw Trey. "Are you happy?" she attacked him as soon as she opened the door. "You took him from me, are you happy now?"

"I'm sorry for what happened, but the truth is, his heart had already left." Trey didn't spare her feelings.

"So you bashed me to your friends like I'm a damn whore, and now you're bashing my husband, who, as far I know it, could be tied up somewhere or maybe dead. I want my husband back. This isn't fair. Why did they take him from me?" Denise put on the waterworks again. It was as if she had slipped into another personality.

Trey embraced her, and she sobbed. Her tears were real because her heart ached for her failed marriage. Her husband was in love with his mistress who was pregnant with his child. The child she so badly wanted for herself.

"What happened after I left, Denise?" Trey inquired, remembering he was there to do a job for Keisha.

Denise's weeping suddenly stopped, and she strolled inside the house with Trey following. "I begged him to stay, but he pushed me out of his way and left." She stopped weeping, and her tone was now stern. "I know he was going to see her." Denise turned facing Trey, whose eyes were searching the house. "Are you looking for something?" she asked, seeing him prying.

"No. Just making sure no one is hiding anywhere." Trey's eyes scoped the room.

"No one like who, and what are you looking for?" her head followed his eyes.

"Well, since Bling is missing and Hype's family was making threats and probably took him, you have to be careful because they could come after you," he warned.

"Why would they come after me? *That* bitch is responsible for all this. Why haven't they killed *her?*"

"I know you're upset, but you should take it easy." Trey took her by the hand.

She pulled away from him. "You are always concerned for my well-being. Weren't you just as concerned that day you showed up with your hidden intentions?" She walked away.

He grabbed her arm. "That's a lie, and you know it. You came on to me."

"I was drunk, but that didn't stop you," she yelled to his face. "*You're* the reason my husband left." Her fists played drums on his chest.

"You can't blame me for this." He held her hands from striking him again.

"Get off me!" She pulled away from him.

"I think it's best if I leave." Trey walked to the door, Denise stopped him.

"I just remembered, I need some help moving some furniture upstairs. Can you help?"

Wanting to investigate he agreed to assist her. "I have a few minutes to spare."

Denise led the way, and Trey followed. She brought him to the bedroom where she held Bling as her hostage. She leaned against the closet door and a sadistic smile appear. "If you could move the dresser over to that side it would be nice," Denise instructed.

Trey complied and relocated the furniture. "I know you're dealing with a lot, but I'm here if you need me."

"I'm sure my husband wouldn't be pleased with you saying that."

"I'm not trying to hurt your feelings, but Bling is in love with Keisha. Why can't you see that?" Trey's tone was harsh because he was annoyed by her denial of the truth.

"No, he's not in love with her," she screamed at him. "He's just upset because he found out that I fooled around with you, but he'll come back to me."

"Before he found out about us he wanted me to seduce you so he could have an excuse to leave you for Keisha," Trey yelled back.

"You're lying! I don't believe you." She covered both ears with her hands like a child.

"How did I end up in your bed, Denise? Your damn husband set it up. What about when you went to Atlantic City and you woke up in bed with another man. Did he tell you what *really* happened?"

"How did you know about that?" Denise asked in a curious manner.

"Think about it, Denise. If you were in the room with the husband, where was Bling?" Trey approached her.

"No, I don't believe you." She covered her ears again.

Trey removed her hands and continued to speak. "He was banging the wife."

"You're making this up. I'm not going to fall for it. My husband loves me. And he's going to come back to me." Denise refrained from believing the truth.

"How can he love you when he arranged for me to sleep with you?"

"How could he disrespect me like this?" Denise broke down again, and Trey was there to console her just like he did the day she opened the door disheveled and drunk, feeling betrayed by her husband.

"Let me love you, Denise. You deserve a man who will always treat you right. You deserve me." Trey was weaseling his way in, knowing she was vulnerable. He made his move. "Let me take away your pain." He kissed her cheek, and she didn't resist. He kissed her forehead, and then her lips. He took her down on the floor and made love to his friend's wife, not knowing Bling was locked in the closet only a few feet away.

***

Bling was seething with anger. He wanted to kill Trey. Denise had tied him up good. No matter how hard he tried, he could not get himself loose. He wanted to get his wife away from Trey. Regardless that he wasn't in love with her, he still wasn't going to let Trey use her for his selfish pleasure.

"Let me walk you to the door," Denise said while getting dressed. She followed him down the stairs, and she had a split in personality again.

"Don't you ever come here again." Her facial expression was of a crazy woman.

"But I thought . . . " Trey was stunned by her attitude.

"You thought wrong. Get out of my face." She slammed the door in his face and stormed up the stairs, opening the closet door and wheeled out her hostage. "How was it listening to me fucking your friend? I was thinking that if I turned into a whore you would fall in love with me all over again, because, after all, you did fall in love with one." She ripped the tape from his mouth.

"Don't go down that road, Denise. Don't wreck yourself."

"Why not? You chose a train wreck over your untainted wife. So I was thinking that if I put some mileage on my pussy I can have my husband back." She took his face into her hands.

"I never meant to hurt you, but my heart betrayed me too."

"Well, she will never have you. I will keep you tied up in this closet until you're old and gray, or until I kill you and bury you in the basement."

Denise left him in the room, and he desperately tried to untie himself. But the duct tape tightly bound his wrists.

Bling clinched his teeth and endured the pain of his skin being cut into. You could see the pressure on his face as he summoned his inner strength and pulled against the tape. Bling folded his lips muffling his moans of agony. Eventually, the taped started to warp and his hands had enough room to maneuver. Suddenly, he heard footsteps coming so he stalled his efforts.

Denise approached him carrying a glass of water, and he welcomed her offering because he needed to refuel, and the water would do for now.

"I thought you might be thirsty." She paused at the doorway looking at him.

"I am," Bling admitted.

"Beg! Beg me for this water."

"Denise, please, I'm thirsty. Let me have a drink."

"Well, drink!" She tossed the water in his face.

In that moment Bling knew he wanted more than ever to be free. He wanted to get away from his wife who he had started to hate. Denise chuckled as she left the room, and Bling was determine to free himself, even if he had to lose an arm to do it.

He gritted his teeth, and the muscles tightened in his jaw. He wrestled with the duct tape, and as if he were Hulk, he pulled both hands in the opposite direction and his eyes bulged—and the tape broke even as it cut through his skin. His hands were free and his breathing was sharp and quick as he held his composure through agonizing pain. Bling knew he had to break out of there because his wife had gone completely cuckoo.

He opened the window and sat on the windowsill and prepared himself to jump. "I just hope I don't break my damn legs." Bling aimed for the grass, hoping not to land on the large rocks that were placed in the front yard as a part of the landscape. He was in motion to the ground, and he knew his landing was not going to be good. He came down hard on his ankle and was in excruciating pain. "Goddamn it!" He grabbed on to his ankle.

"No! No! No!" Denise's voice was heard outside when she discovered that he had escaped.

Bling limped to the side of the house hiding behind the Dumpster because he knew she would be combing the street looking for him, and his injured leg wouldn't take him far. He watched as Denise got into her car and reversed out of the driveway.

"Holy shit!" Bling let out his distress when Denise sped down the street. He limped to the door and went back inside house. "When does it end? Why don't you just take my damn life?" Bling took his keys and like a cripple he limped as fast as he could to his car. He drove in the opposite direction of Denise, blocking out his pain as he stepped on the gas.

Bling pulled into Keisha's driveway and kept his hand on his horn with his body slumped over on the steering wheel. He was weak from not eating, and he was also dehydrated, not to mention being in unbearable pain. Keisha ran out to him, pulling on the car door.

"Where were you?" she asked with fright in her voice.

"Help me inside." Bling's voice was weak. He extended his arm to her.

"Who did this to you?" she asked in a panic seeing his butchered arm.

Bling used Keisha as his crutch as she helped him inside, and then she sat him on the couch. "Water," Bling requested.

Keisha didn't hesitate. She ran to the kitchen and back with a glass of water. Bling gulped the water, and Keisha nervously shook her legs waiting for him to finish.

"Who did this to you?" Keisha reiterated as soon as Bling removed the glass from his mouth.

"It doesn't matter. I'm free now. Can I have some ice for my ankle?" He kept his capture a secret. He couldn't find it in himself to rat on his wife because he knew that her psycho behavior stemmed from his infidelities.

Keisha returned with a frozen pack of green peas, placing it on Bling's swollen ankle. "Do you think it's broken?"

"I'm sure it's just a sprain," he replied after a few grunts.

"What can I do to help?" Keisha fretfully asked, seeing him in such pain.

"You can get me some painkillers and something to eat. I'm starving." His eyes were closed as he spoke.

Keisha was obliging to all of Bling's needs. She was in the kitchen making him a sandwich with urgency. She also poured him a glass of orange juice to wash it down. Keisha set his meal on a tray, but before she served him, she dashed to the medicine cabinet for the painkillers, also placing them on the tray.

"You have to sit up," she instructed, and Bling pushed off his elbows and shuffled to a comfortable position. He awkwardly picked up the sandwich. He was still feeling the pain from his lacerated wrists. Keisha observed him eating. She wanted answers. She wanted to decapitate whoever did this to him.

"Did you know that she reported you missing?" Keisha probed.

"Well, I'm not," Bling spoke with his mouth full.

Keisha was perplexed by his unwillingness to talk about what happened to him, and that led her to believe he was protecting someone.

Suddenly, there was a hard pounding on Keisha's door, but she kept her eyes on Bling as if she was trying to read his mind. *Who did this to you?* Keisha quietly questioned under her breath. The person kept pounding on the door, and she slowly took her attention from Bling and quickly stepped to the door.

"What?" She opened the door, not bothering to investigate who it was through the peephole.

"I'm here to take my husband home," Denise blurted.

"He won't be for long." Keisha rubbed her belly, parading the fact that she was pregnant.

"I think your brain is probably still fried because I remember knocking your feeble ass off your feet the last time."

"You won't be knocking nobody off their feet because I'm carrying your husband's love child, and if you bring any harm to this child, he will personally kill you. Now get away from my door before I push you off my steps."

"I suggest that you go get my husband before I step all over you and your bastard child."

"Go home, Denise. It's obvious that Bling is where he wants to be, and that's with his family."

"Go get my husband. I won't wait another minute, or else I'm going to bulldoze through this damn whorehouse."

"I'll take it from here, Keisha," Bling said limping to the door.

"Babe, are you sure you should be standing?" Keisha asked with concern in her voice.

"Can you give me a minute with her?" he suggested.

"You're dismissed, bitch." Denise waved her off with her hand.

"I'll have the last laugh, bitch." Keisha walked away.

"I should have you arrested, but I'm not, but you seriously need to check into a mental ward," Bling spoke harshly to his wife.

"Speaking of making an arrest, you have a decision to make. You can come home with me or spend a lifetime sentence in jail."

"You need psychiatric help."

"I guess I'll just go to the police with this picture." She brought forth the picture of Jordonna and Bling in bed. "And this note that I found in your pocket, and you will be locked away for murder."

"You wouldn't!" Bling tried to snatch the picture.

"Try me," she threatened.

"I'm not going nowhere with you. Besides, we both know that you killed her."

"But the police don't know that, and this evidence points right to you." She took out her phone and dialed, putting it on speaker for Bling to hear it ring.

"Detective McFarlane speaking." The voice came through the phone.

"I have evidence—," Denise's sentence was cut short when Bling grabbed the phone and ended the call.

"You crazy bitch." Bling was angered by her audacity.

"Are you staying with your mistress or coming home with your wife? I'm sure you'll make the right decision, and I need an answer now."

"Keisha!" Bling hollered, and Keisha came running. "I'm going home with my wife."

"No. You can't do this to me. What about our baby?"

"By the way . . . " Denise addressed Keisha, "we'll be doing a DNA test, so check yourself, bitch."

"I have what you want and it's killing you, so check *yourself*, bitch," Keisha fired back.

Denise threw the keys from her hand, aiming for Keisha's face. Keisha ducked and the key chain hit the door. Bling struggled to keep both women at bay, but Keisha's fist connected with Denise's nose, and blood spurted out.

"You broke my nose!" Denise hollered with her hand covering her bloody nose.

"Don't stop now because I would love to break your neck," Keisha taunted.

"Get inside the house, Keisha!" Bling yelled.

"Not until I beat her to a pulp." Keisha was throwing fists over Bling's head.

"Take me home now!" Denise commanded.

"Don't tell me you're really leaving with her!" Keisha said, locking eyes with Bling.

"I have to." Bling limped, following behind his wife.

"Fuck you and your wife. I don't need you." She slammed the door and found her phone and called Derrick. "Are you at the office? OK, stay there. I'll be there in a few." She grabbed her keys and opened the door, not caring if Bling and his miserable wife were still outside. But they weren't. She reversed out of the driveway in her new pearl color Benz. After someone had carved into her car outside the police station she had to get a new ride. She sped down the road like a NASCAR racer. She pulled up in Top Dot Records and stormed past the receptionist.

"Hello, Miss Burkett," Angela greeted.

Keisha was a woman on a mission, and she didn't acknowledge Angela. She barged into Derrick's office, and he quickly spun around in his chair wanting to see the intruder.

"I'll call you back." He ended his conversation.

"I need to cancel all upcoming events for Bling," Keisha was angry.

"Why? Was he located, and is he in some sort of trouble?"

"Just do it. I also need to push his album back. He's not running shit, I am. Besides, if he wants to go back to his wife, let her push his damn album."

"You can't do that, Keisha!" Derrick pounded his fist on his desk.

"Yes, I can!" Her fist also connected with the desk, and her voice overpowered his. "I need his album pushed back! On second thought, scrap it!" Keisha leaned against the desk for support, her protruding belly had disfigured her hourglass shape.

"I'm a partner in this company too, and you can't mix your personal life with my money." Derick got up from his chair.

"I'm making an executive decision to scrap his album until he produces an album of substance."

"That's bullshit, and you know it." Derrick tossed the pen across the room.

"The only thing I know for sure is that we have a more deserving artist, and I need you to push his album."

"Who is that, Keisha?" Derrick tapped both index fingers together.

"Trigga," Keisha spoke with a straight face.

"You *can't* be serious." He was in disbelief.

"It's about time I light some fire under Bling's ass. He's been having an easy ride, but it stops here."

"I have to agree that Trigga is good, but are you looking to start a war? You know the two have been going at it."

"Exactly. Sometimes you have to sacrifice the good for the bad to get your point across."

"I think the better way would be to have both albums released the same date and see whose album catapults to the top of the charts." Derrick offered a logical solution.

"No, my ruling still stands. I need you to call an emergency meeting to inform everyone of my decision." She proceeded to the door.

"Will you be present at this meeting?"

"No. Fill me in." She kept walking.

"Just like I thought, leave me to do the dirty work," Derrick murmured.

She brought her attention back to him. "You *can* handle the job, can't you, Derrick?"

"Yes, I will deliver the bad news." Derick retreated to his chair.

"Don't forget that it will be good news for Trigga."

"Even so, it's still not fair."

"But I'm justified." She left with her belly leading the way.

"You're playing dirty, Keisha!" Derrick spoke as she walked out of the office.

"Make the call, Derrick!" she hollered back.

Keisha went to her car, and saw a note on her windshield held down by the wiper blade. "What the hell is this?" She snatched the paper, opened the note, and the words were spelled with newspaper clippings.

How I wish you were dead. You should be thankful that my plan was interrupted. But watch your back, bitch, because I'm watching you.

Keisha did another 360-degree turn, knowing her life was in danger. But there wasn't a suspect in sight. She got into her car and drove to the police station. Keisha double-parked her car and quickly opened her door, anxious to get out.

"Ma'am, you can't park here!" a policeman called out to her.

"Tow it then!" Keisha pulled on the door entering the building, and the sixty-degree air from the AC brought her temperature down.

"Detective!" she called out seeing him walking out of his office.

"Miss Burkett, what can I do for you?" He stopped, facing Keisha, who was racing toward him.

"I need you to arrest her." Keisha extended the note forward toward him.

"What's this, and who should I arrest?"

"Denise Mills, for stalking, threatening, and harass-ment."

"I'll take this into evidence, but I can't arrest a citizen on hearsay. You have to file a complaint, and I'll look into it." He walked away.

"What about making a false statement?" Keisha fol-lowed. "Her missing husband is not missing after all. He's at home making a mockery of the police department. How do you feel about *that?*" Keisha tried to find any charge to stick.

"I'll investigate your complaint." He pulled out his chair and sat at his desk.

"I need you to arrest her!" She pounded her fist on the desk causing his family portrait to fall.

"Watch it. You're pushing it, but I'm curious to know on what grounds?" He repositioned the picture frame.

"Assault and battery." Keisha concocted new charges, hoping they would stick.

"Come on, Miss Burkett, now you're really pushing it."

"She assaulted me this morning, and I have a witness so you better go haul her ass in or I'm suing this department for discrimination, and I know you would rather choose to get a hefty donation instead of bringing attention to your corrupt department."

Detective McFarlane closed his office door. "How big of a donation we talking?"

"$10,000. Cash." Keisha knew she got him.

"OK. I'll go pay her a visit." He shook her hand.

"Thank you, Mr. Asshole." She rolled her eyes at him while turning on her heels.

When she exited the building a tow truck was just pulling up to her car. She made it to her car just in time before he hooked her car. "Catch me if you can!" She laughed like a crazy woman.

Keisha went straight home to prepare herself for when Bling came beating down her door. She kicked her shoes off and walked to the kitchen, but before she could open the fridge, the doorbell rang. "I wasn't expecting him to show up this soon." She made her way back to the door, taking a deep breath, then she turned the knob, opening the door. But to her surprise, it was the delivery truck from Baby Depot.

CHAPTER 18

"Hopefully I can get through this meeting without any interruptions, but I highly doubt it." Derrick rocked his chair back and forth. "I see we're missing Trey, but I have to proceed without him. I know every one of you have deadlines for your albums, and a few of you guys still haven't start working on your albums, but we will have everything in order soon."

"No offense, Derrick, but can you get to the point before another brawl breaks out, and we still don't know why we're here," Trigga interrupted.

"You're the one who's always starting shit," Derrick stated.

"I see I'm still the black sheep as usual, but I'll never crown that king." He pointed at Bling.

"Why are you such a hothead?" Derrick got up from his chair.

"Because I'm a man who has to fight for his rights around here," Trigga answered.

Bling was rather quiet at the far end of the table that seated twelve. Both his wrists were wrapped up. He had so much on his plate an overweight man couldn't consume half of it in one sitting.

"Bling, I have to cancel all your upcoming events." Derrick spoke in a low tone.

"I see. But no hard feelings. I need to lay low for a while." Bling nodded his head in agreement.

"And one more thing. We will be releasing Trigga's album, but yours will be pushed back." Derrick delivered the news with disappointment in his voice.

"Did I just hear correctly?" Trigga jumped to his feet. "Has the king been dethroned?"

"This is bullshit! I know this isn't your doing, Derrick. I smell a rat." Bling got up and left the meeting.

Bling drove home with urgency and painfully limped upstairs. He slid the closet door, pushing clothes aside to get to the safe. He entered the combination, opening the safe. "Where the hell is it?" He kept looking hoping to see it, but after realizing that it wasn't there, he turned his anger to Denise.

"Denise!" he called out, limping back down the stairs. "Where is my damn contract?" He found Denise sitting in the kitchen painting her nails. "What did you do with my contract?"

"I burned it." She kept painting her nails without looking up at him.

"You can't be serious." Bling quickened his steps over to her. "Where is my damn contract?"

"That contract was the beginning of the end, so with no regrets, I burned it."

"Do you realize what you've done?" He swept the table with his hand, knocking her nail polish to the floor.

"You've ruined my floor mat!" The pink nail polish splashed all over the floor. "I did you a favor by getting rid of the negative force that drove us apart." She carefully reached for the paper towels and stooped to the floor.

"You've become my worst nightmare." He walked away from her.

"Love you, mean it!" she teased, then laugh a wicked laugh.

Bling wanted to toss his contract in Keisha's face. He didn't want her to think that he was her puppet on a string. The contract didn't mean shit to him, and with his state of mind, he could care less about making music. He opened the door to leave, and found a man standing there.

"Can I help you?" Bling asked.

"I have a delivery for Mrs. Mills," the man spoke, pointing to the Baby Depot delivery truck.

"She has really lost her damn mind." Bling headed back to the kitchen. "What the hell are you up to?"

"I'm just trying to be a good wife by cleaning up this mess you made."

"Stop playing coy with me. Why is there a delivery truck from Baby Depot outside?"

"Are they really here?" She ran past him heading to the door.

"I'm guessing that you're Mrs. Mills," the man said.

"Yes, I am," Denise gleefully acknowledged.

"If you could sign right here, I'll go get the merchandise from the truck."

Denise signed on the dotted line and watched the man walk back to the truck.

"You've really gone crazy," Bling announced his presence behind her.

"I'm not crazy!" Denise was like a vicious pit bull. Her alter ego had resurfaced.

"Where is the baby coming from, Denise?"

"I'm adopting." A smile was plastered over her face again.

"Where should I set this up?" the man asked.

"Upstairs in the bedroom to your left." Denise walked behind him. Bling stepped outside and was almost to his car when a police car pulled up behind the delivery truck blocking the driveway. "Here we go again," Bling spoke.

"I see you're still alive," Detective McFarlane joked.

"I see the disappointment," Bling joked back.

"Your wife reported you missing, but yet here you are." The detective approached him with another policeman as backup.

"What my wife chose to do is none of my business. So are you here to arrest me?"

"No, we're not," the detective spoke.

"Well, you're blocking my driveway, and I need to go about my business." Bling sat in his car.

"I think you might want to stick around because I'm here to arrest your wife."

"My wife? What for?" Bling was baffled.

"For assault and battery on your mistress, Keisha Burkett."

Denise came to the door and the police brought his attention to her. "And there she is." The officers proceeded to the door.

"This is nonsense!" Bling followed behind him.

"I'm only doing my job to protect and serve."

Bling had a sudden epiphany and realized that this was all happening in his favor. Denise going to jail was his ticket to freedom from her.

"Mrs. Mills!" The detective directed his steps to her.

"Yes!" Denise answered. "How can I help you?"

The officers climbed the steps. "You're under arrest for assault and battery on Keisha Burkett."

"*She's* the one who assaulted me," Denise yelled. "My husband will vouch for me."

"Anything you say can and will be used against you . . . " They read her, her rights.

"Don't worry, I'll get you out!" Bling lied because he knew Denise was still blackmailing him and could turn in her evidence.

"I told you she was the devil. She destroyed us. She ruined our marriage! She wants you all to herself. You believe me, now, don't you?" Denise started to cry.

"I do. I'll bail you out," Bling lied again.

The police car drove off with his wife, and Bling let out a loud laugh. *"Ding Dong! The bitch is gone!"*

Bling got in his car and drove to Keisha's apartment. He banged on the door and after a few moments, she opened the door wearing her robe.

"What took you so long? I've been expecting you." She turned and walked away.

"So you think you run my life?" Bling grabbed her arm.

"A small portion, I can admit." She chuckled.

"Well, you're not running shit!" he freed her.

"Come on, Bling, you must admit your livelihood is music, and I'm the deciding factor if you make it or break it."

"That's where you're wrong. My livelihood is my life, and right now, it's nothing but grief, so you can break it because music is the least of my interest at this point."

"But this baby should be of interest because we will not be ignored."

"So do you honestly believe having my wife behind bars will bring me to you?"

"Aren't you here?" she winked at him.

"Yes, to let you know that your little stunt to push back my album doesn't faze me. I have bigger problems."

"What problems? Are you still thinking that Hype's family is after you? As far as I can see, your *wife* is the problem, and I already eliminated her."

"Right now, you're more stress than I can handle." Bling limped to the door.

"You can play tough all you want, but my child and I are your lifeline." She watched Bling drive out of the driveway, and then she went back inside and headed straight for the bathroom.

She stood in front the mirror that was spread across the entire wall and stripped. She encircled her rounded belly, giving comfort to her fetus. "I've been kissed on the inside." She smiled. "Daddy loves us, but he's going through a difficult time. But don't worry, he'll be back before you know it." She put her hair in a bun and stepped in the shower. Wetting her body, she lathered herself with the soft smell of Shea butter body wash. "Finally *you put my love on top, top, top. You put my love on top.*" She butchered the words to Beyoncé's song.

"I see you're trying to break the mirror." Damien slid open the shower curtain.

Keisha almost passed out when she saw him. "How did you get in here?" she demanded.

"Don't worry." He passed her a towel. "I'm not here to hurt you, because in that case, I'll be a baby killer . . . like you."

She grabbed the towel and wrapped her body. "Bling is gonna be home any minute."

"Home? I see you're still living in your fantasy world. You need to realize that Bling will never call this place home or even call you his woman. He might play house, but you will never be anybody's wife." He plopped himself on the granite sink. "Oh, I forgot. I was the only fool to marry a whore."

She took the showerhead and sprayed him. "I'll be filing for a divorce."

He ran out of the bathroom. "I'll be asking for everything, even the kitchen sink."

Keisha closed the door. "Go to hell!"

"Your father owes me money, and I'm here to collect." He jiggled the lock, but he was locked out.

"Well, my father doesn't live here. Your business is with him not me."

"If your brain had remained fried I would be paid in full. So since you're the one who ruined my plan, you have to pay up."

"I would love to know how much you tried to swindle from my father."

"You won't be disappointed; the price was right."

"I'm sure it wasn't."

"He still owes me fifty Gs."

Keisha burst out laughing. "You must be losing your damn mind. On second thought, you have lost your mind, and I've certainly wasted too much time entertaining your nonsense, so get out my house! You know where the door is." She boldly spoke knowing the door was locked and he couldn't get to her.

"You keep thinking that you run the world, but your reign has ended. I need my money or else that love child of yours will be my ransom."

Keisha jerked the door open and spoke without fear. "You will not be getting fifty thousand of my money, and I'll be damned if you're going to stand in my house and threaten my unborn child. Get the hell out." She was like a vicious lioness protecting her cub without fear.

"I would've rather the money, but you've clearly made your choice. You've up the ante, so I'll wait until the devil's spawn arrives to see how much you'll pay then." Damien exited out the back patio door through which he had entered.

"You will not lay one finger on my child!" Keisha shouted, making herself clear. She locked the glass door that gave a clear view of the wooded area in the back. She watched, hoping he would disappear in the woods and get eaten by lions, tigers, or bears. But instead, he made the left, and she knew he had nowhere to go but to the front of the house, so she rushed to the living room and looked out the window and watched him walk down the street crossing the road to his car.

"I need a damn drink." She checked the time on the cable box. It was now 6:30 p.m. She went to the bedroom and dressed herself in a black peplum dress that needed a few more yards of fabric to make an old church lady comfortable. Her Red Bottoms pumps complemented her red Berkin bag. Her fragrance for the night was Coach Poppy, and after several spray she was satisfied. She left the house and made it downtown within ten minutes. The happy hour crowd still lingered, but she found a seat at the bar.

"What can I get you?" the bartender asked.

"A glass of red wine would be fine." Keisha placed her order.

"Coming right up!" the bartender announced.

"I wouldn't expect to see a pregnant lady at the bar," Tina spoke.

Keisha was a little startled by Tina, but she held her composure and spoke with confidence. "But I would expect to see you trying to get a free drink as usual." Keisha plastered a phony smile on her face.

"You never pass up a chance to twist the knife." Tina demonstrated with her hand.

The bartender set the glass in front of Keisha, and she took a sip without delay. "I really needed that," she admitted, then took another sip.

"So you're really going through with this?" Tina curiously asked.

"You've lost me. Going through with what? Drinking a glass of wine? The last time I checked it was fine to do so while pregnant." Keisha knitted her brows together.

"Not the wine, the pregnancy."

"I'm so sorry to disappoint you, but my child is here to stay." She sipped again.

"So who's the daddy?" Tina sat on the stool next to her that was now vacant.

"Get out of my face, Tina, before I wash your face with my wine."

"It's a fair question, but I can see you don't have the answer."

"You've developed some big balls. What makes you think that you can question my child's paternity? From what I remembered, you never had the balls to stand up for your own damn self."

"I was one of your little minions, but my, my, how things have changed. But I see you haven't."

"Why don't you dismiss yourself, Tina, because like always, you bore me?"

"And like always, you're a bitch," Tina insulted her, then departed into the crowd.

"What's new?" She put the glass to her lips and gulped her wine. She swallowed the last mouthful and brought the empty glass back to the counter. "What's happening to me? I'm not supposed to care about her damn feelings. Damn pregnancy hormones." Keisha got up from the bar stool and inspected the lounge trying to locate Tina. She followed her instinct and went to the ladies' room where she found Tina reapplying her red lipstick. "I'm here to call a truce," Keisha declared.

"There's always an ulterior motive behind your actions. So I'm not going to bite." Tina continued to revamp her lips.

"Take it or leave it. But my intentions are genuine." Keisha positioned herself to leave.

"Okay. I'll accept. I'll give it a trial run."

"I didn't say I want to be friends. I'm just saying we can be cordial to each other."

"Cut the act because I know you need a godmother for that little diva you're carrying." Tina rubbed Keisha's bulging belly.

"I don't know about all that because I've yet to see the relevance of a godmother."

"Well, this godmother will spoil her rotten. Assuming she's a girl. Do you even know what you're having?"

"No." She admired herself in the mirror, then fixed her hair.

"Well, in that case, you need to set up a doctor's appointment. I need to know if I'm going to be buying Baby Louboutin for a girl or Ferragamo for a boy. I have a baby shower to plan so I have to get the ball rolling."

"Slow your roll. I don't want to know the sex, and I definitely don't want a baby shower."

"Well, I understand not wanting a baby shower because you would need friends and family to attend, and you have neither." Realizing that her statement might be hurtful Tina tried to retract. "I didn't mean— . . . "

"Get some backbone and stand by your words, Tina. You are such a spineless character. Never apologize for the truth. That's why you can never stand in my shoes." Keisha left the ladies' room.

"I'll meet up with you tomorrow!" Tina pursued after Keisha.

"No, thank you. I can put myself to sleep," Keisha laughed.

"Am I really that boring?" asked Tina, trying to keep up with Keisha's pace.

Keisha ignored her question and went back to the bar. "I'll have another one!" she called out to the bartender.

"I'll have what she's having!" Tina seated herself.

"I so need something stronger, but I will not put my little baby at harm." Keisha turned the swivel stool to face Tina.

"You've definitely made a U-turn because a few months ago you would have abolished kids if it was up to you."

"This child has a purpose, and my baby is the final piece to complete my puzzle."

"Don't tell me you're using this baby as a trap?"

"No. Bling already loves me. My baby will make our family complete." Keisha smiled.

"So is Bling the father?" Tina anxiously inquired.

"And we're back to my child's paternity."

"I didn't mean . . . " Tina was about to justify the intention of her question.

"There you go again. Stop worrying about my feelings. You asked a valid question."

"But you got defensive when I asked you earlier."

"I'm allowed to react however I choose to, but that doesn't mean your question shouldn't be asked. Will you ever learn? Stop being a people pleaser because you allow people to walk over you. But to soothe your curiosity, Bling *is* the father of my child."

"What about his wife?"

"Let's just say, I'm giving him what she can't." Keisha sipped her wine.

"I hope you know what you're doing."

"Trust me. I'm a fighting soldier, armed and dangerous." She gave Tina a wink.

"Keisha, Keisha, Keisha. You never cease to amaze me." Tina raised the glass to her lips.

"Well, I'm going to head home. You don't have a problem paying the tab, do you?" Keisha got up from her seat.

Tina swallowed hard. "Hell, yes, I do!" Her voice was loud.

"I was just testing you. I got this. I know you're pinching pennies."

"And I can see that you're not because you're sporting a ten thousand-dollar Berkin bag."

"You know I am the trend while you have to catch up to it." Keisha took out her wallet and put fifty dollars on the counter and left the bar. On her drive home she let her window down, enjoying the wind blowing on her face.

She would never admit it to Tina, but she did miss their friendship. Tina was the only female who considered her a friend.

She pulled into her driveway, and found Bling sitting on her steps. She immediately cut her engine and exited her car. "What's wrong?" she questioned, hurrying to him. "Why are you sitting outside?"

"I can't seem to find my key," Bling calmly stated.

"How long have you been sitting out here?"

"I'm good, but all these questions are driving me nuts. Can you open the door so I can take a piss?"

"With that attitude I should let you piss your pants. Which one of these many keys is the right one? I don't know." She dangled the keys in his face teasing him.

Bling took the keys and opened the door. Keisha laughed, seeing him wiggling like a child.

"I'll get you for this." Bling ran to the bathroom.

Keisha kicked off her shoes and dropped her bag on the floor and quickly stepped to the bathroom following after him. "I hope you put the seat up."

"Can a man get some privacy?"

"I won't look. Even though I've seen it plenty of times." Keisha cleaned the makeup from her face with a baby wipe.

Bling shook his stuff and returned it to his pants. He turned to see why Keisha couldn't wait until he was finished. She was leaning into the mirror and her ass poked out at him. Her dress climbed up her legs, exposing her ass cheeks.

"I'm almost done, baby." She looked back at him.

"Don't move." He walked up behind her.

"Is there something on me?" she asked in a panic.

"No, but I'm about to be." Bling lifted her dress. She had no panties on. The discovery made his manhood instantly rock-hard. He released himself from his pants and found her wetness. Bling was gentle with each stroke. They watched themselves in the mirror bumping body to body.

It was early the next morning when Bling was awaken by his ringing phone. He rubbed his eyes, dismissing the sleep, and took his phone from the nightstand.

"Hello!" he said. Denise's voice was inaudible, but her terrifying cry softened his hard feelings he had developed toward her. "I can't understand you. You have to stop crying." He got out of bed wearing only his boxers.

"Why aren't you here to get me out?" her somber voice came through the phone.

"I was taking care of business, but I'll be there as soon as I can." He took a seat at the kitchen table.

"Did they bring my baby girl to the house? Did you hear them knocking? Can you listen for their knock? I'm expecting my baby today."

Bling was saddened by her outrageous talk. He could tell she wasn't herself. "Where did you put the picture, Denise?" Bling figured that in her vulnerable state he might get the picture from her possession.

"It's where our love froze in time," Denise giggled.

"Where is that? Tell me!" Bling was furious.

"I'm keeping it in a safe place, baby. I won't let them get it. I'll keep your secret. I . . . won't tell . . . if . . . you . . . don't . . . tell." Denise sang her words, and the line went dead.

"It's *your* secret!" Bling yelled into the phone, even though he knew she hung up.

"Who's secret?" Keisha asked entering the kitchen.

"Not now!" He left the kitchen.

"Is someone blackmailing you?" she followed after him.

"I have to go." Bling hastened to the bathroom where his pants were lying on the floor.

"Go where? Who were you talking to?"

"My wife." He walked out of the door still buttoning his shirt.

Keisha watched Bling drive out of the driveway, then she dashed to the bedroom and retrieved her phone. Her finger quickly dialed and listened as the phone rang. "Detective, I need you to keep her locked up." She spoke as soon as she heard the detective's voice. "Why can't you? I'm paying good money for your services, so I need you to refrain from giving her bail for another day. Yes, you can, for another $20,000 donation. OK. Then I'll settle for a few more hours."

Keisha got off the phone and paced the floor. "I have to come up with a plan. Think, Keisha, think." She kept pacing. "Bingo!"

She moved quickly to the closet and took her jean shirt dress. Luckily, the buttons were already undone, which saved her some time. Her arms went in the sleeves, and she buttoned it, then loosely belted her waist with a tan belt. Her tan gladiator slippers were in reach so she didn't think twice. She wrapped her hair on top of her head in a bun which became her customary look whenever she was on borrowed time. Then she grabbed her bag and left the house.

Keisha got on I-95 heading south. Her phone started to ring, and she answered it. "Yes, Detective." She paused to listen before she spoke. "I don't care if Bling and her sister are there. Hold her for a few more hours. OK. OK. I'll add another ten thousand. What's that, your yearly salary? Just figure it out." She ended the call.

"Why haven't you given up on her, Bling?" she banged the steering wheel. "You have me! You don't need her!" Keisha was now determined more than ever to put Denise away. She floored the gas pedal. Her speed rocketed to 90 mph. "Keep pissing me off, Bling, and you will feel the wrath of Keisha." She maintained her speed not caring if a cop was in range. She made it to her destination and stormed in the building. Karen turned to greet her, but seeing that it was Keisha she clasped her hands and started her prayer. Keisha didn't exchange a word or even look her way. She had tunnel vision all the way to Mr. Salmon's office.

"Not you again. You're making my life a living hell. What is it now?"

"You're a lawyer, and you rub shoulders with the good, the bad, and the ugly, and I know among the three you must know a psychiatrist."

"I'm not getting anyone involved in this mess." He shook his head.

"Do you want to be free of me or not?" Keisha leaned in closer to his face.

"I'm listening." He gave in.

"Good. It's simple. I need a psychiatrist to take a trip down to Bridgeport Police Department. There's a Denise Mills in lockup. I need her committed to a psych ward."

"I'm not getting into that. I most definitely will not." He got up from his seat.

"It's a small deed in comparison to the payoff of never seeing me again." Keisha sat in his chair rocking back and forth.

"How will you guarantee that I will never see you again?"

"My child is your guarantee. I'm turning a new page because I'm going to be a mother."

"I see. But I can't trust that."

"OK, then I'll be a thorn in your ass for the rest of your life." She got up attempting to walk away.

"OK. OK. I do know a psychiatrist in Bridgeport who, in fact, I can call in a favor to."

"I need this done now because the family is there, and I want them to watch as they take her away in a straitjacket." With nothing else to add she left his office.

Karen held her head down, not wanting to make eye contact, but Keisha purposefully stopped at the desk. "Your job is safe, Karen," she idly taunted. But Karen's fingers stroked the keyboard, not giving her the time of day. "I figure a woman of God should let bygones be bygone." Keisha leaned in to view the screen. But Karen gave her the cold shoulder. "How about sending up a prayer for me? Since I'm about to be a mother, I think I might need some showers of blessings. But since the cat got your tongue, I'll leave you to your world of silence." Keisha proceeded to the door.

Mr. Salmon called out to Keisha, and she turned. He was standing outside his office, and she took a few steps toward him.

"He's on his way there right now!" Mr. Salmon announced with excitement.

"Well, for your sake, let's hope everything goes well." She cracked a smile and exited.

Keisha was in a hurry to get back to Bridgeport. She merged to the left lane where her speed almost doubled the limit. She made it back to Bridgeport, but she wanted in on the action, so she drove by the jail and spotted Bling's car. She procrastinated about whether she should go inside, but she wanted in on the drama, so she double-parked her car and dashed to the entrance, and as she opened the door, a loud outburst from an angry woman pointed her in the right direction.

"My sister is not crazy!" You have no right demanding an evaluation of her sanity!" Madison was furious.

"I was informed of her maniacal rants, and we can't have her being a hazard to herself or others," the psychiatrist spoke.

"My sister is not a prisoner, nor is she insane, so I suggest you go find a monkey to do your experiments on."

Keisha cracked a smile at Madison's spunk. She was a woman of her kind. Keisha made eye contact with the detective giving him the signal that he could free the prisoner.

"To end all this madness, I will release your wife," the detective said, removing himself from the ruckus.

"Let the fireworks begin." Keisha was ready for the showdown but she just watched from a distance, not wanting to be a suspect.

"Why are you so damn quiet?" Madison attacked Bling, who was sitting in a chair, visibly caught between a rock and a hard place. Not in a million years would he have expected his life would be this chaotic. But regardless of his anger toward his wife, he still cared enough to get her out of jail.

"I'm here, aren't I?" Bling got up from the chair.

Keisha pulled her head back into hiding. "That was close." She took a deep breath.

"Baby, you came." Denise ran to Bling.

Keisha poked her head out, hearing Denise's voice. She cringed at the sight of her hugging Bling so tightly.

"Did they bring my baby?" Denise released her grip and asked, looking into Bling's eyes.

"Baby?" Keisha repeated.

"There is no baby, Denise," Bling said, looking her in the eyes.

"What is she talking about?" Madison asked.

"I'm adopting a baby, Madison. If she's a girl, I might just name her after you." Denise ran her fingers through Madison's hair.

"Bling, what's wrong with my sister?" Madison looked at him for an answer as Denise continued combing her hair with her fingers.

"Has she already lost her damn mind? She's gone loony," Keisha whispered, observing Denise's childlike act.

"And who are you?" Denise took notice of the psychiatrist.

"Don't mind me. I'm just an observer," the man informed her.

"Is my husband in trouble? You're not going to take him, are you? He didn't do it," Denise rambled on.

"Shut up, Denise! Shut your crazy ass up!" Bling grabbed his wife's arm.

"Let her go!" Madison was in his face.

"What the hell is going on? Why does he seem to be hiding something? What's the damn secret?" Keisha's curiosity was in overdrive.

"*I . . . won't . . . tell if . . . you . . . don't . . . tell,*" Denise sang.

"This bitch is psycho." Keisha peeped from her hiding place.

"I'm taking my wife home." Bling took Denise by her arm.

"Is he going let him take her out of here? Why isn't he stopping them? I have to stop them. I know it will push her over the edge to see me." Keisha came out of hiding and trotted toward them.

"Keisha! What are you doing here?" Bling acknowledged her.

"Hi, honey." Keisha slowed her pace.

"Why are you here?" Bling asked through gritted teeth.

"You will never get my husband. He came here to be with me. Don't you see he loves me and not you?" Denise extended her arms, hugging her husband.

"I'm here to follow up on any leads about who tried to kill me and our child." Keisha rubbed her belly, taunting Denise.

"She took my baby! Give me my baby!" Denise lunged at Keisha, but Bling held her back.

"This woman has gone mad. She needs to be committed. She's deranged," Keisha spoke aloud for the entire department to hear.

"You stole my baby! Bling, she stole our baby!" Denise raged on.

Madison ran to her sister's aid. "Calm down, sis. It's going to be OK."

"Get away from me! You helped her to take my baby! All of you are on her side. You plotted to take my child!" Denise backed away from them.

"Can someone please get a psychiatrist. This woman needs help!" Keisha wanted the psychiatrist to act.

"You don't give a damn about my sister! Both of you did this to her! I'm here for you, sis. I won't let them hurt you." She inched her way to her sister. "Do you remember the song we use to sing as children, sis?"

"Stay away from me!" Denise yelled at Madison.

"You are my sunshine my only sunshine." Madison sang with tears streaming from her eyes. *"You make me happy when skies are gray . . ."* Madison sobbed, unable to finish the song.

"Please don't take my sunshine away," Denise sang, walking to her sister, and they embraced each other. The psychiatrist injected Denise with medication, and she collapsed in Madison's arms.

"What did you do?" Madison screamed. "What did you do to her?"

"It's just a mild sedative. She'll be fine. The ambulance is on its way."

"You are my sunshine, my only sunshine; you make me happy when skies are gray . . ." Madison sang as she lowered herself to the floor still holding her sister.

CHAPTER 19

Five Months Later

Bling opened the steaming pot and the aroma of curried shrimp spread throughout the house. He stirred slowly, adding his tender touch to his special dish. Keisha had a craving for curried shrimp with white rice. He brought the spoon to his mouth and tasted it. "Almost perfect."

He set the dining-room table for two using Keisha's expensive china plates. Next, he set the wineglasses down and stood back to admire his work. "What am I missing? Candles. You can't set a romantic mood without candles. Where do you keep the candles?" he shouted out to Keisha who was in the bedroom.

"In the kitchen drawer," she shouted back.

Bling went back to the kitchen, where the smell of burnt rice was potent. "Oh no, not the rice." He turned the burner off. "I wouldn't want to burn this too." He gave his shrimp another stir and turned the fire out.

"Can I come out now?"

"Be patient, woman, and let me do my thing." He took a bottle of red wine from the fridge and found the candles in the drawer. Next, he brought the two candles and the wine to the table. He removed his apron and his blue polo shirt was spotless. "You can come out now!"

Keisha waddled to the dining room wearing a maxi dress. Her belly was fully grown.

"I'm starving," she proclaimed. Bling helped her to her seat where she struggled to sit.

"Would you like a glass of wine?" he asked, opening the bottle.

"How about a plate of food?" she expressed her hunger.

Bling left the table and brought back two plates of steaming hot food. "Is this what you want?" he teased by putting her plate forward, and then pulling it back.

"Boy, you know that plate is hot. You better stop playing," she warned.

Bling set both plates down and took his seat. "Let's eat."

Before he could take a bite his phone started to ring. "I better get that." He went to the kitchen and retrieved his phone. He didn't recognize the number but decided to answer anyway.

"Who is this?" Bling asked in an aggressive tone. He immediately recognized the voice. "Denise?" he said, startled. "Where are you?" he questioned. "I'm not playing any games with you. Tell me where you are." Bling walked to the living-room window checking to see if she was outside. "Why are you calling me?" He searched for answers because he was skeptical. "Atlantic City? What are you doing in Atlantic City?" He put the phone on speaker.

"I'm in trouble, and I need your help." Denise spoke in a frantic tone.

"Call the police because I can't help you," he instructed.

"They kidnapped me, and I'm scared. I think they're going to kill me." Denise was crying out to him.

"Who kidnapped you?" Bling became concern. Hearing that she was in trouble he couldn't turn his back on her.

"He said he was getting revenge for Hype's death," Denise sobbed.

"You shouldn't be involved in this mess. This has nothing to do with you!" Bling took his frustration out on the chair by kicking it hard.

"Please, Bling, you have to help me. He'll be back soon, and I don't want to die. I really don't want to die!" Denise cried.

"Where exactly is he keeping you?" Bling yelled in the phone.

"I think it's the same hotel we were on my birthday. Room #333. I think he's coming. You have to save me, Bling!" The call ended.

"I won't let you go." Keisha was standing behind him. She forbade him, knowing what he was contemplating.

"I have to. For the simple fact that she has nothing to do with the mess we've created."

"What if they kill you?" Keisha dreaded the thought.

"Nothing you say will stop me, Keisha. I *have* to do this." Bling went to the bedroom and removed his .45 pistol from under the pillow.

"Why can't you let the police handle it?" Keisha still nagged.

"My conscience won't let me."

"Conscience or your ego? You have your child to think about." Keisha grabbed his arm in an attempt to stop him from leaving.

"If anything happens to me, let my boy know that his daddy died doing what was right." He walked away from her.

"Let the police handle this!" Keisha called out to him.

Bling ignored her and ran to his car and drove off. He felt guilty for his wife being in such a predicament. She has already suffered greatly because of his infidelity, and now she's caught up in his battle. Bling huffed and puffed like a blowfish. His adrenaline was pumping. He wanted to end this war one way or another. He was tired of living in fear. Hype was dead, and he wanted this war to be dead too.

Two hours had elapsed before the big sign finally welcomed him to Atlantic City. He sat at a red light and his patience had run thin. He ran the red light, and immediately heard several horns honking, but he didn't give a damn. He pulled into the hotel parking lot and hurried inside. Quickly, he pressed the button for the elevator, but it was taking too long. He opted for the staircase and ran to the third floor like a track star.

He looked to his right, then left, and walked off to his left. Room #333 was three doors down. He took long strides and finally faced the door that held his wife hostage. Bling took the gun from his waist and without a second thought he turned the knob. The door was unlocked. His nerves were a little shaky, but he proceeded on his mission. He slowly pushed the door open, but he could see no visible signs of Denise. His entire body was inside by now, and he took cover between the curves of the wall. Bling poked his head out scoping the room like a trained marksman. But still there was no sign of Denise. He took short steps, placing one foot in front of the other and slowly inched his way inside until the bed was in complete view. Still the coast was clear. As he got closer to the bed he could hear the shower running. He took several deep breaths, then aimed his gun ready to kill. Edging his way to the bathroom with his hand stretched forward, Bling saw that the door was ajar and found it strange. He kept his guard up and pushed it open.

"No!" Bling bellowed from his gut, seeing the white shower curtain stained with blood. He hunched over breathing heavy, as if he was having an asthma attack. "She didn't deserve this. She didn't deserve this." He spoke with hurt, pain, and anger. Bling raised his body and wiped his tears. "Why not me? I would rather die in her place. Why are you sparing my miserable life?" Bling's gun smashed a decorative painting that hung on the wall. Broken pieces of glass scattered on the floor. "This isn't fair!" He wiped his flowing tears and walked into the bathroom, extending his arm forward as he reached for the shower curtain. His arm was shaking uncontrollably. He retracted it, trying to control his nerves. "I have to do this." He tried to calm himself. "I have to see her." He extended his arm once more, and his nerves still took over. But with shaking arms, he pulled the curtain back and couldn't comprehend what his eyes beheld.

She was naked lying in the half-filled tub of bloody-water with her throat slashed. Bling sat on the toilet. "Laura?" He couldn't make sense of why Laura was lying dead in the tub. "But where is Denise?" His phone rang in his pocket. He jumped to his feet just in case it was Denise calling back. And, in fact, it was the same number. "If you hurt one hair on her body . . ." Bling threatened.

"It's me, honey," Denise spoke.

"Did he hurt you? Where are you?"

"Did you like my little surprise in the tub?" she asked.

"*You* did this?" Bling asked, confused.

"Thou shall not touch what's mine." Denise gave her commandment. "Jordonna piqued my interest in the subject of murder, and Laura was my training, and Keisha will be my graduation ceremony." Denise busted out laughing.

"You psycho bitch!" Bling yelled into the phone.

"I'm not psycho! I'm your wife!" Denise shouted back. "I got you." Her voice was now calm. "I bet your fingerprints are all over that room." She laughed a wicked laugh. Bling quickly grabbed a towel and retraced his steps, wiping down everything he touched. He ran out of the room and headed to the stairs. He went down faster than he had gone up. He wanted to get away from the room, the hotel, and Atlantic City. He now knew that Denise's next victim would be Keisha, and he had to get back to Connecticut. He made it to his car and dialed Keisha's number. She answered the phone on the first ring.

"Lock all the doors and the windows and if you hear or see anything suspicious call the police," Bling instructed.

He drove out of the parking lot and exited the hotel. He saw flashing police lights and blaring sirens. They were approaching from both directions. Bling knew he was cornered, so he pulled his car over ready to surrender, but they drove past him pulling into the hotel entrance. He stepped on the gas and pulled off, and as he did so, he glanced in his rearview mirror to see the flickering red, white, and blues decorated the parking lot like it was Christmas. When the police and the hotel were in a distance he let air flow freely to his lungs. He was so tense he hadn't allowed himself time to breathe.

Bling's drive back to Connecticut seemed like a lifetime. His gas gauge indicated that he was almost on empty. A rest stop was approaching, so he pulled off the turnpike. He took the gun from his waist and placed it in the glove compartment. The pumps were all occupied, and he impatiently waited behind two cars. He repeatedly pounded his steering wheel as his mind tried to strategize a plan to defeat Denise without having to put a bullet in her head.

He was next in line at the full service pump, so he rolled down his window and extended a fifty-dollar bill. He uttered the word *super* and his window went up. He watched as the pump ran fast, counting the gallons. When the pump stopped the attendant was tending to another car. Bling didn't have time to waste so he honked his horn, which alerted the man, and he removed the hose, allowing Bling to leave.

After an hour and a half of driving, Bling was at the toll leaving New York and entering Connecticut. He paid his $1.75 knowing he had another forty-five minutes to get to Keisha. His phone started to ring, escalating his anxiety. Keisha's name lit up his phone screen and he quickly answered. "Did something happen?"

"I'm just worried. Where are you?" Keisha asked.

"Did you lock up like I told you to?" Bling questioned.

"Yes, but what's going on? Where are you?"

"I'll be there soon. I have to get off the phone because getting pulled over is the last thing I want to happen right now." He ended the call.

When Bling exited the highway he breathed a sigh of relief. But instead of going to Keisha he went to the house he once shared with Denise, hoping to see her there. Her car was parked in the same spot since she had gotten arrested. The lights were off, but he decided to go inside. There was a picture and a note that he had to find because he now knew for a fact that Denise would indeed use the information to set him up for Jordonna's murder.

Bling entered the house with caution and turned on all the lights as an extra precaution. He went to the bedroom thinking she would be there sleeping so he could suffocate her with a pillow. But she wasn't sleeping in the bed. He rummaged through the drawers and came up empty. He flipped the mattress causing the photo album that was on the nightstand to fall to the floor, but that was also a dead end. He went downstairs and turned the place upside down.

The front door slammed hard, and Bling was almost scared to death. He was so busy searching the house he didn't hear the door open. "What do you think you're doing?" Madison's voice roared.

"This is *my* damn house, and I most definitely don't have to answer to you." Bling continued with his search.

"You had my sister committed to a mental ward, and now you're destroying the place she called home." Madison was enraged. "How can you live with yourself knowing what you did to my sister?"

"I live with myself just fine. But I guess you don't know that your sister escaped and is out committing murder."

"That's a lie, and if so, why aren't you dead?"

"Get out of my way." He took his search back to the living room which he had previously turned upside down. "And don't act as if you don't know your sister was an undercover bitch."

"Where do you get off talking about her like that? She has been nothing but devoted to you."

"Is that so? Weren't you the same one who accused her of being a whore in the Bahamas?"

Madison didn't say a word; instead, she looked at Bling with disgust.

"That's what I thought. Silence means consent." Bling brought his attention to her.

"Whatever she did, you deserved it. God don't like ugly, and your face resembles a monkey's ass right now." She walked away.

"Be nice, Madison! I'm still your brother-in-law."

"I'll put an end to that with or without the law," Madison addressed him.

Bling quit his search for the evidence because his effort was coming up futile. He went upstairs to spy on Madison. "Why are you here, Madison?" Bling barged in the bedroom.

Madison had the wedding album, browsing through the pictures. "My sister thought you were someone special, but you are just a dirty pig in a blanket." She kept turning the pages.

"I am whatever you say I am. But you need to get a life."

Suddenly, the album was making its way to Bling's head, and he ducked. It connected with the wall and a few pictures came loose on the floor. And the evidence was uncovered. The wedding album was where their love had frozen in time, but Bling left the house and went home to Keisha unaware of Madison's discovery.

"Is she dead?" Keisha queried anxiously when Bling came in the house.

"She tried to set me up!" Bling pushed past her.

"But is she dead?" Keisha was impatient to know.

"No!" Bling sat at the kitchen table.

"I was hoping to hear good news," she stated as she passed Bling a Heineken from the fridge.

"She obviously knows what she's doing. I have to outsmart her."

"How did they let that lunatic get away?" Keisha asked as she poured a glass of apple juice. "And why can't you find her?"

"Because I can't think like a damn lunatic, and you need to watch your back because you will be her next target."

"Unlike you, I'm smarter than a fifth grader." Keisha spoke with confidence, then drank from her glass.

"You better take this shit serious. Denise won't hesitate to kill. She's a murderer with a vengeance," Bling cautioned. "And another thing . . ."

"Wait, let me guess. Lock all the doors and windows," Keisha joked, unwilling to believe that Denise could be deadly.

"Her sister Madison is also a threat," Bling informed her.

Someone pounded hard on the door, and they both instinctively looked toward the door.

"That's the police. Shit! They're here for me."

"What did you do?" Keisha asked, seeing him in a panic.

"She killed Laura and framed me for it." Bling paced the floor.

"Who and what?" Keisha wore a puzzled look.

After three more consecutive poundings, Keisha started to the door. Bling knew if he went to trial for a second murder he most definitely wouldn't walk free.

Keisha positioned herself at the peephole the best she could with her big belly. "You can relax. It's Tina," she alerted Bling. "Don't you know what a doorbell is for?" Keisha asked as soon as she opened the door.

"Hello to you too." Tina gave her a stink look.

"What are you doing here?" Keisha scanned the street to make sure Denise wasn't lurking.

"Being that I'm a godmother, I took the initiative of coming up with a plan," Tina gleefully expressed.

"What plan, Tina?" Keisha asked, still standing guard at the door.

"Instead of a baby shower, I convinced a few of your favorite department stores to come to your house and do a fashion expo." Tina clapped her hands, cheering herself.

"It's clear to see that you have nothing better to do. But now is just not a good time."

"I just set up a fashion expo for people to cater to you, and you don't have time? What the hell is so important?" Tina tilted her head, trying to see past Keisha into the house.

"It's just not a good time." Keisha stepped back and closed the door. She rejoined Bling in the kitchen.

"I think it's best for you to go stay with your father," he blurted.

"Say what now?" Keisha couldn't believe her ears.

"Denise would never find you there." Bling couldn't stay still. He started pacing again.

"You must have lost your damn mind. Going back to my father's house will never happen. I'm not going into seclusion. I am not hiding from no one. Never have and I never will." She turned to walk away.

"You will when you are carrying my child!" Bling's voice roared.

She looked back at him and could see the fear in his eyes and realized he wanted to protect his family. "I'll stay at a hotel. Going to my father's is not an option."

"A hotel isn't an option," Bling counteracted.

"If you're that petrified of your wife, why don't *you* go into hiding?" She walked out of the kitchen.

"Why are you fighting me on this?" Bling walked after her.

"Because you're giving her too much credit."

"With two murders under her belt, she's completely insane and totally irrational."

"*Two* murders?" Keisha stopped and faced Bling. "Wait, you mentioned a Laura. So who's the other person?"

"That's not important right now. You need to trust me and know that I want to protect you and my child. I know you don't want to but staying with your father is the safest place right now. She wouldn't be able to find you. Please do this for our child."

"OK. OK. For the sake of our child." Denise untied her robe and climbed into bed. Bling sat at the foot of the bed rubbing her feet. "We have to leave early in the morning." His voice was calm now.

"I need time to pack."

"You don't need much because you have to stay low-key. Just some comfy clothes and you'll be fine."

"How low are we talking?" Keisha asked.

"No malls, not even grocery shopping; more like house arrest."

"You must be out of your damn mind." She pulled her swollen feet from his grip.

"Can you stop being so vain and think about your safety for once? Just let me lead and we'll get through this. Starting with me packing your bags."

"Can I at least give a thumbs-up or down since all my rights have been revoked?"

"Nah. Trust me, I got this," Bling boasted.

Keisha watched as Bling took her clothes from the closet. Her maternity clothes were already separated to the right side of the closet so his task was easy. The thought of going back to her father's house was petrifying. She had left to free herself from rules and regulations, and now she was being ordered to go back. *How ironic,* she thought.

"Where are the granny panties? Because you won't be needing this fancy lingerie," Bling joked, twirling some lace panties with his index finger.

"So you got jokes. It won't be so funny when I wake your ass up to change diapers in the middle of the night. Laugh about that one, baby daddy." She tossed a pillow at him.

Keisha couldn't sleep the entire night. She stayed up repacking her suitcases. The idea of fleeing her home because of Denise made her livid. The only thing that could soothe her was chocolate cookies and knowing it was in the best interest of her love child.

It was 8:00 a.m. in the morning when Bling and Keisha arrived at her father's house. He was standing outside on the porch sipping on a cup of coffee awaiting their arrival. He set the cup down when the car pulled in the driveway and posted himself at the bottom of the steps, not sure of a proper greeting for his daughter. Bling got out of the car and went to help Keisha, who was struggling with her belly.

"Good morning, baby girl." Her father took his daughter's hand into his.

"Is it really a good morning, Daddy?" Keisha redirected his greeting.

"For me it is, for me it is!" He was glad to have his daughter back home. He guided her up the steps.

"It's way too early for all this excitement." Her somber attitude expressed her unwillingness to be there.

"Welcome home, baby girl." Her father expressed his delight when they approached the door.

"This is not my home!"

"But it once was, baby girl." He locked eyes with his daughter.

"I wish you would stop calling me that." She entered the house, but despite her reluctance to be there she was overcome with a feeling of serenity. The décor hadn't changed much except the curtains were replaced. The hardwood floor was well kept, and the house was spotless. The furniture could use an upgrade, but she knew her father was holding on to the memory of her mother. There was an enlarged picture of her and her mother hung above the fireplace. She guided her steps as she walked closer to get a better view. She was sitting on her mother's lap with her ponytails, and her mother's smile was bright. She turned away feeling herself becoming overwhelmed. There was an overabundance of pictures placed throughout the house. It was like a museum in dedication to her and her mother. She took a picture from the coffee table and cracked a smile. Her fashion sense needed some help back then. She went from picture to picture reliving her childhood.

"What's for breakfast?" she asked while turning her head to see Bling and her father keenly watching her. "Daddy in the kitchen, and Bling, my bags to the bedroom since you two have nothing better to do."

"Yes, ma'am." Bling pulled her luggage inside.

"That's a relief," Keisha exhaled aloud, relieved that her bedroom wasn't spread with her pink childhood bedspread. Her full-size bed had been replaced with a queen neatly made with white linen. "How long are you expecting me to stay here?" She sat on the bed and addressed Bling.

"Until Denise is no longer a threat to you and my child."

"Are you coming to see me tomorrow?" she asked.

"It's too risky. I don't know if she's going to trail me, and I won't take that chance."

"So once again she's taking you away from me."

"No one is taking me away from you because you put a spell on me." He kissed her cheek.

CHAPTER 20

Bling called the number Denise had previously contacted him from, but it was no longer in service.

"Goddamn it!" He tossed the phone in the passenger seat. He had no idea where she might be. Even though she had gone psycho, Bling knew she still had a few good marbles up top. "Where are you, Denise?"

He went back to the house, and Denise's car was still there. He parked a few cars down from the house watching to see if Denise would come in or out, but after an hour of staking out the place, Madison's car pulled in the driveway, and his heart was racing.

"What have we here?" He watched intently as Madison exited the car and entered the house. Bling waited for a few more minutes, but Madison reemerged from the house, and Bling ducked quickly, knocking his forehead on the steering wheel. "Holy shit!" He rubbed the aching spot as he slowly raised his head and noticed Madison carrying an overnight bag. "Bingo!" He watched her get in her car and drove out of the driveway, and he followed in pursuit.

Bling trailed Madison, but it didn't lead to a hotel or a safe house. It ended at Madison's house. She brought the bag inside and Bling sat in the car strategizing on how to approach the situation. He didn't want the police involved until the picture of him and Jordonna was back in his possession.

***

He didn't want to intimidate Denise by acting reckless. Regaining her trust was the best way to go. "I can't just walk up and ring the bell. Madison would probably throw piss in my face." Feeling constricted, Bling released his seat belt. "I have to get in that damn house!" Bling didn't want to lurk around the house this early in the day, afraid someone might call the police. He remained his car, not taking his eyes off the door just in case Denise decided to come out for air.

Bling checked the time. It was 1:00 p.m. He was feeling a little hungry, but he would deliberately miss lunch today.

"Oh hell, no." Bling sat up seeing Trigga's car coming from the opposite end of the street and stop in front of Madison's house. Madison came out of the house and Trigga meet her halfway, lifting her off her feet. Bling couldn't believe his eyes, so he briskly rubbed them and refocused. They ended their kiss, and Madison wiped her lip gloss from his mouth. Trigga always portrayed himself to be Mr. Tough Guy, so seeing him locking lips was unexpected. "She's wearing Denise's dress," Bling noted as Trigga escorted Madison to the car. "How long have they been . . ." He dismissed the question.

Trigga reversed his car and headed back in the direction he came from. Bling watched as the car disappeared, then exited his car feeling more at ease because with Madison not being home it was much easier to brainwash Denise. Bling nonchalantly strolled to the door and turned the knob and he had access. The door had been left unlocked, and he cracked a smile. He entered with caution, stepping lightly like a cat. The living room was the first room he cleared, then a few steps to his left and he was in the kitchen. The kitchen was clear also. He wasn't familiar with the layout of the apartment so he was just going off a whim. The next door he approached was the bathroom. He slowly edged his way until he was right by the door. He pushed at the door with his finger, and it slowly opened. No one was in sight. The last door was straight-ahead, and his heart began to race. He turned the knob and pushed hard, hitting it in the wall. There wasn't a scream or a shuffle, and Denise didn't put up a fight—because the only sign of Denise was her clothes scattered on the bed giving Madison options for her date.

Bling kicked the empty travel bag that sat on the floor, landing it in the corner of the room. "I can't believe this shit!" He left the house, slamming the door behind him. Even his car door felt his anger when he closed it with force. He drove off with speed, pissed that he had wasted his time. "Where the hell could she be?" he asked out loud, not knowing where to begin his search. Ten minutes into his driving Bling couldn't ignore his growling belly any longer so he decided to settle for lunch at the diner. But he quickly lost his appetite when Damien blindsided him at the table.

"How does it feel playing daddy to another man's child?" Damien approached.

"This is the wrong time to do this!" Bling warned.

"Don't tell me the thought never crossed your mind?" Damien invited himself to the available seat.

"Yes, the thought of breaking your neck just crossed my mind!"

"You might want to bring it down, besides, you don't want to disrupt these people trying to enjoy their meals." Damien turned his head viewing the room.

"The day I sit down to a meal with you will never come." Bling got up from his seat.

"I just wanted to discuss visitation rights to my child." Damien raised his voice.

"I see you're still delusional from the last time I knocked you out." Bling dropped a twenty-dollar bill on the table and walked away.

"What about Hype? He's another candidate. Oh wait, you killed him!" Damien called out to him.

The thought of the baby not being his never crossed his mind, but now it was burning a hole in his brain. Not wanting Damien to know he had gotten to him, Bling held his composure until he got to his car.

"How much more can a man take? What's next? The sky's falling down on me." Bling sat for a few seconds processing his thoughts, but he needed answers. He reversed out of the parking lot with Keisha as his main focus.

Bling made it back to Keisha's father's house, and her father was sitting on the porch enjoying a cigar.

"You're back so soon?" He released the smoke from his mouth.

"Not for good reasons." Bling climbed the steps to the porch.

"Is there more trouble?" He took another pull.

"Where is she?" Bling stopped to ask.

"You know she's in there waiting for you to take her away from here."

Bling went inside. Keisha was in the kitchen enjoying a bowl of fruit salad when Bling appeared in front of her.

"Is she dead? Are you here to take me home?" Keisha was elated.

"Is the baby mine?" Bling promptly asked.

"What did you just say?" She pushed the bowl aside.

"You heard me." Bling didn't enter the kitchen. He stood by the entrance looking in.

"Did your wife send you here to question the paternity of my child?"

"Just answer the question!" Bling raised his voice.

"You answer this question! Do you believe Damien is the father of my child?"

"Is Hype the father?" Bling's voice was still on high.

"Is Hype still a threat to you, Bling? You can't be serious."

"Why are you evading the question? Or maybe you don't know who the father is."

"That's enough!" Keisha's father's voice roared like a lion. "You don't come in my house and insult my daughter! Get out." He pointed to the door.

"Are you going to answer the question or not?" Bling still pushed for an answer.

"You heard my father, get out!" Keisha backed her father.

"I went through all this shit just to be deceived by you? I ended my damn marriage for you! And now the baby isn't mine." Bling was no longer yelling. He spoke with sadness in his voice.

"Who said it wasn't?" Keisha's tone was stern.

"You didn't say it was." Bling left the house.

Keisha remained at the table feeling insulted and humiliated at the fact that her father had to witness Bling's behavior. Her father turned to walk away, but she stopped him.

"Don't walk away. Look at me!" She banged her fist on the table.

He faced his daughter with sadness in his eyes. "What can I do to ease your heartache?"

"I'm a strong woman because I molded myself into one. I'm not a weak woman like my mother!" Tears ran from her eyes. "I can take care of my child without the help of a man." She pointed her finger at him. "So don't you dare feel sorry for me!"

"I see your strength, baby girl, and am proud of you." He walked closer to her.

Keisha was astonished to hear those words because she thought she was a failure in her father's eyes. "Are you really?" She wiped her tears.

"In you I see your mother's strength. I know you thought she was weak, but she was a fighter just like you. You are my everything, baby girl, and I'm sure your mother is smiling down on you."

He kissed her forehead and turned to leave, but she took ahold of his hand. "I love you too, Daddy."

He fell to his knees, and Keisha embraced her father.

"I think I'm having a heart attack," he suddenly said, his face turning pale. He let go of his daughter and placed his hand over his heart.

"Daddy!" Keisha called out to her father as he lowered his body to the floor. "You will not die on me!" she yelled at him.

"Baby girl, call 911." Her father's voice was low.

"Hold on, Daddy!" She took the phone from the countertop and dialed 911. "I need medical help! My father is having a heart attack! Please hurry!" She awkwardly scooted down to her father. "You can't die! You're all I've got!" Keisha protested.

"Be strong for your baby," he whispered to her.

She looked up to the ceiling. "God, please don't take him from me! You keep taking and taking. My mother, Uncle Patrick, and now you won't allow me to have my father! Yes, I've made mistakes, but my punishment is unfair." She brought her attention to her father. His eyes were closed. "No!" she bellowed from the pits of her gut.

The EMT rushed in, and she moved away, giving them access.

"One, two, three. Breathe." They administered CPR.

Keisha watched in horror as they pumped his chest. She slowly walked away, giving up hope. She had come to her father as a safe haven, but death still followed her. Her steps had no haste. There was no motivation as she walked away.

"We have a pulse!" one of the EMT called out.

She turned quickly, finding the energy to rush back to the kitchen. "Daddy, I'm here!" she ran to him.

"Get out of the way, ma'am! We have to go."

Keisha pulled herself together and found the key to her father's car. She drove to the hospital and wobbled inside. "Can you tell me what room Mr. Burkett is in?"

The nurse did her query by typing in the name. "Let me get Dr. Edwards."

"Is he not assigned to a room yet?"

"Dr. Edwards will answer your questions," the nurse calmly spoke.

"I don't have time for this. Just tell me what room my father is in!"

A tall, slender man wearing a white overcoat made his way toward Keisha, and she shortened his journey by walking to him.

"Dr. Edwards, is something wrong with my father?"

"I'm sorry to break this to you, but your father passed."

"Did he put you up to this? Is he's trying to pay me back for giving him hell for the past fourteen years? Go back there and tell him I'm not falling for his prank. Now tell me what room is he in so I can go suffocate him." She cracked a smile, but the doctor maintained a straight face. "You're not kidding, are you?" Keisha fearfully asked.

"He suffered another heart attack on the way here, and he didn't make it."

"No! I don't want to hear it." She poked his chest with her finger. "You better take me to him now!"

"I understand your pain, but you have to be careful about stressing for the sake of your baby," the doctor warned.

Keisha slowly backed away from him.

"Is there a preferred funeral home you would like to contact for transporting your father?" The doctor took a few steps forward.

"Burn him." She made a dash for the exit.

She wasn't going to allow herself to be vulnerable or grieve her father's death. She went back to the house and dragged her suitcases to the car and drove back to Connecticut to her apartment. Her neighbors couldn't get rid of her, and she wasn't going to give Denise the privilege, regardless of how crazy she might be.

"Keisha!" a voice called.

She looked toward Tammy's apartment, but there was no one at the door. She started to walk to her door, but the voice called her again so she detoured to Tammy's apartment. The door war ajar, and she barged inside.

"Make it quick, Tammy," she said with an attitude. But Tammy wasn't in view. "Where the hell are you?" Keisha looked toward the living room.

"In the kitchen," Tammy's somber voice indicated.

"Are you hurt?" Keisha hurried to her, but she suddenly stopped. "Who did this to you?" she proceeded toward her. Tammy was tied up to a chair in the kitchen. Her eyes were speaking but Keisha couldn't break the code, and she rushed to Tammy.

"Hello, Keisha." The voice came from behind. Keisha spun her head—and beheld her arch nemesis. "I've spend two days and ten hours torturing your neighbor. I hope you didn't consider her a friend because she filled me in on how much of a bitch you are just so I would set her free. But I didn't. It gives me pleasure to hear her beg for her life." Denise slid her index finger on the long, stainless steel knife. Keisha shielded herself behind Tammy.

"I sat by that window and watched my husband go back and forth from his mistress's house, and I patiently waited for you to come home, and bingo, here you are. You couldn't stay away, could you? You had to come running back to him. Did you miss the way he touched you, or did you miss him rubbing your feet? Does my husband tell you that he loves you?" The knife sliced her finger, and she watched the blood drip on the floor.

"See what you did. You will pay for this." She stuck her finger in her mouth. "Eenie meenie minie mo, catch a puppy by its toe." She waved the knife back and forth pointing it at the two women.

"You can have your husband back." Keisha tried to defuse the situation.

Denise laughed a loud laugh. "No, thank you. I have my heart set on someone more pure and tenderhearted, and I'm going to cut it out of you."

Keisha cradled her belly. "I would rather die before I let you take my child." Keisha gave her word.

"That's exactly what I planned to do because you have my baby, and I want what's mine."

"You don't want to do this." Keisha stepped back and grabbed a knife. "You can threaten me all you want, but you do not fuck with my child."

"Why don't you put that knife to good use and cut me loose?" Tammy pleaded.

"Shut up!" Denise screamed. "You think you're running this, Keisha? No, you're not!" She threw the knife, and it landed in Keisha's arm causing her to drop her knife.

Tammy screamed, thinking the knife was aimed at her. "I'm not ready to die!"

Keisha pulled the knife from her arm without flinching as the blood ran down her arm. "What don't kill me only makes me stronger."

"I wasn't trying to kill you. That was just to show you that I'm not here to play. But now I am ready to kill you." Denise pulled the gun from her waist.

"I don't know why I'm in the middle of this shit. Denise, I'm on your side. You have all right to be mad as hell. She stole your husband, and I would want to kill her too, but I had nothing to do with it. So if you untie me I can help you tie this bitch to the chair." Tammy begged for her life.

"If you kill me, the baby will die, and then all this would be in vain." Keisha retreated behind the counter.

"My plan is to cut the baby out of you, then watch you bleed to death." Denise walked closer.

"Well, put the gun down. You don't want to hurt my baby," Keisha charmed.

"That's my child! "Denise yelled. "The gun is to keep your ass in check because as bad as I need my baby, I'm not afraid to kill you."

"If you put the gun down, I'll just lie right here and let you take the baby," Keisha baited.

"You won't give that baby up because that's the glue to you and my husband."

"Well, I have news for you. He's not the father," Keisha goaded.

"Now you're lying. You think I'm stupid!"

"No. Do the math, Denise. Hype is the father, so I have no hold on your husband. If you want the child of a murderer, you can have it." Keisha noticed that Tammy had freed her arm. "You can do it, just grab it." Keisha sent a subliminal message to Tammy.

"You will always be a conniving bitch." Denise inched closer to Keisha.

"Now!" Keisha called out to Tammy, but Tammy was shaking uncontrollably.

"What the hell are you yelling about? You think someone is going to come save you?"

"Keisha, you better do what she said because I can't risk my life," Tammy recoiled.

"You better listen to what she said." Denise took aim.

"At least I'm willing to die with dignity." Keisha messaged back to Tammy.

Denise kept her focus on Keisha, and Tammy summoned the courage to tackle her. She took Denise down to the floor, and Keisha ran out of the house leaving

Tammy and Denise wrestling on the floor. She went to her apartment, and Bling came out of the bedroom to see who it was.

Keisha couldn't breathe. She braced her back against the door. Bling rushed to her seeing her bloody arm. "Denise, next door. Tammy."

A loud gunshot echoed, and Bling's eyes widened. "That's a gunshot."

"Oh God, no!" Keisha screamed.

"What the hell is going on?" Bling shouted.

"Denise is next door. She tried to kill me, and I escaped. Tammy had nothing to do with this, and now she's probably dead."

Bling ran to the kitchen and took his gun from the table and hastened to the door. "Lock the door behind me," he instructed as he ran to Tammy's apartment where he found Tammy on the kitchen floor with blood gushing from her arm.

"Where is she?" Bling asked lifting her to the chair.

"She went out the back," Tammy answered through her pain.

Bling took off his shirt and wrapped her arm. "Call 911. I have to get back to Keisha." Bling raced to the door.

"Drop the gun!" the police called out to him.

"I didn't do anything!" He slowly put the gun down.

"Get down on your knees!" the cops yelled with their guns drawn. Bling did as he was told, and two officers rushed over and cuffed him.

"What are you doing? He didn't do anything!" Keisha said.

"Tell that to a judge," another cop chimed in.

Bling took his seat in the back of the cop car and lifted his head looking at the ceiling. "Here we go again."

***

Bling sat in the interrogation room with his head on the table when a detective barged in. He raise his head. "It's either you're going to charge me or let me go." Bling's temper flared.

"You should just make this place your home. You're here on a regular basis."

"This place will never be my home."

"How do you explain this?" the detective asked, placing the evidence on the table.

Bling couldn't believe his eyes. The picture of him and Jordonna in bed just sealed his fate. His heart was racing. He was having flashbacks of the cell door slamming behind him when he was tossed in the first and second time, but this time he knew he wouldn't be walking out. The detective banged his fist on the table causing Bling to jump.

"Cat got your tongue?" the detective spoke again.

"No matter what I say you already think I'm guilty." Bling didn't try to defend himself; instead, he lowered his head to accept guilt.

"Why is my client being interrogated without his law-yer present?" A woman entered the room speaking with a Jamaican accent. Bling raised his head and laid eyes on a woman wearing a tight, fitted, royal blue pantsuit holding her pose at the door.

"I need to speak to my client in private." The woman's heels clanked on the tiled floor as she approached him, slamming her briefcase on the table.

Bling wore a puzzled look on his face knowing he didn't hire a lawyer.

"Young lady, your client is no stranger to the process." The detective rose to his feet.

"You will address me as Mrs. Patrina in and out of this building."

The detective left the room, and Bling got up from his chair. "Who hired you?" he questioned.

"Keisha hired me, and trust me when I say I'm the best. So what am I dealing with?"

"My wife is trying to blackmail me, and it's working." Bling reclaimed his seat in defeat. "She killed Jordonna, and now she's trying to pin it on me."

"Whoa. Hold on now. Bring it back. I thought this was about illegal possession of a firearm?"

"Initially it was, but Denise gave them a picture of me and Jordonna," Bling explained.

"Who is Jordonna?" Patrina asked.

"It's a long story."

"Well, you better cut it short because I need to know what I'm up against."

Bling filled her in but made a long pause before deciding to spare the details of his wife's involvement. Regardless of him despising his wife, his heart wouldn't allow him to incriminate her. "I saw what happened on the news, but I had nothing to do with it." Bling ended.

"If that's the only evidence they have, that's dismissible. You in bed with a woman simply means that you had a night of passion. About the gun, you wrestled it away from your wife who was about to kill you, and you chased after her, forgetting you still had it in your hand." Patrina gave him an alibi.

"But her fingerprints aren't on the gun," Bling added being doubtful.

"Simple. She was wearing gloves." Patrina closed her briefcase.

"Damn, you are good," Bling acknowledged her crafty lie.

"I'm not good, I'm the best. Now sit tight while I go demolish the weak case they're trying to build." Patrina exited the room.

Bling got up from the chair and patrolled the small room. His palms were getting sweaty knowing his fate rested in his lawyer's hands. Shortly, Patrina reentered the room, and Bling's heart started to race.

"I have bad news," she uttered.

"I knew it. I'm going to jail." He scratched his head in defeat.

"The bad news is that I didn't bring a shirt for you to wear when you walk out of here," she smiled.

Bling ran over to her and gave her a tight hug. "Thank you! Thank you!" he shouted.

"You better get off me! I have another case to defend in this expensive suit."

"I'm sorry." Bling stepped back.

CHAPTER 21

"Hold on, baby, Mommy is almost at the hospital."
Keisha was having contractions but instead of calling the
ambulance she decided to drive herself. "Ugh!" She bit on
her bottom lip as the pain shot through her body. "I'll just
call Tina and have her meet me at the hospital."

She took her eyes off the road trying to find her phone,
unaware that she was drifting to the wrong side of the
road. An oncoming car started to honk, trying to get her
attention. She brought her attention back to the road just
in time to swerve away from the car, but she lost control
and went off the road.

The car flipped, and she couldn't free herself. She
had blood all over her face from being cut by broken
glass. She was also in and out of consciousness. "Help!
Somebody help me!"

Someone came to her aid, but Keisha could barely see
the person's face her vision was so blurry. The person
released her from her seat belt and lay her on the ground.

"I'm in labor. My baby is coming!" Keisha declared.

"Push!" the person instructed.

"You have to take me to the hospital. I can't have my
baby here." Keisha spoke through agonizing pain.

"I would suggest that you push," the woman ordered in
a firm voice.

"*Ahhh!*" Keisha screamed.

"That's it. Keep pushing."

"I can't!" Keisha stopped pushing.

"You better push!" the woman raised her voice.

Keisha conjured up her strength and gave several hard pushes. She heard the baby crying, and she also cried. "Is it a boy or girl?" she anxiously asked.

"A handsome baby boy," the woman informed her.

"He must look like his daddy." Keisha said her last words and fell unconscious.

Keisha woke up in the hospital, and her head felt heavy. She touched her forehead. It was tightly wrapped with a bandage. The door opened, and she assumed it was a nurse. "Nurse, can you please bring me my baby?"

"I came as soon as I heard." Bling rushed to her.

"Did you go to the nursery yet?" Keisha asked.

"No. I wanted to make sure you're OK." He sat on the bed gently rubbing her foot.

There was a knock on the door, and Bling instructed the person to enter. A nurse joined them.

"Can I see my baby?" Keisha asked.

"I don't know how to say this, but we think whoever delivered your baby kidnapped your child."

"What?" Bling jumped to his feet.

"When the paramedics arrived, she had already given birth but there was no baby."

"This can't be true; you need to bring my baby to me." Keisha sat upright in the bed.

"I'm sorry to tell you the bad news, but your baby isn't in the nursery," the nurse reported.

"If you won't bring me my baby I will go get my child." Bling helped Keisha off the bed.

"Can we have a chair?" Bling asked. The nurse left the room and came back with a wheelchair. Bling pushed Keisha to the nursery. Keisha eagerly peered through the glass but none of the four blond-haired babies could be hers. She broke down in tears. Bling hugged her, trying to console her.

"Who would do such a thing? Who would take my child?" Keisha cried.

"Denise would." Bling gave her the obvious answer.

"You have to find her. She can't have my damn baby!"

On the way back to the room they ran into the detective who was on his way to Keisha's room.

"Did you find my baby, Detective?" Keisha eagerly asked.

"We haven't located your child as yet."

"He needs his mother. He needs me," she cried.

"I'm here to ask you some questions that can better help us to locate your child, but I can come back if you need some time."

"I'll answer all the questions you have. I need my son home instead of with a lunatic."

Bling pushed Keisha back to the room.

"Can you think of anyone who would want to kidnap your child?"

"My wife, who I keep telling you, is a nut job," Bling spoke.

"You have reasons to suspect your wife of doing this?"

"Really, Detective, what more proof do you need? You already know she's insane. You were a witness to her madness." Bling helped Keisha back into bed.

"I will follow up on this lead, but in the meantime, please don't do anything drastic that will hinder the safe return of your child. Meaning, do not try to confront your wife and accuse her of this kidnapping."

"I won't promise anything," Bling stated.

"This is police business. Do not interfere." He moved to the door.

"Wait!" she stopped the detective. "Damien. My husband had threatened to take my child."

"When did that happen, and how come you didn't tell me?" Bling, upset, asked.

"Let me get this right. Your wife," he pointed to Bling, "and her husband," he faced Keisha, "are suspected of kidnapping your love child? This would make a good book."

"This is not a damn joke, Detective!" Bling raised his voice.

"And what makes you suspect your husband of doing this?" he questioned Keisha.

"My father owed him money, and he wanted me to pay. I told him no, and he threatened to take my child for ransom," Keisha explained. "I need my baby!" she sobbed.

"He will be home soon." Bling hugged her, but she pushed him away. "Can you guarantee that we will ever see him again? How do you even know if he's OK? He's probably hungry. He's probably dead!"

"Don't talk like that! He's not dead." Bling stormed out of the room.

Bling showed up at Damien's restaurant and approached a waitress who was coming his way after taking an order. "Excuse me, I have a meeting with Damien. Is he here yet?"

"Yes. I'll take you to his office." She led the way, and he followed. They went through the kitchen to the office in the back. "You can take it from here." She tried to walk away, but Bling stopped her.

"Why don't you knock on the door?" he suggested with a smile.

"Are you a Germaphobe or something?" she asked.

"Yeah, something like that," he replied.

The waitress knocked the door, and they both waited for him to answer.

"Who is it?" Damien's voice sounded a little irritated.

"It's Jessica. There's a . . . " Bling shook his head no, and she ended her sentence.

"Just a minute." Damien's activity sounded suspicious.

The door opened, and another waitress came out of the office with her hair out of place. "Simone, I thought you were on your break." Jessica went after her.

Bling went inside. Damien was sitting on the couch buttoning his shit, not paying attention. "What is it, Jessica?"

But Bling ran up on him, putting him in a choke hold. "Where's my child?"

Damien's eyes widened as Bling tightened his grip. "I don't know what you're talking about." He spaced his words as he spoke, trying to get air.

"My son was kidnapped, and I know you set it up!" Bling squeezed tighter.

"I wish I did, but I didn't." Damien could barely speak.

"You're a damn liar! Where is he?" Bling squeezed harder.

"Let him go!"

Bling looked up to see the detective with two other policemen. "Didn't I tell you not to interfere with police business?" the detective said, walking in the office.

"Well, if you're dragging your feet I have to take matters in my own hands."

"Release him now and let me do my damn job." The detective hardened his voice.

Bling released Damien, who was like a fish out of water trying to get air in his parched lungs.

"Where is my son?"

"Isn't Karma a bitch? She killed mine, and now some-body took hers. If only I had the privilege of doing the job," Damien chuckled.

Bling rushed him again, but the officer pulled him away. "You don't want to do this," the cop warned.

Bling left the restaurant on a mission to solve the mystery on his own. He showed up at Denise's house, and before he could park his car, a patrol car was right on his tail. Bling procrastinated, wondering if he should leave it up to them, but then went with his gut feelings and got out of his car.

"I told you to stay out of this!" the detective called out to him.

"You didn't tell me I can't go home," Bling said sarcastically.

"If you jeopardize this search I will throw your ass in jail. Now step back! " The detective marched to the door, followed by the same two officers.

"This is the police, open up!" They banged on the door. After a few seconds they repeated themselves, but no one came to the door.

"I have a key," Bling announced, dangling the keys.

"Let him open the door," the detective stated, annoyed by Bling's antics.

Bling opened the door and ran inside. The house was neatly put back in order. He had left the house in a disastrous state when he was there last. He ran upstairs to the nursery Denise had prepared, but she wasn't there. He went back downstairs. Meanwhile, the police had located Denise in the living room. She sat in a rocking chair rocking back and forth, holding a baby wrapped in a pink blanket.

"I will always keep you safe, and no one can ever take you away from me." Denise's voice was calm.

"Hand over the baby to us!" an officer said.

But she was incognizant of their words. She got up from the chair dressed in a long white nightgown. She swayed from side to side with the baby in her arms. *"You are my sunshine, my only sunshine. You make me happy when skies are gray, so please don't take my sunshine away."*

"Hand over the baby!" they called out to her again.

"You are not going to take my baby," she finally acknowledged them.

"Give me my son, Denise."

"This is my little girl. Our little princess. You can't let them take my child! This baby belongs to me." Denise held the baby tightly.

"Calm down, Denise." Bling walked slowly toward her. "Give me the baby. I'm not going to let them hurt him."

"She's a girl. Her name is Joy. I told you that she would make us happy again. You came back. She needs her daddy to tuck her in at night." Denise smiled.

"Give the baby to me. I will tuck her in at night, but right now she needs her mother."

"I *am* her mother! Don't come any closer." Denise took a couple steps backward.

"We need to take the baby to the hospital to make sure she is OK." Bling stepped closer.

"She is just fine. She has your eyes."

"Hand over the baby! This is your last warning." the officer informed her.

"You brought them here to take my baby? Don't you love me anymore?" Denise asked with sadness in her voice as she looked into his eyes.

"Yes, I still love you. Now give me the baby." He stretched his hand forward.

"*Liar!*" Denise screamed at him.

"I'm not lying. I want to make things right and get you the help you need. I love you."

"Promise that you will never leave us."

Bling was hesitant to answer.

"Promise!" she screamed at him.

"I promise. We could change his diaper together." Bling said what she wanted to hear. At this point he would do and say anything to get her to trust him.

She looked down at the baby, and Bling inched closer.

"Daddy promised that he will never leave us. Daddy is home to stay." She kept her eyes on the baby.

Bling rushed to her and grabbed the baby and quickly walked away.

"*Liar!*" She grabbed the gun from behind the cushion and aimed it at Bling.

The police also aimed their guns at Denise. She fired one shot and missed.

"No!" Madison ran inside, but she was too late to stop the bullets from piercing her sister's body. The room fell silent as Denise fell to the floor. Even Madison froze in the moment. Bling dropped the baby, and it didn't cry.

"What are you doing?" The detective gently picked the baby up . . . only to realize it was a doll.

"I'm here, sis." Madison ran to her sister crying. Madison placed Denise's head in her lap.

"I feel like I'm stuck in a horrible dream and I can't wake up," Denise spoke. Her nightgown was stained with blood seeping from the multiple bullet holes in her body. "I keep fighting, but as soon as I'm about to break free, it starts all over again. No one knows my struggles, no one knows my pain. When will it end?"

"I know your pain, sis. My heart aches for you." Madison rocked her back and forth. Bling got down on his knees and crawled to Denise. "Get away from her!" Madison screamed at him.

"I'm being tortured, used and abused. I'm a prisoner of love, and love has no mercy, conscience, or guilt. It keeps feeding me hate, and I'm starting to digest it."

"It's gonna be OK." Madison kept rocking her sister. "Call the damn ambulance!" she yelled, looking at the officers.

"Whenever I free myself from this horrible dream I will run as far as I can away from love because love isn't a friend of mine. It's a predator, a parasite, and an intruder that I will never allow to prey on my heart again. I will break free from this dream, and I will purge myself of hate and inhale freedom." Denise painfully coughed up blood from her mouth. A moment later, she closed her eyes, and died in Madison's lap.

"Nooooo!" Madison let out a sorrowful cry.

Two weeks had passed and the police still had no leads on who kidnapped her baby. Keisha was on the verge of going crazy. She stayed in bed taking pills of all kinds. Tina pulled the curtains back, letting the sun in.

"Rise and shine," she sang.

"What for? I have nothing to live for." Keisha covered her head with the blanket.

"Yes, you do. There's still hope of finding your baby."

"Why are you here, Tina?"

"I brought you coffee and donuts." Tina pulled the sheet from her head. "And there was a package left outside for you."

"Leave me alone. Let me grieve in peace." She covered her head again.

"If you don't get up, I swear I'll nominate you for the ice bucket challenge, and trust me, I'll dunk you in the bed."

"No, you wouldn't." She pulled the sheet, covering her entire body.

Keisha could care less what Tina had to say. She was going to grieve in her own way. Suddenly, Keisha screamed when the ice-cold water touched her body.

She jumped out of bed, running from the room with no destination in mind.

"That ice bucket will have a sinner catching the Holy Ghost." Tina followed after her.

"I'm going to die of hypothermia," Keisha yelled on her way to the kitchen.

"Now drink some coffee to warm you up and have a donut. You have to eat something."

"I can't eat. I can't even think straight." Keisha sipped the coffee.

"I know. But you need your health for when your baby comes home." Tina was optimistic. "There are sick people in the world who do crazy things, but the police will bring your baby home. Then you will be one big happy family."

"I'm not too sure about that." Keisha set her coffee down.

"What do you mean by that?"

"Bling hasn't been coming around. I think he blames himself for Denise's death, and it's as if he gave up on finding our son."

"He didn't give up on finding your son. He's just taking some time to mourn his loss. Everybody grieves differently."

Keisha laughed out loud. "Is this my punishment for sleeping with a married man?"

"Don't say that. This has nothing to do with you."

"Are you sure about that? Look at my track record." She took a pen out of the drawer and wrote Hype's name on the package that was sitting on the counter. "He's dead because of me."

"Stop it. Stop this nonsense!"

"Johnny." Keisha wrote his name.

"You killed Johnny?" Tina was in complete shock.

"Nikki." She wrote the name on the box. "She died because of me. Her baby also died because of me." She stabbed the box with the pen and ripped it apart. "This is my punishment! This is my punishment! My baby is gone because of me!" A picture of a baby and a note fell out of the box.

"Keisha! Look!" Tina pointed the items out to her. They both stared at the picture. Keisha slowly picked up the picture off the floor. Tina reached for the note.

You didn't deserve this baby! The words were typed in bold letters.

"This is my baby boy. This is my baby!" Keisha cried.

"You should call the police," Tina instructed.

"Look at his smile." Her finger traveled across his mouth. "My baby is alive."

CHAPTER 22

"Show your face, you damn coward." Bling spoke aloud so his captor could hear. He was sitting in the middle of an empty room with his hands tied. "My hands are tied, and you're still scared of me? You're nothing but a damn punk! Asshole Jackson, I know it's you. Your brother was a punk just like you!" Bling taunted, hoping Officer Jackson would show his face. Bling waited for him to come rushing in the room, but nothing happened. "For a cop, you shoot like a bitch. Aren't you supposed to be a straight shooter? You couldn't kill me at the church, I'm still alive."

Bling could hear someone's heels clunking on the hardwood floor, then the jiggling of keys at the door. He knew the person was coming to him. The door opened, and a woman wearing dark shades dressed in all-black strutted toward him. "Who are you?" Bling curiously asked. But the woman kept walking. "Let me guess . . . Hype's damn sister."

The woman paused at his feet looking down at him. "Let's just say I'm your savior."

"How ironic, because you're the one holding me hostage. I need saving from you and your brother?"

She stooped down to his level, screwing the cap off the bottled water she was holding, then extended the water to his mouth, but Bling refused to drink. "You need to drink."

"You've been holding me hostage for almost two weeks, and I need to know why."

"I'm trying to save you from a life of misery." She elevated herself and backed away, sitting on the lone chair in the room.

"What's in this for you? Why am I here?"

"I told you, I'm protecting you!" she crossed her legs.

"You and your brother kidnapped me. How are you saving or protecting me?" Bling screamed at her.

"I'll return when you've calm down." She gracefully strutted out of the room.

"Asshole Jackson, you can't fool me! I bet you're sitting in front a camera watching." Bling turned his head, viewing the four corners of the room. "I'm not a punk like you. I know you're waiting for me to accept defeat and beg like bitch to be set free, then you'll get pleasure out of putting a bullet in my head. But I'm gonna go out like a man, so you might as well kill me now! As a matter of fact, put a bullet in my head; after all, I did blow your brother's brains out." Bling knew that should get his attention, but the door remained on its hinges. He sat in the corner waiting for the showdown.

Soon, he heard the clinking of the woman's heels coming back, and he knew for sure she was going to kill him this time. The woman opened the door, but she didn't carry a gun or a knife.

"I'm gonna run out and get dinner, but I think it's wise for me to check on you just in case your arms came loose." She walked behind him and retaped his arms and legs. "That's better."

"Why don't your brother show his face? What's he waiting on to kill me?"

"You have this all wrong. I'm not Hype's sister." She patted his head.

"Then you must be Officer Jackson's wife."

"Wrong again. I happened to save you from Hype's brother, and I must tell you, he was going to blow your head off your body, but I got to you just in time. You see, Bling, when you went to the bathroom at the bar after you had drunk yourself in oblivion, he was rounding up his crew. If I hadn't taken you out of there, you would be dead by now." She walked away.

"So are you still holding me here for me to say thank you? Well, thank you! Now let me go!" Bling called out to her.

"I'm afraid I can't." She closed the door behind her.

Bling desperately tried to untie his arms, but he was getting nowhere. He badly needed a drink of water and the bottle was left on the floor, but with bound hands, it was impossible to get it. "When does it stop?" He lay on the floor staring at the ceiling until he fell asleep.

The aroma of fried chicken raced to his nostrils. He slowly raised his head to a plate of fried chicken with mashed potatoes.

"I think you should eat something." The woman spoke with a gentle voice.

Bling didn't refuse the meal because he knew she wouldn't save him to poison him. She raised the chicken to his mouth, and Bling took a big bite. The woman watched him eat like a wild caveman. "I see you were hungry."

"Water, I need water," Bling expressed.

She brought the bottle to his mouth, and he gluttonously drank. "There's more water where this came from."

"So, if you're not Hype's family, who the hell are you?"

"Let's just say I'm your guardian angel here to save you from Keisha, but don't worry, I'm not going to kill you unless you cross me."

"I don't understand. What good am I to you?"

"The better question is . . . What good am I to *you?* And to that I'll say, think of me as your therapist."

"I don't need a damn therapist. I need to be out there searching for my child. I need to fix my family." Bling became angered.

The woman also became riled. "Keisha isn't your family. She brainwashed you with sex to leave your wife. She doesn't deserve you!"

"She's mourning our son, and I need to be with her!" Bling's temper flared.

"She's not going to win!" The woman smashed the plate into the wall. "I'm going to make her suffer the way I did."

"This isn't about me." Bling slowly spoke, realizing this woman had unsettled business with Keisha. "Who the hell are you?" His eyes searched her face for clues.

A baby's cry came through the wall. Bling curiously scoped the room, then looked back at the woman. "You woke the baby up. Mommy's coming." The woman scurried off.

"Wait! Is that my son? Is that my son?" Bling scooted on his ass attempting to follow her. "Wait! Is that my son?"

The woman locked Bling in the room and hurried to the kitchen where she took a bottle from the bottle warmer and quickly walked to the crying baby that was lying in the crib surrounded by stuffed animals. "Mommy is here with your bottle. Give me a minute. If you keep eating like this you are going to be a big boy." The baby continued to cry until the woman took him from the crib. "What's the matter? Mommy's right here." She put the bottle to his mouth, and the baby greedily sucked from it, and the woman laughed. She brought the baby to the room where she had Bling tied up. *"Hush, little baby, don't say a word, Mommy's gonna buy you a mockingbird,"* she sang. "Maybe not a mockingbird, maybe a little puppy."

"Let me see him, please!" Bling begged.

"Maybe later, he's sleeping now."

The baby's eyes were closed, and she removed the bottle from his mouth. "Look how precious you are. She didn't deserve you. I deserve to have you, not her." She kept her eyes locked on the baby.

"Now I remember your face." Bling was in a state of shock.

"Do you?" The woman became irate as she addressed him. "So you should know that she messed up my life for her own selfish pleasures. She took my child from me. Now I have to replace mine with hers." Her attention was back to the baby. "You are not going to miss her at all. I'm your mommy now and look." She positioned the baby to face Bling. "Daddy's here."

Bling got to see his son for the first time. "That's my boy. That's my boy." Bling cried.

"I know you're a good man, but you got corrupted by Keisha. So I'm granting you the pleasure of raising your son . . . with me. You deserve to see your firstborn grow into a man. But you will have to understand that Keisha brainwashed you. But I'll fix you. I'll undo her spell. *We* are a family now. So dismiss the thought from your mind of going home to that bitch." She brought her attention back to the baby. "I love you. You love me. We're a happy family with a great big hug and a kiss from me to you. Won't you say you love me too?"

"I remember who you are. I remember seeing your picture on news, but you're supposed to be . . . " Bling couldn't get the words out.

"Dead." Nikki finished his sentence with a smile.

ORDER FORM
URBAN BOOKS, LLC
97 N18th Street
Wyandanch, NY 11798

Name (please print):_____

Address: _____

City/State: _____

Zip: _____

QTY	TITLES	PRICE

Shipping and handling: add $3.50 for 1st book, then $1.75 for each additional book.

Please send a check payable to:
    Urban Books, LLC

Please allow 4-6 weeks for delivery